WHITE

Also by Elias Khoury in English translation

The Little Mountain
The Gates of the City
The Journey of Little Gandhi
The Kingdom of Strangers
Gate of the Sun
Yalo (MacLehose Press, 2009)
As Though She Were Sleeping (MacLehose Press, 2011)
Sin Alcool (MacLehose Press, forthcoming)

Elias Khoury

WHITE MASKS

Translated from the Arabic by
Maia Tabet

MACLEHOSE PRESS
QUERCUS · LONDON

First published in the Arabic language as *Al-Wujûb al-baydâ*
by Dâr-al-Adâb, Beirut, in 1981
First published in the English language
by Archipelago Books, New York, in 2010
First published in Great Britain in 2013 by

MacLehose Press
an imprint of Quercus
55 Baker Street
7th Floor, South Block
London W1U 8EW

A CIP catalogue record for this book
is available from the British Library

ISBN (TPB) 978 0 85705 212 4
ISBN (Ebook) 978 1 78087 609 2

Designed and typeset in Cycles by Libanus Press, Marlborough
Printed and bound in Great Britain by Clays Ltd, St Ives plc

And when, in the course of his journey through the wilderness, Jesus came upon a decaying skull and beseeched God that it should speak, the Lord gave it to utter thus: "I am Balwan bin Hafs, king of Yemen. I lived one thousand years, sired one thousand offspring, deflowered one thousand virgins, defeated one thousand armies, and conquered one thousand cities! But all of this was like a dream, and may he who hears my tale not be deceived by the world." And Jesus, peace be upon him, did so passionately weep that he fainted.

AL-ABSHEEHI, *Al-Mustatref*

Prologue

This is no tale. And it may not be of particular interest to readers, as people these days have more important things to do than read stories or listen to tales. And they are absolutely right. But this story really did happen. The truth is that it did not happen just like that. One morning, I saw in the paper a short piece entitled "Dreadful murder in the U.N.E.S.C.O. district" and, don't ask me why, but whenever I see the word "dreadful", the word "wonderful" springs to mind. So the phrase stuck in my mind like this: "Wonderful murder in U.N.E.S.C.O.". My eyes skipped from this "wonderful" crime to a photograph of the victim: a man in his fifties, with traces of bruising on his chest and puncture wounds to the face. I didn't linger over the picture – the terrifying visions that fill my nights are enough for me, I do not need new nightmares. Although I tried, I could not place the man's name, but I seemed to remember that I had come across him somewhere. Turning finally to the report printed alongside the photograph, which was very brief, I read the following: "The corpse of an unidentified man has been found in the U.N.E.S.C.O. district of Beirut, near the Habib Abi Shahla statue, bearing gunshot wounds, abrasions and bruises. According to the forensic pathologist's report, death occurred three days earlier."

Before I knew it, I was following the story of this corpse, step by step. I have admired Habib Abi Shahla, one of the architects of Lebanon's independence, ever since I was a boy – besides which, of all the monuments commemorating the leaders of the independence movement, his was the only one that had not been felled in the civil war. The statues of both Riad al-Solh and Beshara al-Khoury had been destroyed, leaving Habib Abi Shahla the sole remaining witness to our independence. What is more, in addition to being a rather extraordinary figure, it is rumoured that Habib Abi Shahla also died an uncommon death, expiring in the arms of a woman as they made love.

As a boy, I was absolutely enthralled by this – what a way to go, I thought! And though I later learned that it happens to a lot of men, this did not diminish Habib Abi Shahla's standing in my eyes: to me, he remained a trailblazer, and certainly the most illustrious of men to have met with such an end. When our neighbour, Saïd al-Sabbagh, passed away, a rumour went around the neighbourhood that he died making love to his wife. Now that is a beautiful death, I said. When I asked my father about it he gave me a scathing look, but I knew that he knew the details – our late neighbour's wife was one of his many mistresses. He denied it, and did so vociferously, but I caught him – no, of course I never told him, I would be too embarrassed – with the laughing young widow in his arms, as they stood waiting for the lift one day.

So I followed the story of the corpse out of plain curiosity, but also because it provided me with this link to Habib Abi Shahla. I had graduated in political science from Lebanese University in 1974, just a year before the start of the civil war and, owing to "prevailing circumstances", had been unable to find a job to match my ambitions – as a journalist, for instance. So I worked in a travel agency, where all I did was sit for hours on end at a computer that looked like a calculating machine, issuing tickets and waiting. I thought the story of the corpse would help me pass the time, especially after it turned out that the victim, Mr Khalil Ahmad Jaber, lived in our neighbourhood in Mazra'a. He was a Lebanese citizen, born in 1928, employed at the Lebanese post office – the Post, Telegraph and Telephone department, or P.T.T., as it is known.

The murkier the story got, the more my interest grew. Thanks to a variety of sources I was able to contact, as well as my daily perusal of the papers, I was able to collect a vast amount of information pertaining to the murder, which, according to medical reports, took place on the morning of 13 April, 1980.

So I am setting out to tell this story, which is really not a story, as the discriminating reader might observe, and which I am aware might be of no interest to anyone. The reader could simply refer to the forensic pathologist's report and dispense with all the attendant detail; alternatively, he might find it sufficient to read the widow's statements or those of the municipal workers – they were the ones to discover the naked corpse dumped on the roadside. Indeed, the reader might even regard this introduction as sufficient, and leave it at that. Every one of us has a story, after all, and that's more than enough. We have no need of other people's.

The information I have been able to collect about the deceased is highly contradictory. Some say he had amassed a considerable fortune during the war, thanks to his "martyred" son, Ahmad. Before his "martyrdom," Ahmad had been a boxer and a contender for Lebanon's featherweight title, but then he joined one of the militias – whence the alleged fortune, which he would have kept at his parents' house. After he died in one of the Qomatiyyeh skirmishes, his comrades-in-arms went to his father demanding the treasure. Khalil Ahmad Jaber told them he knew nothing about it. He said he had no knowledge whatsoever of a stash of money that they claimed was in his son's possession. This could be the motive for his murder. But the evidence strongly suggests otherwise; Mr Khalil Ahmad Jaber's house was not searched or ransacked, either before or after his murder, and neither Mr Khalil Ahmad Jaber, nor any members of his family, exhibited any sign of conspicuous wealth after the son's demise.

Another avenue of thought regarding motive for the murder might link Khalil to some woman. However, he had no history of drinking or womanizing, and all who knew him could attest to that. He was, on the contrary, a real home bird, his only pastimes being an occasional game of draughts or backgammon, and watching T.V. Such a hypothesis, therefore, appears altogether improbable.

A final hypothesis remains, that Mr Khalil Ahmad Jaber was the victim of a case of mistaken identity, a common occurrence these days. But the likelihood of such an error is remote given that the victim had his I.D. card on him: while it was retrieved far from the body, it appears that it was thrown there by the criminals in their attempt to muddy the evidence and obstruct the inquiry. So that this was simply a sectarian killing seems highly unlikely, or even impossible, as Mr Khalil was known to all the militiamen of his neighbourhood and would have been able to prove at any checkpoint that he was the father of Ahmad, the "martyr" – and checkpoint personnel are compelled to treat a martyr's father with the respect that is his due.

Who then killed Khalil Ahmad Jaber, and why?

The truth is that after collecting this vast amount of information, I find myself quite baffled – there seems to be neither rhyme nor reason to this dreadful, wonderful murder, and no motive for it.

Mr Khalil Ahmad Jaber's disappearance three weeks prior to the crime may, however, hold the key to the mystery. On Thursday, 20 March, 1980, the deceased left for work and did not return. People attributed his disappearance to kidnapping – they thought he might have been on his way to visit his daughter, Su'ad, who is married and living in Tripoli, when he was kidnapped on the Jounieh–Tripoli road. This supposition remained firm in everyone's mind until the body was found at the U.N.E.S.C.O. roundabout. Should one conclude then that Khalil Ahmad Jaber was indeed kidnapped on his way to Tripoli and that his corpse was only later dumped beside the Habib Abi Shahla statue, as the forensic pathologist's report surmises?

To tell the truth, I find myself mystified, as nothing wholly substantiates or refutes any of the hypotheses. That is why I have chosen to leave the last word to the documents themselves and not to weigh in any further. These documents and the information I have gathered might provide a key to understanding Mr Khalil Ahmad Jaber's case; they might also help us understand the many other similar cases that we are unable to explain, in terms of both their widespread occurrence and their underlying causes.

In closing, I wish to state unequivocally that I am pointing a finger at no-one, and that my aim is not to level accusations. It would be meaningless to do so in these fair times of ours, and the whole affair warrants no more effort than that required to read about it.

CHAPTER I

The Boxer-Martyr

*The victim's wife: Mrs Noha Jaber, née al-Hajj, born in Beirut in 1938.
The following fragments of her account were gathered from a variety
of sources, including: the preliminary inquiry carried out by the
head of "Popular Security" in West Beirut, a "comrade" of Ahmad, the
martyr; the investigation of the examining magistrate; scattered bits of
conversations and the wife's responses on various occasions, particularly in the course of condolences following the funeral, or in discussions with friends and neighbours, as well as with the author of this
document, who made several visits to Mr Khalil Ahmad Jaber's home.
The author made his first visit on the day of the funeral, 17 April, 1980,
and returned three times after that, posing both as a friend of the
martyr and as a journalist who wished to cover the event.*

Oh, Lord, Lord, this is it, the final reckoning, the Day of Judgement, the day we always feared and expected . . . and now it has
come. First, Ahmad died. He just slipped through our fingers. We
thought life was over – life as we knew it had come to an end. But
base as we human beings are, we got used to it. The boy went and
we carried on! Before he died, I could never have imagined – and
neither could my late husband, Khalil – that we'd be able to live on
after him, not even for a minute. But he went, and we just carried
on . . . oh Lord! . . . And now, dear God, how do you expect me to
manage – me a poor widow, all alone? What will people say? . . .
The devil take them! . . . Forgive me, God!

Just like everyone else, my father always said: "Dear Lord,
let me not perish by fire or by drowning, nor destitute and

wandering." And now, dear God, the country is on fire and the city is drowning in rubbish and he died destitute and wandering the streets. They just left him there . . . dumped him naked in that empty lot after killing him. He died on the street, and then they brought him to the house, him and that smell . . . May the Good Lord forgive me . . . I couldn't go near him, my own husband, I just couldn't! Lord, have mercy! What fault of mine was it, what fault of his, of anyone's? May God have mercy on us all and preserve us from earthquakes and other calamities . . .

This is the final reckoning . . . not just mine, but everybody's . . . And you, Abu Ahmad, how could you leave me and go like this? You left the house never to return . . . I'm sure they kidnapped you, and they killed you . . .

Before that . . . ? Nothing; nothing special . . . Of course he was upset, he was prostrate with grief – what would you expect when your own son dies? He was beside himself. But he survived, we all did, and we said, that's our lot, that's our fate, and afterwards everything went back to the way it was before. In fact, it was as though he were born again – he was rejuvenated somehow. Then, one day, suddenly, it was all over: I no longer understood him – or him me – and then he disappeared.

Where shall I begin?

We've turned into a story, a tale people tell.

Khalil was a nice young man, and one day he came to our house with his late father to ask for my hand in marriage. My father said he's a nice boy, he's twenty-five years old – I was ten years younger, so that was a good age difference – he's from a good family, he's educated, and a government employee – you know, a civil servant. Our destinies were joined and I never had cause to complain. Every day, he'd come home from work, wash, and sit quietly in front of the T.V., like a child; I never felt his presence he was so softly spoken. There were no worries or anything, even though his salary was only just sufficient – but he was an easygoing man.

14

When I bore him our first child and it was a girl, he didn't mind; it's God's grace, he said, and he named her Su'ad: Su'ad for happiness, he said, and he wasn't the least bit upset. When the second child came, and it was another girl, he didn't come to the hospital for three days. He looked sad, and I told him he had a right to feel that way, though when I came home, he treated me the same as always. But he wouldn't pay any attention to baby Nada – I was the one who named her – and he started going to the café every day, to drink tea, smoke a hookah and play draughts. He no longer spent all his spare time at home. Well, he's a man, I thought, men can't spend all their time at home, they have to go out, it's only right that they should do what they feel like. My mother said I was lucky, and I was, because then Ahmad came along. When Ahmad was born, everything changed. The man was transformed: he started to take an interest in the children's upbringing and to share my domestic concerns. He would come home from work, play with the little one, and tell me about his day, about his problems at work, all the cheating and corruption. Listening to him crowing about not taking bribes, I felt upset – bribes are better than nothing, you know, with children and school fees and the cost of living, but he wouldn't hear of it.

"I won't take a penny from anyone, I am above that. Taking bribes is dishonourable."

That's what he said. He got neither a raise nor a promotion, and I didn't like to ask why not, but people said that he wasn't conscientious, that he spent most of his time doing the crosswords in the paper, drinking coffee and smoking. I don't believe any of it. I'm sure he was a model civil servant, but he just wouldn't suck up to the bosses, that's why they didn't like him. Anyway, how would I know . . . we never socialized with any of his colleagues, and only ever visited my mother-in-law! That was it – every Sunday. It was our only ritual.

And so the days passed . . .

It's unbelievable how life goes by – in the blink of an eye, like a dream, and then it's over. Ahmad grew into a fine young man – handsome, his grandmother said, like her brothers. Actually, he looked more like my brother, may he rest in peace, but I didn't like to say so. Fortune smiled on Su'ad and she got married, then it was Nada's turn, with the grace of God. I had only three children. Khalil would say he wanted another boy, one more boy and that would be it. But it was God's will, and I wasn't blessed with another child, *al-hamdulillah*! Ahmad grew up and we grew old . . . he did alright at school, but sports were his thing. He would sit in front of the T.V. for hours on end watching wrestling matches: the Saadeh brothers, Prince Komali and the Silver Monster. Sometimes, I'd be lying down in the bedroom, and I would hear Khalil and Ahmad in the living room getting louder and louder as the matches progressed. Then Ahmad joined the Sports and Fitness Club. I told Khalil this would distract the boy from his studies, but the father had become even more of a fitness fanatic than his son. He told me he was going to start exercising every morning, and that when he was younger he'd wanted to be an athlete and hadn't had the chance. Except that Khalil wasn't consistent with his morning exercise: some days he'd get up early and lift small weights before taking a cold shower and going to work; but then several days would go by without him doing anything . . . he wouldn't exercise, or wake up early, or take that shower. And with time, his resolve faltered, but he never lost interest in his son's career . . .

The boy had taken up boxing – you should have seen what a figure he cut – and said he wanted to go professional. Khalil pinned all his hopes on him: "Why shouldn't he become a great boxer, why not, like Muhammad Ali Clay, or even better?"

With these words, the woman looks across at the photograph of her son in his boxing gear, walks over to it, wipes her palm across it, and stands silently for a moment.

May God rest your soul in peace, Ahmad, if only you'd lived . . . He took part in several tournaments, and he won! I went to a fight once, and you should've seen how he leapt around the ring, like a real boxer, delivering punch after punch! When he took one in the face and I saw the blood, I dashed towards the ring, I wanted to tell him to get down from the ring, but Khalil grabbed hold of me and began swearing, so I went back to my seat and, in the end, Ahmad won the fight! He knocked down his opponent, and the guy just lay there motionless while the referee slowly counted to ten and Ahmad looked on. Then the referee lifted Ahmad's hand in the air and I saw Khalil thrust his own arm up and run to embrace him. Ahmad competed in several championships and won every one of them – he was always telling me how he was going to take part in the national championships, featherweight class. I'd laugh to myself at the expression, as if a feather weighed anything. Really, men are pea-brained, they're like little children! Still, it was our lot, the luck of the draw, and there was nothing we could do about it.

No, the war didn't have anything to do with it. Nothing changed during the war – it had nothing to do with it. Khalil stopped going to the main post office down in Riad al-Solh Square, and joined the Mazra'a branch instead – he couldn't bear to sit at home like a housewife, he said. But later he had to, with the shelling everywhere, there was no way to go out, and after I begged him to stay at home, he agreed. His salary went on being paid and we lacked for nothing. We thanked our lucky stars, disaster never struck, just the one shell landing nearby, but we were in the shelter and nothing happened, *al-hamdulillah*! I said to Khalil, why don't you do the same as our neighbour Abu Tareq? You know, selling cigarettes from a makeshift pavement stall? His salary was no longer enough, you see.

"No," he said, "I am a civil servant and I won't work anywhere else than at the post office, handling calls and telegrams. I am not about to sell cigarettes . . ."

Ahmad went on training regularly, and we steered clear of politics. Khalil always said: "When the winds of change are blowing, keep your heads." And we kept our heads pretty well. Even the newspapers didn't cross our threshold – Khalil got them only at work; and anyway, he didn't read them, it was only for the crossword puzzles and the sports page. But then, they did . . . you know how it is, a man, at home all day long, with nothing to do, helping out with chores like fetching the water – the water supply was cut off – going off every morning with big plastic containers and coming back all breathless. Ahmad never helped out; and besides, Khalil wouldn't have let him. "No," he'd say, "Ahmad must concentrate on his training, leave him alone." And so, with nothing to do at home, he started reading the papers, even though he always said he hated politics.

"It's nothing to do with us," he'd say. "We are just the play-things of foreign powers . . . kicking us around like a ball! It's nothing to do with us."

You know how it is . . . I mean with the war and everything, it's inevitable, isn't it . . . all the young men in the neighbourhood were donning uniforms, *mashallah* . . . When Ahmad told me he wanted to join up, I begged him not to, I told him, no, you're our only son and only sons don't go to war; our only son, and you're going to die! Then these words reeled off his tongue, I don't know where he got them from, he said all these things I didn't understand. And one day he vanished. Khalil was so upset, he stormed into the kitchen swearing and smashed all the plates; then he made the rounds of all the political party offices, asking after him and plead-ing, but all they said was that Ahmad was going through military training in the mountains and that he'd be back.

And so he was . . . After three long weeks of sorrow and grief and penance, he came back, strutting around in his fatigues with a rifle slung over his shoulder, all puffed up with pride. I caught him one day admiring himself in the mirror, in his high combat boots and his khakis, caressing his rifle! In the beginning, Khalil refused to speak to him, and just sat by the radio, muttering to himself. Then we got used to this new state of affairs – the Devil's curse on us humans, how we get used to anything! Even the death of our sons! Then Ahmad started bringing money home; he'd give some of it to his father, who was on speaking terms with him now, and they would have political discussions.

I, for my part, was worried. But Ahmad's father, may his soul rest in peace, seemed unconcerned, and he became interested in what the boy brought back – nothing very valuable, mind you, a bracelet here, three gold rings there, and other useless trifles. But it helped his father cope with the terrible price increases that were breaking us. Khalil stopped muttering to himself, but he was always worried about the boy and waiting for him to get back.

And poor dear, how he got back . . . !

No, no, Ahmad's death didn't change anything. He was killed in combat in 1976, four years ago now, but no, nothing changed. Khalil was just the same as always. Yes, of course it was a crushing blow, and he began to show signs of ageing – his hair went completely white – but he didn't change.

It was ten in the morning that day, Khalil wasn't home. They had knocked at the door, but I hadn't heard them – the power was off, the doorbell wasn't working, and I was in the kitchen with the racket of the Primus stove. Then I heard shouting and clamouring at the door, so I opened up. Three young men in fatigues stood there and I told them Ahmad wasn't home. I was about to shut the door but they insisted on coming in. What's going on? I thought, and then my heart started pounding, and I knew that Ahmad . . . When I asked about him, one of them said, "Steady now, Auntie."

"What happened to him?" I screamed hysterically, as they trooped into the living room. The three of them sat down, I remained standing, and the oldest one did the talking.

"Sit down, Auntie, we need to speak to you," he said. I burst into tears.

"Ahmad's dead!" I cried.

They nodded, and, overcome with the shock, I began to wail and scream and tear at my clothes. Then Nada was there, though I hardly even noticed, and then all the neighbours came, men, women, crying and ululating and carrying on – nothing made any sense. They said he died far away – in Qomatiyyeh – and that his body was in the morgue at the American University Hospital; he's a martyr, they said, he was killed in combat. Khalil, who had come home to all the screaming and wailing, sat in a corner, speechless. He just nodded silently as the three young men informed him the funeral procession would go directly from the hospital to the Martyrs' Cemetery, as they weren't able to retrieve the body immediately, and Ahmad had been dead for more than forty-eight hours.

"You know how it is, Uncle," one of them said, "the body won't last. It's best that way."

Khalil went to identify the body, and when he came back he said nothing, just ground his jaw and recited Qur'anic verses under his breath.

Then we went to the American University Hospital – that is to say, they went – and brought the coffin home. They took him to his room and opened the coffin for a minute so I could see him, but I never saw him. Everyone saw him but me. Then they hoisted him up on their shoulders and carried him to the cemetery, firing in the air, chanting slogans and singing. The whole time, Khalil muttered and talked to himself, saying that was the way they wanted to do it. They wouldn't let us wash him – a martyr shouldn't be washed, they said, he is cleansed by his own blood – and they buried him just like that . . . doing exactly as they pleased! Then they lined up beside me and received condolences while I stood like a stranger in their midst, as if it had been their son. Afterwards, they brought food over to the house, and milled about, doing everything themselves . . . as if we didn't exist, as if Ahmad hadn't been our son.

If truth be told, Khalil found some consolation in the posters plastered all over the walls in the neighbourhood. They had produced a colour poster, in red and blue, with the words "Ahmad Khalil Jaber, Hero and Martyr" printed under his picture, and there was an obituary of him with photographs in all the papers. Still, Khalil grieved, and so did I.

Then those three young men came back one day and handed my husband four thousand lira and told us we would be getting four hundred lira each month. Khalil told them it wasn't necessary. They insisted . . . they were the ones to insist: they said it was the martyr's stipend and we must take it. So we took it. It was bad enough that the boy had died, were we also to die of starvation and grief? No way! I told my husband he should accept the money. It's not dirty money, I told him; it's our due.

That's when the posters of Ahmad became Khalil's main preoccupation, before it turned into an obsession. He was upset whenever it rained. They'll be damaged, he'd say. So he brought home about a hundred of them and went around putting them up on the walls of the neighbourhood whenever the old ones peeled off, or when children tore them down or they were covered over with advertisements. Then they began to disappear – no, not disappear, there were just fewer of them; it was only natural, the war was over, and the walls were being covered with new posters for films and plays. Still, he insisted on going around putting up the posters of Ahmad. At the beginning of every month, he would go to the local party office to collect the stipend, and they would make such a fuss of him as the martyr's father. He got on with them famously now, and slowly these new relationships filled our lives – and Khalil was his old self again.

The war stopped, or subsided, I'm not sure how to put it . . . but anyway Khalil was going down to the central post office again, playing draughts at the café, and watching T.V. I'm not sure why, but it seems his relationship with the "boys" began to deteriorate. He stopped dropping by for visits and then one day he asked whether I would go and collect the stipend. When I went, I didn't notice anything wrong, but he told me that the last time he'd been there, he had asked the apparatchik in charge to reprint the poster because we only had ten of them left. The rain and little fingers were ripping up Ahmad's pictures, he said, so he needed a new printing. The "officer" apparently didn't receive him at all well, and in fact started yelling at him, telling him the war was over, and three years had gone by since Ahmad's death. I could see the man's point of view, and I told Khalil, it's over for the one who dies. But he got all upset and said that they were dishonouring Ahmad's martyrdom, that he no longer felt welcome, and that they had changed their attitude. If truth be told, they weren't the same as before – in the early days, they visited us regularly, bringing little gifts with them, but now . . . well, they were probably right, the war was over, and more than half of them had quit and gone back to their jobs. Some had even left the country to work in Saudi Arabia or the Gulf, and the "officer" had more important things on his mind now.

While it was Khalil who told me this, I knew it made him sad. He hung a poster of Ahmad up in our bedroom and carried on as before, going to work and to the café, and then coming home and watching T.V. He didn't say very much, but I certainly didn't sense there was anything wrong. That was about a year and a half ago, in 1979. Khalil seemed reconciled to the situation: there were still a few posters in the wardrobe and there was the one hanging in our room.

But then the fighting started – the war, it's started up again, I told him. There was shelling everywhere, but he didn't seem concerned. Even the newspapers had stopped being brought into the house, as if he'd gone back to his old self. Only that smile of his was gone. Everything was the same as before, except for the smile and the white head of hair.

But then, how shall I put it . . . strange things began to happen whose meaning I couldn't grasp . . . I just didn't understand anything anymore. All of a sudden, Khalil started to change . . . it must have been about three months ago. He just completely changed. Nothing specific happened. Our daughter Nada had a little boy; he was happy about the boy and he went to see her. Nothing happened, but he changed, he became another man. I did everything I could to understand him but he wouldn't tell me anything. He simply said nothing. Then, one day, he left the house, saying he was off to work. He went and he never returned. Whether they kidnapped him or murdered him, I don't know – all I know is that he never came back, and he was killed.

I'll have you know, young man, we don't have any enemies . . . no-one hates us, why should this happen to him? I swear I have no idea. No, no, he wasn't the foolhardy type, even our visits to our daughter in Tripoli were few and far between. We're not the adventurous sort, and since the safe route to Tripoli was too long, we simply didn't go.

Honestly, I don't understand how everything happened, I really don't. I neither see nor understand, all I know is they killed him, they dumped him there, dear God, just like that, naked to the waist . . . and the rubbish . . . Oh Lord, I can't understand it . . .

The story? There is no story. Everything happened so suddenly. We woke up one morning, and he wouldn't get out of bed. He told me he wasn't feeling well and wouldn't be going to work. I went out to buy a few things, and when I got back I found he'd locked himself in the bedroom. I knocked on the door, and when he didn't open, I started to scream, I thought something terrible had happened to him. But then I heard him speak, and he sounded quite normal, saying, everything's alright, I'm just a bit

23

busy. So I left him there and went to attend to things in the kitchen. Then it was lunchtime. I knocked again, and again he didn't open. He said he wasn't hungry; then it was dinnertime, and he still didn't come out. I asked him to please open the door because I wanted to go to bed, but he asked me to sleep in the other room. I tried to peep through the keyhole to see what he was up to, but I couldn't make out anything. So I went out on the balcony – but all I could see from there was that the lights inside the room were switched off. What to do? I said my prayers, asked God to give him guidance, and went to bed in the other room – Ahmad's, I mean – but it still had his smell and I couldn't fall asleep there, so I went to the living room and slept on the sofa.

The next morning he came out to go to the bathroom. I went into the bedroom, cleaned and tidied it, and when he came back, he asked me for a bottle of water, and told me to leave. You must be hungry, I said, and told him I would make him a bowl of *foul*.‡

He just shook his head to say no. I went and fetched him a bottle of water and when I came back he was in bed. I asked him if he felt ill, whether he needed me to call the doctor, but all he did was shake his head and motion with his hand that I should leave the room. Then I heard the key turning in the lock behind me. It went on like this for about five days, with Khalil spending all day – and night – in bed, neither eating nor sleeping, and only coming out of the room to use the toilet. I was beside myself with worry, and though I tried to be helpful, I just didn't know what to do. I'd stand outside the bedroom door for hours pleading with him to come out and have something to eat.

Then, one day, he opened the door. It was dusk, almost dark but not quite, and there he stood wearing the same pyjamas he'd had on for five days. "Alright," he said, "I'll eat." I went straight to

‡ A Lebanese meze dish made from fava beans, garlic and parsley

the kitchen and got him a plate of rice and spinach stew, a loaf of bread and a raw onion.

He gestured that I should leave the food at the door. I did as he asked, and went back to the living room, and there I slept soundly for the first time in days. I said to myself that if he was eating, the worst of the crisis was over.

In the morning, when he went to the bathroom, I discovered that he had only eaten the bread and had left the rice and spinach, and the onion. I removed the plate, took in some fresh bread and some cheese, and left again. When he returned to the room, he locked the door as usual. I felt completely lost . . . and I had no-one to turn to . . . I was afraid of a scandal, and of him too. Abu Ahmad would surely get angry if I told anyone, and his condition would worsen, so I didn't tell anybody except our neighbour, Imm 'Imad al-Kaadi. She's an older woman, she's someone really special, and I was sure she'd keep my secret. So I went to see her. When I got to her house, there she was sitting alone in the living room wearing her white headwrap with little wisps of grey hair escaping from underneath. She looked really concerned when I told her about Abu Ahmad. She sidled up to me on the sofa and dropped her voice.

"Listen, dear," she said, "these things happen. Exactly the same thing happened to Hajj Abu 'Imad, God rest his soul and the soul of your departed. How old is your husband?" I told her he was about fifty.

"That's what it is, dear," she went on. "It's the difficult age. May the Lord spare your husband, dear child. That's exactly what happened to Abu 'Imad. He was forty-seven and one morning, all of a sudden, he woke up and wouldn't get out of bed, he said he wasn't going to work. He stayed in bed for two weeks. He didn't lock the bedroom door, we could go in and see him, but he hardly spoke or ate. Then, God be praised, one day he got up. As far as I can see, my dear, your husband's case is very similar to that of mine. It's a difficult age, you know, men feel they're past it, that life has passed them by and that old age is around the corner. They feel they're no longer men, you understand what I'm saying, don't you? But it's just a phase, a short phase, and things will move on, *inshallah*, with the help of God. My dear, you should be thankful. Other men . . . do you know what other men do? They go after cabaret girls. No, this is good. Still, my dear, you just pray to the Good Lord to have mercy on him, and don't burden him with anything."

I understood Imm 'Imad to be saying that Khalil was . . . But no! There was no doubting his manliness! That's not at all the case, I told her. She carried right on, as if she'd been expecting me to say that.

"Don't you worry, my dear, it's a phase, just a little phase, it'll pass, with the Good Lord's help. Now, you be good to him, and don't you worry."

I felt confused as I left her house, thinking maybe she hadn't understood. I called Nada, my daughter, and went to see her to tell her about it. She and her husband came around that evening, but as hard as Nadeem tried, Khalil wouldn't speak to him. He had loathed his son-in-law ever since Ahmad had gone, and how likely was he to answer Nadeem when he wasn't even talking to me, his wife! All the same, Nadeem knocked at the door for ages, he really tried, and after expressing his astonishment, he said he'd come over with the doctor the following day.

The next day came, and the doctor with it. I described Khalil's symptoms to him, and we tried to get Khalil to let him in, without success. I begged the doctor to return in the morning, when Khalil normally opened the door to go to the bathroom, but this made him very angry.

"I'm not your servant," he snapped. "And in any case, your husband is having a nervous breakdown."

Then he started asking me all sorts of questions to which I didn't know the answers. He asked me about his situation at work, about our relationship and our financial circumstances. The truth is, I didn't answer him honestly. How could I? Telling him about such private matters, when I hardly knew him! In any case, the doctor handed me some pills to give him – to "calm his nerves," as he put it – and he left.

I tried to persuade Khalil to take the pills but he just ignored me. All he would have was a little bread and some water. Oh, God, what was I to do? Nothing was helping . . . well, almost nothing . . . I have to admit, the doctor did write a sick report so that my husband wouldn't lose his job – what on earth would he do, if he no longer worked at the P.T.T.? So we thanked our lucky stars, and thanked the doctor for his trouble.

To this day, I don't know how the story got out and made the rounds of the neighbourhood. Maybe it was Imm 'Imad, or maybe even our daughter. But I discovered that everybody was talking about my husband and his condition. Many people thought that he had cancer – God forbid – and that I wouldn't take him to the hospital because, the rumour was, I didn't want to spend the money! Shame on them for thinking that I would scrimp and save where Abu Ahmad was concerned! Shame, shame!

Then, one day, Sitt Khadijah appeared. You know, the famous Sitt Khadijah, the one everyone's heard about – she makes amulets and summons spirits, and can talk to djinns and demons. It turned out that she'd come at Imm 'Imad's insistence.

"It's only because Imm 'Imad has such a place in my heart that I've come, dear," she said, adding that she didn't usually go to the homes of the afflicted. I told her I thought very highly of Imm 'Imad and expressed my profound gratitude to them both. She read my fortune in some coffee grounds and told me I had a long journey ahead. Naturally, I didn't believe her: how would someone like me ever get to go on a journey?

Then she drew up her legs beneath her and sat cross-legged on the sofa, like this, and started making strange sniffing noises, as if she could smell something. I asked her if something was wrong.

No, she said, nothing. Then she pulled out some dried twigs from under her long baggy shift, struck a match and lit them. The smell of incense and other strange aromas filled the house.

And then she started saying in this throaty voice: "Hmm . . . I smell something, my dear . . . I can smell . . . I smell . . . this house . . . I smell . . . I can smell djinns! This house is inhabited, my dear, your home is possessed . . . the djinn . . . the Good Lord protect us . . . The djinn, he's in another room, such a strong smell he's got . . . he's inside a man . . . it's your husband who's inhabited by the djinn! And it's an evil djinn . . . I've got to see the man and talk to him, then the djinn will leave, he'll have to leave him . . . Hmmm . . . Oh, the smell of the djinn . . . O-o-oh!"

By now, I was well and truly frightened. Djinns are terrifying, and it seemed that this one was right there before me, just as she was. She blew out the incense sticks, put them away inside her shift, and asked me to open the windows and air the room. I told her that it wouldn't be possible for her to see my husband, that he refused to open the door.

"The djinn, dear Sitt Noha . . . Oh, if you only knew . . . I see them, I can feel them, with my own hands, every day . . . It's as if Beirut were overrun with these evil and godless demons, Lord have mercy upon us . . . They have come here from the very ends of the earth, they don't know the Arabic language, and they speak in strange tongues that we don't understand . . . but, with God's grace, I shall overcome the djinn that is here. Go and tell your husband that I want to see him for five minutes – five minutes and everything will be alright. You know," she went on, "this city is full of strange things . . . and now this demon, this alien, is in our midst . . . and we've got to find a way to get rid of it, or else we're done for! The very moral fibre of our society is at stake! Get up now and go to your husband, go on, go and tell him just five minutes. The djinn, oh my, the djinn . . ."

Even though I knew he wouldn't agree, I got up and went to his door. She came with me, and we stood there, together, knocking on the door, over and over again, to no avail. She started speaking to him in that throaty voice of hers, begging him to open and let her in just for five minutes, but he wouldn't. She reminded him that he had once asked her to summon the spirit of our boy, Ahmad, and that she was ready to do so now, provided that he opened the door. Just five minutes, she insisted. There was absolutely no response, we couldn't even hear him: he was probably sitting up in bed, stock-still. We went back to the living room. Sitt Khadijah was clearly disheartened.

"The situation's desperate," she said. "Let's try something else. Although I haven't ever before come across the particular djinn that's possessed your husband, we'll try another way. You know, don't you, that djinns love to inhabit cats; they prefer cats to people, don't ask me why, I couldn't tell you. What do you think of this? I'll go and buy him a cat, a completely black cat, and I'll make sure it's not possessed, and then we'll slip it into his room . . . Then, hopefully – there are no guarantees, you understand – the evil djinn will leave your husband and enter the cat, and you'll be relieved and so will he, poor man."

I said I agreed, but what if Khalil didn't?

"Well, at that point only God can help," she replied.

She sat down and began to fidget, as if she wanted to get up again, and added, "Let me have a hundred lira, dear, and I'll get the cat."

"One hundred lira for a cat!" I exclaimed in astonishment.

"If not more," she said. "But I'm mindful of your circumstances. I've got to find a cat that's not possessed and then I have to make sure that it's receptive to the djinn. Some cats resist, you know – and that's all very costly. Well . . . it's as you wish, please yourself . . ."

Sitt Khadijah got up as if to leave. I went to the cupboard, got a hundred lira, and gave it to her.

"The cat will be here tomorrow, by the grace of God."

The next evening, she brought me a little black kitten with shiny eyes and a coat like charcoal, so glossy and lush it practically glowed in the dark. She handed me the cat and left.

I held the poor creature in my arms for a moment, but then it scurried off and hid under the sofa. After a while, I heard some mewing and saw the cat creeping out from its hiding place – and it frightened me! It seemed to me that the cat was the djinn! Dear Lord, how was I to sleep that night? I gave him a bit of bread dipped in some leftover *labneh*, and he ate hungrily, stopping every now and then to look up at me, as though afraid the bread would vanish. Imagine that! The kitten was afraid, when it was me who felt petrified! Anyhow, I left him to eat by himself, and slipped off to Ahmad's room and went to sleep. Ahmad's room, with all the memories and grief it brought back, was preferable to being in the same room as the black cat.

In the morning I looked for him and when I found him, he came to me; he was strangely docile, so I took him with me when I went in to do my husband's room. I also took in a cardboard box with some sand in it, and a small carton of *labneh*. I thought to myself, Khalil would know it was for the cat.

When Khalil came back from the bathroom and locked the door behind him, there was no indication he had noticed anything different. I stood listening behind the door but I didn't hear any unusual noises – just the cat mewing softly and the sound of Khalil's footsteps padding across to him, and little murmurs of "Puss, puss, here puss," as if he were trying to beckon the cat. Then, nothing, just silence, and the rustle of paper . . . nothing out of the ordinary. The next day, I left the bedroom door open while I cleaned inside, and to my great surprise the cat didn't want to leave the room. Thank God, I thought, soon you'll be well, Abu Ahmad.

But in fact nothing changed. Except that the room started to smell. I would clean and change the litter every day, but the smell wouldn't go away. And then it happened . . . I don't know exactly what it was that day, but it was around four o'clock in the afternoon, and I was sitting in the living room by myself, knitting – my daughter Nada was expecting her second child, and it would be a boy with the grace of God. She said she'd call him Ahmad, so that once again I would have a little Ahmad to play with, just as I did with my own little one – so I was knitting, something out of blue wool, in anticipation of his arrival. That's when I heard these strange noises coming from my husband's room: things falling on the floor and the cat wailing. Then the mewing became frantic, I heard Khalil shouting and something crashing to the ground. When I put my ear to the door, I could hear him panting and jumping up and down on the bed, so I knocked and told him to open up; I was really frightened, and I fell to my knees, and begged him to open the door, for me, your wife, I told him. But there was no answer, just the sound of his panting and shouting and crashing objects. Dear God, preserve us from your wrath, I said, and then I heard this almighty racket. It must be the chair, I thought, he must have hurled it across the room, I'd better break into the room. I wanted to break down the door, but the noises coming from the room paralysed me . . . He's going to die, I thought . . . it's the djinn, that's what it is. And then, just like that, everything went still. There was dead silence, I knocked at the door once again, I heard him coughing, and I went back to the kitchen.

I don't know what happened that day, but things basically reverted to how they were, nothing really changed. Well, except for the cat. I could see that he'd changed . . . how shall I put it, I mean he began changing colour. Even though he was a black cat, his blackness began veering to white, it was closer to grey, a dirty sort of grey. The fur on his neck was all puffed up. And he'd stopped mewing – he just sat in a corner of the room and didn't move. But it was the smell . . . That smell became unbearable, even though I did everything under the sun to get rid of it. What was I to do? And him – Khalil, I mean, he seemed oblivious . . . he didn't seem bothered by the cat, or by the fact that it had changed colour, or even by the smell. So I still don't really know what happened that night. I asked Khalil, and I asked the cat, did they have a fight? I didn't think so, the room was just the same as before, there was nothing different about it, and there was no evidence of any fighting. It must be the djinn, I thought. But do djinns make those kinds of noises? I don't know, I swear to God I no longer understood anything.

And then he died. The cat, I mean. He died without a name – in our preoccupation with Khalil and the djinn, we never gave the cat a name, so he died nameless.

When I went into the room that morning, I found the poor scrawny-necked thing lying on the floor, motionless. I wrapped him in a newspaper and threw him out on the street where we dump the rubbish. When I got back, Khalil was sitting on the edge of the bed. I asked him to leave the room so that I could clean. He did, and after I was done I found him sitting in the living room in his usual corner, listening to the radio. Seeing me come in, he smiled and asked me what I was going to cook. I told him I was making macaroni.

"That's great," he said.

Al-hamdulillah, it had worked, Sitt Khadijah's plan had worked! I asked him to come with me and we went into the bathroom, where I got him to change his pyjamas. He washed for the first time in days and then I dressed him in fresh pyjamas, sat him in the living room, and went into the kitchen to prepare lunch. Although he went back to his bed, he left the door open. When I went in and sat beside him and asked him if he was hungry, he said yes, and I brought him a plateful of macaroni. He polished it off, eating with his old gusto.

"I want to sleep, leave me now," he said.

So I did, but the door remained open all that day and all night. I didn't dare sleep by his side, I was afraid, no, not of him, but . . . oh! I don't know, I was just afraid . . . But I thanked God that the djinn had departed and Khalil was himself again.

In the morning, my husband got up, dressed, and said he was going to work. I can't describe to you how happy I was. But then he switched on the radio and sat in the living room.

"What about work?" I asked.

"I'm just going to listen to the news before I go," he replied.

I rushed over to Sitt Khadijah. I told her the whole story and kissed both her hands. Khalil's cured, I told her, and asked if there was anything else I should do. She advised me to burn incense in the room. She gave me some – only after I'd paid a pretty penny for it, mind you – and I went back home.

When I got there, I found him in the room, sitting on the edge of the bed, staring into space . . . I spoke to him, but he didn't even turn round . . . so I started on the incantations and the incense-burning. His face was furrowed with wrinkles, and he seemed totally absent. Oh Lord, Lord, what is going on, what is happening to us, I said to myself . . . his face . . . that's not a face . . . so thin and wrinkled, and with those big dark rings under his eyes. He gestured for me to leave the room, so I did, and I heard the key turn in the lock.

He went back to his old ways, and nothing did any good any-more. To tell the truth, I'm not one to believe in djinns and demons, this cat business was all nonsense, as far as I could tell, sheer superstition, just a ploy to make people part with their money! Still, what is it, I thought, what is he doing to himself acting like that, I really didn't understand . . . and what made it worse was that I didn't know what I could do to help him. Honestly, it's wretched being a woman, putting up with a man's every whim! I couldn't go on like this much longer, with no-one to turn to – it's as if there weren't a soul in the city left! Where were my neighbours! Where was everybody? Why had they left me all alone with a sick man and abandoned me?

What can I say, we'd become a story, a mirror. We'd become . . . Oh, Lord, I thought, preserve us from prying eyes . . . People looked at me and recoiled, as if I had the plague. It was all Khadijah's fault, she was the one who spread rumours about the djinn, and no-one would come to visit us anymore.

And him?

Well, he lied when he said he was going to work. I'm telling you, before my very eyes, he stood there and told a barefaced lie: he didn't go to work at all. He went somewhere and bought these useless things, these pencil rubbers . . . All sorts of rubbers, little ones and big ones, yellow ones and white ones and grey ones. There were rubbers everywhere . . . what for? I found them scattered around his bed one day, and when he came into the bedroom and saw me looking them over, he swept them all up and cradled them in his arms like you would an infant, shaking his head back and forth. He leaned down to pick up some rubbers that had dropped to the ground, and dropped a few more; I bent down to help him, and then when he had them all securely in his grip, he laughed, and these great big yellowed teeth filled his face – it was the first time I noticed that he had such large teeth – and I felt afraid all of a sudden. He could attack me, I thought. Imagine, feeling afraid of my own husband, after a lifetime spent together . . . but, there it is, I was afraid.

"Khalil, what are all these for?" I asked. "Please answer me, and let's be done with all this."

But answer me he wouldn't . . . He just laughed . . . No eating that day, no leaving the room, just laughing . . . My goodness, even his teeth laughed!

He stopped locking the door – so I could go in whenever I felt like it – and started doing these strange things: he'd take a rubber and rub it over the skin of his hand, as if he were trying to erase something written there. He just muttered at me when I asked what he was doing, he'd taken to muttering constantly. Sometimes he played with the rubbers: he'd line them up along one side of the bed, or gather them all together and hurl them against the wall.

Then I discovered that this rubber business wasn't a joke, it was serious. I found him one day working on the newspaper cuttings about Ahmad. Naturally, like any other family, we'd kept all the news reports about our dead son and put them in a big manila envelope – we never looked at them, though, just kept them as mementos. He had pulled out the envelope and, seated on the floor, spread all the clippings around him. He rubbed out tirelessly.

"What are you doing?" I asked him.

"Working," he answered, looking up.

Not another word. Just "working" . . .

He worked, let's call it that, all day long. I couldn't bear to be in the same room with him anymore, I was really fed up, and I just let him be. To begin with, I had tried to steal the cuttings away from him, but that had driven him wild, and he'd thrown himself over them on the ground and refused to move. He could always go out and buy another lot, so I relented.

Rubbing out, that's what he did: at first, it was just the pictures, photographs of Ahmad. He'd start with the eyes, go down to the chin, and then work his way up to the nose – even when the paper tore, he just carried on. All day long, he worked feverishly, constantly muttering, as if possessed, or something . . .

I didn't tell anybody. I certainly wasn't going back to Khadijah, and he flatly refused to see the doctor. At least he was eating now, even if it was only once a day; and I could go in to him whenever I wanted.

Then he began rubbing out the newsprint. He'd erase Ahmad's name: first the surname, Jaber, then the word Khalil, then Ahmad, then the word martyr, and then everything written about him.

All day long, he rubbed-out, and then at night, I suppose he was having trouble sleeping because he'd sit up in bed absolutely still. He didn't turn on the lights, but he wasn't asleep either – he simply sat up against the headboard, eyes wide open.

Once he was done with the newspaper cuttings, he moved on to the posters. He had stashed away about ten of them in the wardrobe, after he had stopped pasting them up all over the neighbourhood following the rejection of his request for reprints from the local party cadre. There was only the one hanging on our bedroom wall, and he never again brought up the subject of the posters.

Now the posters were scattered all over the room, and he was kneeling over them on the floor. When I asked him what he was doing, it wasn't so much a question as a hysterical outburst. "I'm working, this is work," he said. His "work" consisted of rubbing out the blown-up images of Ahmad's face: first the eyes, then the chin, and then, when nothing but grey was left and the paper started to tear from all the rubbing, he moved on to the print. I lost my temper.

"You can't do that," I shouted. "He's our son, you brute! First they killed him and now you want to wipe him off the face of the earth!"

I don't know what got into me, but I was screaming like a madwoman. He stared at me vacantly, as if he hadn't heard anything, and went back to what he was doing: muttering and "disappearing" the words methodically, holding the poster down with one hand, rubbing with the rubber, and then softly blowing away the debris. Seeing him like this – looking up at me, eyes dilated, still blowing at the paper – just made me angrier, and all of a sudden, I found myself hitting him. As I pummelled his head and face he stood completely still, but when I grabbed the posters and tried to wrench them from him, that's when he began shouting at me to get out.

"Give me the posters!" I shouted back, trying to pull them from his grasp, but he held on tight. As I tugged at them again, the posters tore. The sight of them ripped was like an electric shock for him: as if the demons had departed all at once, as if . . . how can I put it . . . He stood there staring at the posters, and as his whole body shook, great big tears rolled down his cheeks, glistening in the white growth coming through his beard. Straightening up, he teetered and made his way over to a corner of the room, where he crouched down with his face in his hands.

I went to him. "Khalil, forgive me," I said to him.

He did not lift his head, and his body was wracked with sobs.

To be honest, at that point I got scared. Dear God, what have I done? I thought. The man is sick and I'm just making him worse. Damn the posters! Let him tear them all up if it makes him feel better . . . what's it to me?

No longer knowing what to do, I left the room and didn't go back in for several days after that, leaving him alone to do as he pleased. I would just take in a plate of food, some bread and water, and leave them for him. Even cleaning became impossible: what was there to clean anyway? I was afraid he'd get upset and start crying again if he saw me removing the shreds of torn paper. I left everything as it was, with him between the corner and the torn posters. The rubbers had disappeared, except for a small one lying on a torn poster; and now there were knives scattered over the ground, along with a straight razor and some tiny blades.

And he started all over again, except that now he wasn't rubbing out anymore, he was shredding the posters. He sliced the paper into tiny shreds that he dipped in water, kneaded into little balls of brownish dough, and then lined up all along the wall chuckling quietly to himself.

37

I tell you, these things happen . . . The man was sick, his nerves had given out and he was at the end of his tether. No, his job had nothing to do with it. Perhaps Imm 'Imad was right after all, maybe she was, but I wasn't asking for anything, I swear I made no demands on him – sex isn't everything, you know, and anyway what would I want with sex after all that had happened?

Days passed like this, with him holed up inside the room and me going along with whatever he did, so there was no more tension between us. But then he was finished with the newspaper cuttings and the posters, and there was nothing left for him to do. I told him one day that I wanted to remove the little "dough" balls from the room but he wouldn't let me.

"I need them," he said. So I left them.

Gradually, he stopped spending all his time in the room. He started walking about the house and opening drawers, as if he were searching for something. When I asked him if I could help in any way, he simply replied, "No."

He'd open a drawer, rifle through its contents, close it, and then open another one. I followed him around and found him carting off all our family photographs: pictures of him as a little boy, of his mother and father, pictures of me and of our wedding, and snapshots of the children – Ahmad in his school uniform, Ahmad the boxer, Ahmad in fatigues. He gathered them all up with this almost childish joy, and carried them off to his room. There he laid them on the floor and set them out ever so carefully . . . into, sort of, crescent shapes. He'd make one crescent, then another, and another, until he had a whole array of identical shapes.

Then he sat down and started: using a bottle of white nail polish, he painted the face over in white and then cut off the head with scissors. He worked carefully and methodically to separate the head from the body. Then he gathered up the severed white heads, shuffled them, and combined each head with one of the decapitated bodies, so he had all these white-headed photographs . . . then he gathered up all the heads again and stacked them next to the crescents of photographs.

"What are those?" I asked him.

"They're everybody's heads," he said; then he began giving them strange names.

"But they're our heads," I said.

"No, no, you don't understand, these are other people's heads. Look, this is the head of Ahmad al-Houmani, and that's his mother's, and that's Munir al-Kaadi's head." He was quiet for a moment, and then, looking at me strangely, added: "I killed them. I killed them, I had to . . . They're the people . . ."

"But who are they?" I asked him.

"They're people from here," he replied, "from Beirut, they work with me at the post office, and I caught them making fraudulent phone calls. I don't know what they were saying, they were speaking in French, but I'm sure about it."

"But they're our heads."

"No, no, no, woman! I'm sure they're the ones behind the disappearance of Jameel Hamdan."

"And who is Jameel Hamdan?"

"Oh, you don't know anything. No-one does . . . but I know. He's a colleague of ours, the one who disappeared. He's my friend, who was hanged."

But no-one was hanged, what was the man talking about? It was true that Jameel Hamdan had disappeared during the war and his body was never found – the young men said he'd disappeared at the Aadliyyeh checkpoint. He was executed, for sure, but he wasn't hanged. In any case, no-one was hanged during this war, there wasn't ever any time: you were kidnapped, tortured – there was a lot of talk of torture, but I never believed a word of it – and then you were shot. And you know how fast a bullet is. But it had nothing to do with me, or my husband, it wasn't any of our business. So why was he talking like that and cutting off those heads? He always said it had nothing to do with us and he was against killing.

Then he set to the hands: he painted them white, cut them out in small rectangles, and stacked them in a pile. Then it was the thighs, until gradually, all that was left of our family photographs was this huge collection of white photograph fragments, stuck to each other with nail polish.

Once he was finished with the family photographs, he again had nothing to do – so he just sat silently, and hardly even walked round the house. I tried to clean up the white fragments strewn across the room, and to tidy up a bit, but he wouldn't let me. I suggested that he shave, since he hadn't in ages, and after hesitating for a long time, he agreed. I heated up some water for him and laid out his razor, shaving cream and brush. When he went into the bathroom, however, he was holding the scissors.

"What are the scissors for?" I asked.

He stood in front of the mirror and began snipping at his beard. As the hairs fell into the basin his face was slowly transformed, but he didn't seem to notice. In fact, he barely glanced at the mirror.

"What are you doing?" I asked.

"Working, working."

He carried on trimming his beard like this, with the tap turned on full; the hairs cascaded down, while he sprinkled the sides of the basin from the cup of hot water he held in the other hand. Then he took the brush, smeared on some shaving cream, and started shaving with the razor, while whistling a Fayrouz tune. I stood watching him.

He finished, and dabbed some aftershave on his cheeks. Then he coated the brush with more shaving cream and began smearing the mirror. As he covered the mirror with foam, little gaps would form, so he kept going over them again and again to make sure everything was covered in white, all the while whistling that little ditty "*Ya Dara Douri Fina*".

He was at it for two hours, and still the gaps kept on appearing, while I stood there watching him without knowing what to do.

"It's over, everything is over," I thought I heard him say.

"What's over?" I asked.

"Nothing, nothing . . . I'm working," he replied.

Then he grabbed a red towel and, after drying his face with it, wiped the mirror clean. He covered it with the towel and then just stood there, as though looking at his reflection.

Then he went to his room and began to rearrange all the bits of paper, the dough and the severed limbs that were scattered over the floor. After laying them all out neatly in a corner of the room, he opened the wardrobe, took out his suit, got dressed, knotted his tie, and went out.

No, before he left he told me he was hungry. He stood in the doorway of the kitchen in his suit and tie and said, "I'm hungry." I noticed how thin he'd grown, and that he looked older. So I sat him down in the kitchen to a plate of fried eggs, which he ate in total silence.

"I'm going," he said, getting to his feet.

"Where to?"

"Work."

"But it's three o'clock in the afternoon. You'll go tomorrow."

He stepped out of the kitchen, got his overcoat from the wardrobe, opened the front door, and hurried down the stairs. I never saw him again.

At first, we thought he'd been kidnapped. I was really terrified – I knew the man was at the end of his tether and might even harm himself. But there was nothing I could do but wait, he never came home, until that day when they turned up with him inside a wooden coffin and that overpowering smell . . . Dear

God, may we be delivered from evil . . . The Day of Judgement was upon us, the final reckoning . . .

Actually, I didn't do a thing with his belongings. While I was waiting for him I didn't do a thing with them. I left everything – the shredded paper and the whitened heads and limbs – just as it was. I thought he'd be back and might get upset.

And now, I don't know why, but I don't dare go into the room. It smells of blood . . . blood and cat! Maybe the blood is from the pictures . . . Oh, Lord . . . I don't know what's happening to me . . . But it smells of blood.

After he died, I threw everything away. I scrubbed the room with soap and water and had it whitewashed. But it still smells, and that frightens me. No, I don't go in now. You can go in if you like, but I won't.

CHAPTER II

Perforated Bodies

Mr Ali Kalakesh, architect at the National Architecture Company in Beirut. Born in Saida, in 1940, married with three children, resident of the Mar Elias district of West Beirut. Known for his social activism – he headed a "popular committee" for the distribution of flour to local bakeries – and for his good-neighbourly relations with everyone. The only blemish in this otherwise perfect picture is the rift with his wife, which, for reasons unknown, almost resulted in divorce. However, they patched things up after she returned from a brief stay with her parents. By his account, he leads a happy family life. He has often visited the home of Khalil Ahmad Jaber to offer his condolences to the victim's wife. He has volunteered to forward any information he gleans to her and to the security authorities concerned, but he is convinced his efforts will be to no avail. He recounts quite spontaneously all that he knows about the deceased, to whom he refers at times, with some reservation, as "the martyr".

What is happening to us is very strange . . . One wonders if it is the result of unexplained mental disorders . . . No-one is able to control all the crime . . . It has grown into an epidemic, a plague devouring us from within . . . I suppose that is what is meant by social fragmentation in civil conflicts – I've read about it, but somehow this seems different . . . you would think they positively savoured murder, like a sip of Coke. Poor Khalil Jaber! But it's not just him . . . he, at least, has found his rest . . . what about the rest of us, the Lord only knows how we will die . . .

Imagine, that Armenian doctor, Dr Khatchadourian, a seventy-

43

year-old man with nothing, or very little, to his name . . . You can't
be a doctor and have nothing . . . but, as I was saying, nothing of any
consequence. They broke into his house . . . What for? . . . Probably
to rob him, which they did, but listen to what else they did . . .
Apparently, he had heard them, he heard their footsteps and
the sound of their voices, and he decided to pretend that he was
asleep, since there wasn't much he could do anyway. But he was
afraid of his wife; she wouldn't stand for it. It had been that way
ever since he'd married her, she wouldn't stand for anything. And
now, if she heard their voices she was sure to get up and start
wailing. So Dr Harout Khatchadourian lay there in bed shivering
with fear, not just because of them, but because of her. She had
already caused trouble with them at the beginning of the war,
strange woman that she was.

She was lying beside him in bed, breathing rhythmically, as
he tried to peer into the dark. But he couldn't see a thing; all he
could distinguish was their voices. He tried shifting his position
slightly, but his limbs felt leaden. Then he turned to her – she was
sure to wake up, she could hear a pin drop in her sleep. Her hearing
was acute, as indeed were all her senses. He used to tell her that
she was all senses, nothing but a bundle of nerves. But she slept
on peacefully and everything was alright.

Dr Harout closed his eyes . . . they were getting closer, they
were bound to find something to take in the living room; now
they were in the other bedroom. He could hear them, why were
they talking so loudly? Usually, robbers speak softly and wear
rubber shoes so no-one can hear them, but this was a reckless
bunch. And then they switched on a light! He could see it,
filtering in through the crack in the door from the room across
the hallway . . . She's going to wake up . . . she's waking up now
. . . and she'll do what she's always done during this war. I told
the woman to keep quiet, but all she said was, "This is our home,
they're robbing our home." So what? Doesn't she understand

44

that our home means nothing when our lives are in danger!

"They'll kill us now, woman, be quiet."

"This is your own home, what kind of a man are you!" she answered me and got ready to go and confront them. In the end she didn't go out, though, it was the gunmen who made *us* leave . . .

It was like this. We were at home that day and there were a lot of explosions going off nearby. I wasn't frightened. I was sitting quietly listening to the radio, and she was reading in the dining room, when we saw them. They had appeared out of nowhere – as if they'd seeped through the walls – with sandbags to stack against the windows.

"What's going on here?" she asked.

They didn't answer her. They were scurrying around the house, bent over double under the weight of those sandbags. She went up to the window where they were stacking the bags.

"What is this?" she asked.

"Shoo," one of them answered. "Go on! Get out of here!"

"What do you mean get out? No, this is our house. You get out."

The man speaking was holding a machine gun pointed at me. I did nothing, just stood there in the corner of the room. He came towards me.

"Take your woman and get out of here."

I did as I was told. I could feel their hands propelling me along from behind, then she fell into step beside me, and they shoved us both outside. They left us in the lobby of the building with a gunman and went back upstairs.

The gunman came up to me and said, "I.D.s." I gave him mine, and after examining it closely, he handed it back.

"And what, if I may ask, do you do for a living?"

"I'm a doctor. A surgeon," I told him.

"Well, good day to you, Doctor, and forgive us but it's for your own sake we're doing this."

"You mean it's for the sake of robbing our house," my wife said.

"And who is the lady?" He was looking at her angrily.

"My wife," I replied. "She's my wife."

"Your I.D., please."

"It's upstairs."

"Go and get it."

To be honest, I was afraid for her at that moment. I told him she was my wife, that she was a little overwrought, because of the situation . . . that she meant no harm.

He said nothing, maybe he believed me, I don't know. Then he started talking, and telling me how they needed doctors, how they were fighting on behalf of the poor and the dispossessed, and how it was my duty as a doctor to collaborate with them. He was genuinely trying to convince me . . . imagine, me practically at death's door and him rattling on about social justice!

I told him I was all for justice and for their cause. But I'm a doctor, I said, and it's my humanitarian duty not to make any political distinctions and to attend to anyone in need.

Then he started telling me how their cause was similar to that of us Armenians . . . and how this and how that . . .

I told him it would be better for them to leave the house and set up their barricades elsewhere, as we had nowhere to go to. He nodded, as if he agreed, but when I tried to go back upstairs, he stopped me.

We stood around like this for about two hours. Then another gunman came and asked us to follow him, and they led us to a nearby building. When we went in, we heard all this screaming and commotion coming from the floor above. Then we saw a boy enter holding two men at gunpoint; he was limping. The men were shaking and they kept glancing back at us over their shoulders as they went, in a silent plea for help. They came to a halt at the end of the hall, and I heard the young gunman with the sore foot asking:

"Which one of you is collaborating with them?"

"Neither."

"You," he said, looking at the fat one who seemed the older of the two.

"No, really, we've nothing to do with it; I swear it's nothing to do with us."

The other man kept looking back over his shoulder, his mouth quivering with fear.

The gunman said that he was going to detain them both, as there were reports that someone from the Fakhoury family, living in Kantari, was collaborating with them. And he told them that if he wasn't able to work out which one of the two was the collaborator, then "over there", at the party office, they surely would. And only the innocent one would be released.

The fat detainee asked the gunman if his foot hurt. Surprised by the question, the gunman said, "It's O.K. It's just a sprain."

That was when the woman appeared. Tall and dark, with a baby in her arms, she goes up to the three men and speaks to them in faltering Arabic, then sinks down to the ground and begins to weep. The gunman is visibly bewildered. She tells him that she's going wherever her husband does, that she has no-one else in this world but him and that she won't let him go alone. The gunman tries to talk her out of it but in fact he has no idea what to say; his shoulders slump in discouragement.

I decided to intervene. I told the gunman that I was Dr Harout Khatchadourian and that, as a local resident, I knew them both and could guarantee that they had nothing to do with politics whatsoever. He looked at me sympathetically.

"But I can't let them go," he answered me, "I just can't. Those are my orders." Resting the rifle on his lap, he squatted next to the woman as she wept and said, "Listen, sister, what can I do? I simply can't . . . you must understand my position. Please stop crying and try to understand."

But her weeping only increased. The two men looked at each other, at her, at us, and at some other people who had also been gathered and brought in. In the end I saw the gunman leading them all away – the two men, the woman, and the child – and showing them out to the street. Before he left he turned to me:

"I swear I did it for you, Doctor."

I thanked him and asked him to take us home.

"Honestly, if it weren't for that woman," he went on . . . "She's just a foreigner and has nothing to do with all this . . . poor woman, I had to release them . . . don't you think . . ."

Then he left. He said he'd be back but I never saw him again during any of my frequent visits to the apartment. I couldn't ever ask after him because I didn't know his name.

As for this wife of mine, she's going to be the death of me. Another man came that day and told us we would have to leave the neighbourhood because the area was now a war zone. I believed him – the gunmen were ducking and weaving across the streets and running for cover; how could we continue to live here?

When I told the man that I agreed, and we would leave, she lunged at him, screaming. He stepped back, grabbed his rifle, and started shooting in the air. It was the first time I had heard a machine gun at such close range – the sound of the Kalashnikov ripped through the air, blasting our ears, and the shells tore from it and hit the concrete floor in a rapid, brassy yellow flash. All of a sudden, I had this urge to urinate. She froze and then fell to the ground.

And ever since, whenever I remember that incident, I feel thirsty and need to urinate. You should have seen those shells . . . I didn't realize that they were empty, I don't know what I thought they were, but it never occurred to me they were just blanks.

Whenever we talk about the house in Kantari nowadays, I always say the machine gun was urinating. She smiles and says I'm good for nothing but passing water anymore! And I can hardly manage even that with my wretched prostate problem! Even though I'm a doctor, and a surgeon to boot, I'm frightened of going under the scalpel. I tell her I'm no longer a real man – if I were, I would have made sure she left quietly without all that hollering and screaming and carrying on. I feel an odd sort of tenderness for her, though, as if she were my sister, as if we'd been born together, and I fret that she might die. She's obstinate, you know; she always made me go and check on the apartment, even though we were living with our daughter on Hamra Street by then, and we lacked for nothing. I used to go, hear the gunmen hurling insults at each other across the barricades, and come back. She only ever asked about the furniture, and I would make up some lie – I never went upstairs, they wouldn't let me and I didn't insist . . .

And now here she is again, in this same house with a whole set of new furniture that she went out and so painstakingly bought – as though we were newlyweds – and I'm feeling frightened . . . she's bound to wake up and cause another to-do . . .

The sound of their approaching footsteps grew louder. The door was opened quietly and he clamped his eyes shut. The woman stirred, awoke, and then started screaming. He would have liked to tell her to be quiet, he would have liked to say that he was the man and that she should therefore listen to him, but the hot liquid just burst forth from his entrails. He didn't even hear the gunfire, all he felt was this sudden thirst tearing at him, he remembered that he hadn't had any water to drink before going to bed, and now he was desperate for some water . . . he didn't want to die of thirst like they do in films. It was only when he tried to get out of bed that he heard the gunfire.

Now tell me, how is it possible . . . I read about it in the paper, as I did with poor Khalil Jaber . . . how can they do such things?

Three gunmen breaking into an apartment, murdering a doctor, raping his wife and killing her, then robbing the place and leaving! A nineteen-year-old raping a woman of sixty-five! How have we come to this? That poor Khalil, God rest his soul, how they tortured and then finally killed him – at least that's what they said in the papers . . . I always used to see him wandering around, he was perfectly harmless, he wouldn't hurt a fly – yes, he loitered on the pavement, looking this way and that, but that's hardly an offense warranting such a grisly death.

I followed the story of Dr Khatchadourian's murder in the press, and found the confessions of the perpetrators after they were arrested truly mind-boggling. Imagine, three young men, Sameer as-Samad, Ahmad al-Husseini, and Assem Kallaj – respectively, nineteen and employed in a novelty store on Hamra Street; twenty and unemployed; and the third, a twenty-four-year-old card-carrying member of one of the political parties – committing a crime of that magnitude and then being exposed because they fell out over a bracelet that belonged to the doctor's wife. Could it get any more disgraceful? This Sameer fellow, in particular, made my blood boil. The way he recounted it was that they were all from the same neighbourhood and that they plotted the crime after Assem had gone to take a look at the apartment under the pretext of seeing the doctor about an inflamed appendix. Then one night they went up to the apartment armed with pistols and knives. After breaking in through the front door, they began searching the living room for silver, but then they heard footsteps: it was the doctor shuffling to the kitchen in his slippers. When he switched on the light, the three of them looked at each other uncertainly. Assem Kallaj was the first to react: he leapt into the passage between the living room and the kitchen; there he watched the old man panting as he filled a bottle with water from the plastic measuring jug on the kitchen floor. His bottle filled, the doctor poured himself a glass of water and drank; then, taking the bottle and the glass with him, he left the kitchen. He turned off the light and went towards the entrance hall, feeling along the wall with his left hand for the light switch. Unable to locate it, he lost his balance and the bottle of water fell to the ground and broke. Instinctively stepping back, he then dropped the water glass, and it too shattered. So then he made his way back to the kitchen. There he switched the light on and found a pistol aimed at his face as Assem clamped a hand over his mouth, hissing "Shhh!" Absolutely terrified, the doctor shook from head to foot. He sagged over the water jug, straightened up, and tried to make a run for it. Stumbling across the broken glass, he felt his way down the hallway once more, halted an instant, and then dashed for the door. Just as he got there, Assem fired a shot. Hit in the back, the doctor staggered and sank to the ground, into a pool of blood.

"He's dead!" Assem cried. There was the sound of a stifled moan.

"Not quite." Sameer came over and shot the doctor in the head at close range. "Now he's dead. Come on, let's get out of here."

"But we didn't take anything."

"Everything's in the bedroom and the wife is in there. Let's go!"

Ahmad went towards the room, they followed behind, and as he flicked the light on, his gun pointed straight ahead, the white-haired head of a woman rose from the pillow. "What is it? What's going on? Why all this shooting? Out, do you hear me! Get out! Out of our house! This is our home!"

Ahmad, gun in hand, tells her to be quiet.

"Where's the jewellery?" he asks.

"We don't have anything left, you people have taken everything. There's nothing here. Where's Harout? Get out, get out of here!"

As Ahmad takes a step towards her, the woman tries to jump

out of the bed. Just then Sameer enters the room and, as he makes his way towards her, he knocks over all the water bottles lined up along the side of the bed. The bottles break, both the empty ones and the full ones. The woman tries to get to her feet; Sameer sits on the edge of the bed removing the shards of glass caught in his trousers. Ahmad approaches the woman clinging to the blanket, and he clamps his hand over her mouth to silence her and immobilize her on the bed. Pushing the blanket off to free herself, the woman exposes her thighs, and at that instant Sameer throws himself on top of her to pin her down. Later, she is found murdered, with injuries from stabbing and gunshot wounds. According to the forensic pathologist's report, she was raped before being killed.

The bodies were discovered two days later in the caretaker's room, on account of the putrid smell in the building's lobby.

The investigating magistrate was apparently flabbergasted by the way the three young men conducted themselves after they were arrested. Evidently, they exhibited no feelings of remorse and were not the slightest bit fearful of the investigation and the prospect of imprisonment. They responded to his questions in a calm and matter-of-fact way, and even told jokes, as he tried to establish the motives for the murders and the rape.

Assem's account: Sir, it's quite simple really. Everyone else has got rich in this war, and we were down and out, so when we discovered that the doctor owned some valuable jewellery, we thought we'd rob him. We had no intention of killing him. But he got up just as we were getting started, and when he turned on the light and tried to run, we got scared we'd be found out. So we killed him. Then we went into the bedroom, and before we had even taken anything worth mentioning, the woman started to wail and scream. She tried to get out of bed, so we did what we did and fled. You can't trust anyone these days, it's a disgrace! We told an old friend who works in a pharmacy what happened, and he's the one who snitched. And it's only because we have no connections in high places that we've been arrested. That's all there is to it.

Sameer is quiet and then recounts how he raped the woman.

"How could you rape a woman your mother's age, if not your grandmother's?" the magistrate asks.

Sameer says he hadn't thought about it beforehand, it just happened, by accident.

"Ahmad had covered her mouth to stop her screaming, and I was sitting on the edge of the bed in case he needed help, and when I saw her trying to struggle out of the bed, I jumped on her. Holding her head down with one hand, I put my other hand on her thighs so she would stop her kicking, and when I felt her naked skin under my hand all of a sudden . . . I don't know exactly how it happened . . . but I felt incredibly aroused, as if I had desired this woman forever. I didn't even take off my pants: I just pulled out my member and let it find its way. I didn't have to undress her, either, I slid right in, and the strange thing is that she didn't say anything or try to resist – well, yes, she pulled at my shirt and the buttons all ripped off, but she didn't struggle – or maybe she couldn't. Anyway, after I finished and got off her, I felt really sick. I was so disgusted with myself that I pulled out my knife and stabbed her. And then, seeing the rivulets of blood seeping into the room from the hallway and the kitchen, I took a step back and fired one shot at her. Then we ran. No, before that, I pulled off the gold bracelet glittering on her wrist covered with age spots.

"Don't ask me why, but they tried to take the bracelet from me, and I wouldn't let them. It's mine, I told them, and mine alone. I was the one who did everything. Then they went and told that dog of a pharmacy boy . . . I'm gonna kill him."

Ahmad interrupts and recounts how he was caught off guard, how he had his hand clamped over her mouth, and then all of a sudden, Sameer was on top of her and he began to take her while I looked on. I could hear him panting, or was it her . . . no, it wasn't her, she wasn't panting, she was as stiff as a corpse. I couldn't see her face – he was going at it like a billy goat. Naturally, I felt a little excited too, I'm only human, I'm not made of stone, but I was scared at the same time: I was afraid that someone would come and see what we were doing, so I yelled at him to finish so we could leave. But he didn't hear me: he was writhing on top of her like a fish. Then he straightened up and stabbed her. The strange thing is she didn't fight or even try to get out of the bed after Sameer was done with her. Then, when the blood gushed out, he shot her with the pistol, grabbed the bracelet, and we took off.

Assem was waiting for us at the front door, gun in hand. He wanted to know what had taken us so long, and then, seeing Sameer's blood-spattered clothes, he asked us what had happened.

"We killed her," I answered.

"Did you find anything?"

"Sameer has the jewellery."

Then we went to my house and Sameer took off his clothes and showered. He said he felt nauseous, that the smell was killing him, and he needed a 7-Up. When we went out in the morning, he got his 7-Up, and we all had some *foul*. But he refused to give us the bracelet. Then I told the pharmacist – not on account of the bracelet, it wasn't worth the trouble – but I told the bastard for laughs, how Sameer had screwed a woman his grandmother's age, and he went and squealed! He claims it's because the doctor was his friend and he felt sorry for him. That's what he says, but I'm sure it's just because he used to get a cut on the prescriptions the doctor wrote . . . the medication mafia . . . you know what I mean. And because we don't have connections in high places, nobody's got our back – actually everyone turned their back on us – and we're not regarded as "part of the bedrock of society" . . . meaning that we're expected to do the shit work while they reap the benefits . . . that's why we're being investigated . . . well, I have my pride, and I'm not willing to be someone else's skivvy!

The magistrate was speechless as he watched them reenacting the crime with the utmost matter-of-factness; they showed him how they carried the two corpses out of the apartment, took them down in the lift, dumped them in the empty caretaker's quarters, and then locked the door behind them and pocketed the key.

Such a heinous crime – it makes you shudder just thinking about it . . . And Khalil, poor man, he hadn't done anything . . . I told you I used to see him out and about – he was completely harmless, just an ordinary man. Only now do I understand what was ailing him . . . it was his nerves . . . all these wars had shattered his nerves . . . honestly, we're all at the end of our tethers. So what if he stood on the pavement in his suit and tie as if he'd lost something? Why kill him? . . .

Dr Khatchadourian's son, a young man in his thirties, was finishing medical school in America. He was at Georgetown University, in Washington, D.C., when he had to come back for his parents' funeral. He told anyone willing to listen that he couldn't understand how a nineteen-year-old was capable of raping a sixty-five-year-old woman.

Poor Father, the bane of his existence was that he could never quench his thirst! There was never enough water as far as he was concerned. He'd drink and drink and was always afraid of water shortages and the dark. He'd collect all the bottles and put them by the side of his bed, as if the water might run away. Whenever I came back to Beirut on short visits, he'd talk about how the water was contaminated and how you had to boil and filter it thoroughly because it was full of germs. I used to tell him he should drink the mineral water you could get in plastic bottles, but he wouldn't: he said those bottles were tampered with, that the water wasn't pure, and that it was probably even more polluted and dangerous than tap water.

I felt sorry for him in his old age because of the way he used to forget things. He'd fill one bottle and then, forgetting the first one,

55

he'd fill another. My mother barely looked after him anymore. She gave the impression that she couldn't stand him and was always making fun of the way he urinated, standing in the bathroom for hours with the water running. My advice to him was that he shouldn't drink so much water. Where was it to go after all? I told him if you need to drink that much water, why don't you go ahead and have the prostate operation? But he'd just get angry and go and sit alone in a corner of the living room, refusing to speak to me.

I don't know what happened to my mother . . . She wasn't looking after the house anymore, or cooking the delicious, spicy food that I miss every single day in America. No vegetables, no meat, and no eggs for her: the days of eating are over, she'd say. She had taken to drinking vast quantities of milk – and Father did the same. The house stank of milk, but whenever I tried to suggest that they should have something besides that, my mother wouldn't hear of it.

"I like milk, my son. And your father, he too can drink milk. It's better than water."

Milk was everywhere: the milk in glass bottles, and the powdered kind, in tins. The kitchen floor was littered with empty tins mother wouldn't throw away. "I never throw anything away," she'd say.

Now they're dead, and there's no longer any reason for me to come back to Beirut. I'm just going to leave – the house, the furniture, everything. Let them have it, all of it, I don't want a thing. I used to beg them to come with me to America, but they never would. You'd think Beirut was Armenia! I told Father that he was entitled to leave without feeling guilty. Leaving Beirut isn't an act of treason, I'd tell him, but he'd say, "What about our home? People shouldn't abandon their homes!"

I think I'd like to meet their killers . . . Well, maybe not . . . I wonder why they did that to my mother . . . No, no, I'm leaving and

I don't want to see anybody . . . They all despise me anyway: I saw how they behaved at the funeral, sniggering and grimacing, and then sitting in our house drinking coffee and smoking cigarettes, making conversation and laughing! You'd think we were having a party they were having such a good time! A funeral a party! No, no, I don't want to see anybody, I just want to leave.

Ali Kalakesh recalls:

I remember the first time I met Khalil. I don't recall the exact day, but I was on my way home one evening, slightly breathless from the load of fruit and vegetables I was carrying, when I saw this man standing on the pavement across the road from our building. He greeted me, or I thought he did . . . In any case, he nodded and muttered something; dressed in a well-cut suit, he looked as if he might be waiting for someone, but he had this bewildered air about him – unshaven, a vacant look about the eyes, a mouth that seemed to be quivering. Come to think of it, I don't think he said anything to me, it was just his mouth quivering.

Climbing up the stairs to the apartment, I didn't give him another thought – there wasn't anything to think about. I went in, washed my face, and, as was my habit, slumped down in front of the T.V. with a glass of whisky and started telling my wife about my day. At about ten o'clock that evening I heard gunfire on the street, so I went out to the balcony to see what was happening, and there he was again, facing the wall with his back to the street, his hands moving up and down as if he were plastering something onto the wall, or taking something down. I couldn't quite make out what he was up to. I remember being puzzled and thinking to myself that it was strange. But I went back inside and thought no more of it – I didn't even bother telling my wife about him, I just went to bed and fell asleep.

Things began to get complicated, at least from my point of view, when my friend Musa Kanj came to visit. We go back a long way, Musa and I. I first met him when he came to our office seeking help with the redecoration of his apartment. I went to see the place and met his wife, Nadia. She was a pretty brunette with long hair, who seemed to be twenty years younger than him; she was the one who discussed all the details of the work with me. At my suggestion, they bought some fairly expensive furniture, for which Musa paid quite happily – he had his heart set on pleasing his wife in whatever way possible – and the work was completed swiftly. Nadia was a divorcée, and it surprised me that a man of Musa's wealth who owned a fabric store in Souq Taweeleh would marry a divorced woman with two children. But, I guess those are love's hidden ways and love overcomes all things . . . Then we all became friends. One day my wife went to Musa's store to buy some fabric, and he wouldn't take any payment from her. We exchanged visits, and the two women grew close; over time our relationship deepened and grew stronger.

The war didn't seem to affect Musa. The store burned down, but he opened another one, on Television Avenue. To tell the truth, he wasn't really working anymore – the sales clerks were the ones who ran the store, he just dropped in at around ten every morning to check up on things and have some coffee, then he headed home. He really didn't do much at all and behaved as if there was nothing wrong.

I found out from my wife that Nadia had come into a lot of money – I mean millions – after the death of one of her uncles in the Congo. It seems that my friend Musa was looking for ways to spend this windfall, so one day he came to see me and told me that he had bought a new house. "But you've already got a really nice place," I said.

"Oh, but this one is much better, with both sea and mountain views. It's amazing!" And he asked me to help him refurbish the place.

"I want parquet everywhere – we'll rip out all the tile floors and replace them with parquet! No tiling anywhere! And all the furniture must be Italian. Cost is not an issue. I want a stupendous house!"

I agreed, and we set to work. When I went over to the new house, I was dumbfounded: marble floors stretched all the way from the entrance to the end of the living room!

"It's a pity, Musa, a real pity to replace this marble with parquet," I told him.

"No, that's how I want it. All wood, just like houses in Europe," he insisted.

I was baffled. I said, "I don't agree with you, but will do whatever you wish."

Musa's eyes danced with delight as he looked over at his wife, who was there in some tight-fitting black trousers with one of her sons, wandering around the apartment. And so we set to work. Nadia was at the site every day, and Musa came past once in a while. The fact is that nothing happened between us, nothing at all, the thought didn't even cross my mind, nor hers I am sure – and in any case, the place was teeming with workmen! Nevertheless, somehow or other, the devilish thought took hold of him.

He came over to our apartment one day and asked to see me alone. After my wife left us in the living room, he got up and closed the door.

"It's about Nadia," he said.

"What about her?"

"You and her – I know everything!"

What was this man talking about? His face had gone crimson, and he had this glazed look in his eyes.

"Nadia and you," he repeated. "I know about it . . . But you're a friend, how could you?"

I tried to explain, but it didn't do any good. "Honestly, Musa, there's nothing like that going on. Your wife is a respectable woman – she's like a sister to me. I don't know how you got that idea into your head – it must be all the stress . . ."

"It's true I'm very tired," he answered. "I'm at a loss, at a complete loss what to think . . . but you're a friend . . ."

Then he asked how the work was progressing at the house, questioning Nadia's frequent presence there, our long conversations, and our visits to furniture galleries and cafés together. I told him that when she went to the Italian furniture dealer – because she liked to pick things out for herself – she requested, indeed demanded, that I accompany her. I assured him that he was my friend, and that nothing had happened, I swore, nothing.

I'm not sure why he believed me so quickly, but it must have been because it was the truth – the truth is quick to convince, apparently. "You're a real friend," he said, patting me on the shoulder. I offered him a drink and he asked for a whisky. I got up and opened the living-room door, and my wife brought us two tumblers of whisky on ice. We drank under her questioning gaze, and as soon as he'd downed his drink, he got up and announced he was leaving. I tried to keep him but he insisted on going. After shutting the front door, my wife asked why he had come.

"No reason in particular . . . He just wanted to find out about the new house."

"You're lying! I heard Nadia's name being mentioned; what did he say about her?"

"Nothing." And I picked up the paper and pretended to start reading.

"I heard everything! About you and Nadia," she said, bursting out laughing. Sitting down beside me, she added, "Poor guy! I know what's going on, Nadia tells me everything!"

No, it wasn't Nadia that caused the tension in our relationship, nor the car accident.

"I know everything, Nadia tells me everything," she repeated. "She's told me that her husband can't . . . he can't . . . do it! You know what I mean . . . I mean . . . get it up . . . !"

Nadia had apparently been over one morning and, in a flood of tears, told my wife that Musa was impotent. "It's been like this from the night of our wedding," she had said. "He married me even though he knew he couldn't do it and was taking all sorts of medicines and potions. He said he couldn't help himself, he was haunted by the idea that I was going to cheat on him with every man I saw! Imagine that, me only twenty years old, still studying for my Baccalaureate, with my newly wed husband sitting on the edge of the bed, his back turned to me, puffing angrily on a cigarette, what was I supposed to do? I put on my nightgown and went to sleep – I was tired and went out like a light. In the morning, he told me he hadn't slept all night, and that tonight he would do it. But he never did . . . I spent the day in tears . . . and now he wants me to stop going to the worksite, telling me it's a woman's duty to stay at home! All I feel like doing is crying, but I can't leave him: I was already divorced once and went back to school . . . It's all my parents' fault, they married me off to the first one when I was only sixteen and if I divorce the second one now, people will say I'm a whore . . . No, I won't leave him, I can't, but I want what everyone else wants, just like you."

I told my wife that I didn't understand how Musa, broad as he was tall, and in good health, couldn't do it. And that's when all the trouble started.

My wife and I never had any disagreements until the car accident. It was horrible: that car accident frightened me more than all of the insane shelling that brings down entire buildings. I was driving home from work one day, not far from the U.N.E.S.C.O. roundabout. It was dark and the rain was really coming down. Just as I put on my windscreen wipers, a car appeared out of nowhere, cut in front of me and came to a screeching stop. Several gunmen – I don't remember how many exactly – spilled out, pistols and machine guns raised. I don't remember what they looked like, but I do recall one of them had a gold tooth that glinted in the dark. He came over and banged on my window with a pistol aimed at my face, so I rolled the window down.

"Switch off your lights," he barked. I did as he said. "Get out, get out of the car!"

I was gripping the steering wheel hard, and even though I didn't really want to stay in the car I found myself clinging on, unable to release my grip. Their guns still pointed, one of the gunmen hopped into the front seat, and another one climbed into the back. The barrel of the gun held against my neck was pressing hard into my skin.

"Follow the car in front of you!"

As I switched on the engine and started the car, the gunman in the back seat hit me across the head with his pistol. "Faster," he screamed. "If you try to escape we'll kill you. Not a word out of you. Come on, faster than that!"

I hit the accelerator and, as the car picked up speed, they spat out directions, and I tried to follow the speeding car in front of me. It came to a sudden stop and I had to slam on the brakes to avoid a collision. As soon as we stopped they fell on me, kicking and punching.

"Your money . . . everything you've got!" I gave them everything I had: one thousand lira in cash and a cheque for another fifteen hundred. "More. Come on now!" And they took my watch, my wedding ring, my papers – my I.D. card, passport, and address book – as well as the car keys.

I stood there, with the roar of the sea and the rain all around . . . and nothing, just me, the roiling sea, and the raining sky . . . and them . . .

When I tried glancing over towards the sea, one of the gunmen – the one with the gold tooth, I think – grabbed me by the collar, practically strangling me.

"We're letting you go," he said, "but only because you're a coward and an idiot. You be very, very careful, now . . ."

I told him I hadn't done anything and that the car was new, I hadn't even finishing paying for it.

"Very careful, you hear," he said. "Not a word . . . Next time, we'll kill you!"

"Please, the car . . ."

The gunman got in, turned the ignition, and the two cars sped off. I ran shouting behind them, while they were probably looking out of the rear window and laughing.

Nothing but rain and that surging black sea. I leaned against the railing of the Ouza'ï Corniche and let the water soak my hair and dishevelled clothes. I felt sorry for myself at the thought of walking all the way to Mar Elias through the rain, and I was on the verge of tears. There wasn't a taxi for miles around.

I don't know where I found the strength to do it, but I walked all the way home. And as I did so, I could hear the surging of the sea, and I felt myself surge and fall in unison with it, floating in the air one instant and plunging into the depths the next. Then I began to run, crying and laughing at once, like someone in a dream. When I reached the crossroads, I took shelter from the rain in the doorway of a building and started thinking about my daughter.

"Your Aida's a real problem," her teacher, Madame Helen, had said. "She's seven and still wets herself in class."

The teacher had pursed her lips tight, retouching her lipstick, and claimed the problem had started when Aida refused to sit at her desk, preferring to crouch underneath and bark, like a dog. I had noticed that she'd taken to sitting under tables pretending to be a dog at home, but I hadn't given the matter much thought.

The problem was serious, Madame Helen said, and it was no longer possible to take such a thing lightly, because the habit had begun spreading to the other students. One of the nuns had instructed her to call me to discuss the problem, she said. I told the teacher that I would look after it . . . but really, what could I do? When I broached the subject with my wife, her reply was, "It's normal, the child is frightened." And she said I was to blame; she claimed that it was my way of racing down to the shelter under the building whenever the shelling started that was causing the child's anxiety.

So what was I supposed to do? Still walking in the rain, I thought maybe I should go and see our doctor, and I resolved to call him the following day. And ever since, Sitt Inaam – my wife – hasn't been the same.

First of all, she telephoned all her friends and told them what had happened. Then she said I should report the incident to Comrade Ayyash: "He's a friend of ours and one of the city's prominent leaders."

So I called him, and he came over to hear my story. He listened attentively, drank three cups of coffee, and promised my car would be returned. He took notes as I talked, showing interest in the men's appearance. I told him that all I recalled was the gold tooth on one of them. He scribbled that down and drew a circle around his words. Then he put his notes on the coffee table, next to his American-brand pistol, lit a cigarette, made a call, and issued some vague promises. And that was it!

Then he rose to take his leave, tucking away the pistol; I saw him out to the lift. When I came back into the living room, I found the sheet of paper with his notes detailing the particulars of my Renault – registration number, colour, and so on – and the location of the incident. I tore it up and didn't tell my wife.

Really, that is how all our problems started. I don't know what got into her, but she was transformed overnight, it was as if she had become a completely different woman: she took to praying and fasting and reading religious books; then she started hiding away any alcohol that was in the house, burning incense, and doing other such nonsensical things.

And because I drank – yes, I admit, I drink, and I can't stop . . .

How else are we supposed to put up with all this horror, how does the stupid woman expect me to sleep with her if I don't have a couple of glasses of arrack beforehand – she left the house and went to her parents. But her father just made fun of her, and he was the one who brought her straight home. Since my wife still had her keys on her, they just walked in, the two of them, her father leading her by the hand.

"It looks as if your wife has seen the light," he said as she slipped off to the kitchen, leaving us alone in the living room. The old man looked at me long and hard, and then gave me a pat on the head.

"You're like a son to me, Ali, you know that. I told her that all men drink – how could we not? God created evil and man drinks so we can learn to distinguish between right and wrong!" But then he asked me not to drink at home. He told me how all his life he had drunk alcohol but he never let it into the house.

"It's not proper, my son. Evil must not be brought into the home. When a man comes home, he cleanses himself of evil and treats his wife the best way possible."

So after that I began drinking outside the house, but everything changed. She used to be like a real partner, we discussed everything together. Not anymore. And now, she'll turn her back to me and say no – she flat out refuses me, and the loneliness is practically killing me . . . not even my wife understands me anymore.

Now I really can feel for my friend Musa, even though our problems are not the same. My situation is different from his, but I understand his feelings a little better. Anyhow, that evening I was . . . well . . . you know, I don't frequent such places, but he does . . . I was leaving my office on Makdissi, the street parallel to Hamra; it was about seven o'clock in the evening, and I was thinking about getting my arrack at Baron's after a hard day's work, when I saw him in front of the Beirut-Life bar; he was teetering about next to a slim, blonde bar girl, and was clearly drunk. I didn't meet his eyes, I couldn't, I just went on my way. But then I heard a voice calling from behind, "Ali! Ali!" and when I turned, he waved at me. I gestured to him that I was on my way home, but he was indignant: "What's this? You see me and don't even say hello?"

The street was bustling with people, the scandal there for everyone to see. So, I crossed the street and we shook hands – the girl didn't even turn around, she was indifferent.

"What do you say to a drink?"

I told him I was tired, but maybe some other time.

"Come on, have a drink with me!"

And he pushed the two of us, the bar girl and me, inside the bar. We sat at a table in the corner and after ordering a bottle of whisky, he turned towards me.

"All the girls here are at your disposal," he said. "Take your pick!"

"No, Musa, that's out of the question. I don't go in for this kind of stuff."

"Just one, my good fellow . . . Think of it as an appetizer!"

He gestured towards a mini-skirted blonde casting us sideways glances.

"No, not that one . . ."

"Alright, the brunette then . . . You like brunettes!"

The idea grew on me: a whisky and an appetizer! Why not? So I agreed. He got up and brought her over to our table. She sat down next to me and I poured her a whisky while he dived into some amorous banter with the blonde. He gesticulated and laughed raucously, but the girl was impatient, and her eyes kept flitting towards us. My brunette was gulping her drink fast.

"Careful, that's not tea you're drinking!"

"No, it's whisky."

I told her how I'd read in a cheap magazine that bar girls

drank tea with their customers. But this girl was drinking real whisky, strong stuff, and the magazines were lying. Musa ordered another bottle.

"But we haven't even finished the first one," I pointed out.

"Oh, but this is going to be the mother of all nights! *Ya hala wa ya marhaba* – a warm welcome to all friends – *ya akhi*! You're my friend and I want to celebrate . . ."

I asked the brunette what her name was.

"Anastasia," she said.

"You're not from here, are you?"

She answered in a strange and lilting Arabic, part Egyptian and part Lebanese, that she was originally Greek, but born in Alexandria. I drank to that and told her that Greek girls were famous in Lebanon, and we talked about Marika Spiridon, the ruling madam of the red-light district. My friend raised his glass and offered a toast to Marika and to all the women of the Third World. Then he leaned towards me and whispered that we should drink to Nadia's health.

"Shame on you, Musa . . . How tasteless!"

"Ah, come on, man! Women are like that . . . they're all whores at heart. There is a whore lurking inside every woman, is there not?"

"That's just stupid drunken talk!"

"Ah, 'women, women . . . their cunning is great indeed'!"[‡]

I asked the brunette what brought her to Beirut. She told me that during the war, she'd moved to Cyprus, but that she preferred Beirut. "Even with all the shelling and the fighting, Beirut is still better than any other place."

She edged a little closer and laid her hand on my head, but I was watching my friend and beginning to feel concerned about

---

[‡] An allusion to a verse from *Surat Youssef* in the Qur'an, rendered somewhat inaccurately by the speaker. The original statement speaks of a specific woman rather than all women.

him: he was so drunk, he was about to keel over, and the girl sitting beside him was taking absolutely no notice whatsoever; she was busy following the comings and goings of the other patrons – a couple of young thugs in particular who had just walked in with their pistols displayed for all to see. We seemed like strangers in this world, my friend and I.

As Musa slumped over the tabletop, breathing heavily, the girl looked over the rounded hump of his back and said to me:

"Your friend here, he isn't good for anything."

"What's that?"

"He's useless. I don't know what his story is, but the poor man's useless. Only yesterday . . ."

"No, no, you're wrong . . . He's just . . . tired."

"Uh-oh, don't tell me you're the same!"

"Shut up, bitch!"

"Listen, yesterday we went together but he couldn't do it. He put on some music, then he started drinking – all night long, he wouldn't do it and kept saying he was tired. Let's leave it till tomorrow, he said. And now here we are tomorrow . . . we were just leaving, he and I, but as soon as he saw you coming, he latched on to you . . . only God knows what's the matter with him. He looks healthy enough."

Then she turned to a uniformed man hovering next to her, took his hand gently and winked at him. The man left the bar.

"Mmmm . . . God is my witness, there's nothing like an officer – now there's a real man! Not like your lot!"

I strained to see whether my friend was aware of anything that was going on, but he seemed to be in a stupor. I grabbed hold of him and pulled him to his feet; just then the waiter came with the bill, and Musa, appearing suddenly to regain consciousness, fished out his wallet and insisted on paying.

We walked out into the dark and empty streets. Musa staggered and almost fell, and then began to throw up. After wiping his face with a tissue, he stumbled alongside me.

"The bitch! . . . Says I'm useless . . . eh? Bitches, all of them . . . and now the other one wants to travel!" He told me how Nadia wanted to go to Paris for a fortnight and that he felt obliged to agree. "What the eye doesn't see the heart doesn't grieve over. Let her sleep with dogs, if it pleases her!"

We got a taxi; Musa was maudlin by now. When we reached my house and I asked him in for a cup of coffee, he was quick to accept the offer. Stepping inside the building, we found a man asleep and snoring: wrapped up in a winter coat, his head resting on his left arm, eyes shut and mouth hanging open.

"What's this?" Musa said. "You've got a tramp sleeping in the entrance hall of your building! Come on now!"

"He's a very odd man," I replied. "I often see him wandering the streets, fiddling with bits of paper, and hovering around the walls of the neighbourhood."

"And you let him? He's disgusting and disease-ridden. And what do you mean, he hovers around the walls? You should throw him out!"

Awoken by my friend's voice, the man jumped to his feet and scuttled away. We went upstairs, and I went straight to the kitchen to make the coffee; when I returned to the living room, I found Musa asleep on the couch. I left him there, tiptoed to my bedroom, and went to sleep. When I woke up the next morning he was gone – he had probably woken early and left.

As for the late Khalil, I saw him again that same afternoon. I was walking down the street when I caught sight of him in his overcoat; he was feverishly shredding posters and trying to remove the graffiti from the wall. A bucket of lime by his side, first he'd strip off whatever was on the wall, then whitewash it. I thought maybe he worked for an advertising firm, taking down old posters and replacing them with new ones. But when I got close, I was shocked to see he was stuffing the shreds of paper into his mouth and chewing them. I also realized that he wasn't sticking anything new up on the wall: he was just whitewashing it. After brushing the wall with lime, he wiped his palm across the freshly painted surface, leaving traces of his handprints and splashing white drops of paint onto the pavement.

I tried to speak to him, but as soon as he saw me he started, hastily gathered his things, and ran off, as if he had remembered the incident of the night before. When I got back home, I found both Aida and her mother in tears.

"What's going on?" I asked. My wife led me to the bedroom and locked the door behind us. "It's that man," she said.

"What about him?"

She told me that Aida was frightened by him, that she'd seen his member when he was urinating against the wall, and then he turned in her direction and she saw something black. "I don't know if he took a step towards her or not, the girl won't say, but, damn it, who is this man sleeping on our street, and what's he doing there anyway?"

I raced downstairs to find him, and decided to go and ask Comrade Ayyash to put a stop to this. But then I remembered that he wasn't in charge of our neighbourhood anymore, and as I retraced my steps to the house, there was the man again: sitting on the pavement by himself, looking frightened. He didn't stir when I approached, as if he hadn't even noticed me. I asked him what his name was. He didn't answer. I raised my voice.

"Can't you hear?"

He looked up at me, wide-eyed.

"What are you doing here?"

He shrugged.

"Why do you rip the posters from the walls? Is it your job? You're nothing but a pervert, aren't you? Why did you scare my daughter? . . . You know, I could – I could have you locked up . . . I'm going to tell the militiamen about you and you'll see . . . You don't believe me? Come on, get out of here, brother . . . just leave us alone."

I watched him get up slowly, he seemed not to have heard me: he just stood up, gathered his belongings – the paintbrush, the bucket of lime, the torn papers – and walked away. And I never saw him again.

Poor Khalil Jaber! I swear I didn't know he'd end up being murdered. I'm sure he meant no harm, either to me or to Aida. I just happened to tell Comrade Ayyash about it . . . I ran into him on the street one day and told him. I was trying to be funny, but Ayyash took it seriously and said he'd let the officer in charge of our neighbourhood know. He also asked me about the car. I told him it had never come back but that I'd begun to get used to living without it.

When I told my friend Musa Kanj that the man had disappeared, he seemed relieved and said we shouldn't allow beggars like him to "deface our city". I told him he wasn't a beggar.

"Khalil Ahmad Jaber is no beggar," I said. "I tried to give him money once and he refused. He's just a man of strange ways."

Musa, who wasn't really interested in what I was saying, told me that his wife had come back from abroad and that everything was going according to plan. And he thanked me for my good taste in refurbishing his new house.

"Excellent job, my friend . . . Even nicer than what one finds in Europe . . . !"

Poor Khalil Jaber, I wonder who killed him? I can't imagine that anyone had anything to gain by his murder. He was just a poor guy, looking like one of those beggars, he had nothing – and he would not have hurt a fly!

It's true we found him annoying, but these days one's annoyed with one's own self. Such dreadful times we live in . . . all we hear about are crimes and stories of murder . . . Is there no end to this?

My wife says the only solution is prayer and so I pray. But

praying isn't everything. There are other things, real problems I mean, and I don't know the solution to those.

And the poor martyr, Khalil . . . I swear he's a martyr . . . I feel ashamed of myself . . . but I didn't know that he was the Khalil Ahmad Jaber who would be murdered and whose picture would be in all the papers. I swear, had I known, I would've taken him in and cared for him . . . What can we do? It was God's will!

CHAPTER III

White Walls

Fatimah Fakhro, 42, widow of Mahmud Fakhro, the deceased care-taker of the Peace Towers Building at the end of Mar Elias Street overlooking Mazra'a Avenue. After her husband's death, Fatimah was able to stay on in the building thanks to numerous interventions on her behalf – in particular, the intercession of Professor Nabeel Assi, a member of the Arts Faculty at the Lebanese University, and one of the cadres of the National Movement in Beirut. The landlord, Mr Basheer al-Harati, agreed that Fatimah could stay in the caretaker's quarters and collect her husband's salary – but only, it is alleged, after receiving threats moving him to understand that it was in his best interests "not to cause any trouble". Fatimah gave him her word that her children would not be allowed to play in the lobby of the building because that "would just cause too much noise and disturb the tenants."

Following the discovery of Khalil Ahmad Jaber's body, Fatimah was repeatedly detained for questioning, and, while she eventually admitted to her relationship with the deceased, she denied any involvement in his murder. Given the lack of solid evidence against her, and also because of her genuinely cooperative atti-tude, the strongmen in charge of the local party office concluded she was innocent.

"Now what! ... If it's not one thing, it's another ... nothing but trouble, from the day we are born!"

Fatimah Fakhro doesn't understand what is happening to her ... This man had nothing to do with her, nothing whatsoever ... First her eldest, Ali, had fallen down outside and pierced his skull

73

with a nail, then her old man's grisly death, and the hullabaloo over Professor Nabeel's intercession on her behalf, and now this . . . It was just one calamity after another! When she asks them why they've dragged her here, her question is met with scowls and a barrage of questions.

But how did they find out? She didn't tell anyone, she didn't even know anything about the man's death until Sitt Elham, the landlord's wife, told her the body had been found; then it turned out that their neighbour, the engineer Ali Kalakesh, also knew the dead man – he'd seen him around the neighbourhood, she said.

That was the day she told her. Sitt Elham was standing in the doorway of the kitchen, puffing on a cigarette and gossiping, as Fatimah cooked. She told the lady that she too had seen him around, and that she had even spoken to him. Sitt Elham said that was a rash thing to have done.

"Yes, and I wept, even though I didn't know him."

The men in the party office glower at her. One is smoking; he exhales right into her face and says: "We know everything, every single thing that goes on around here. Nothing escapes us."

So she confesses. She feels that since they know everything there is no point in lying. She tells them how she had noticed him sitting on the pavement and asked him what he was doing in their neighbourhood; and how he had asked for a piece of bread, and she had given it to him. She is frightened, these men know everything . . . still, she does not tell them every last little thing. And they believe her! So they don't know everything after all, and she can get away with a fib!

Fatimah tells them that she saw him sitting on the pavement and told him to go away. Then she finishes her testimony by saying that she never saw him again, that this man surely had nothing to do with her husband's murder. And besides, she had never seen him before.

Then they set about beating her; one of them, however, the tall

74

one, after raising his hand as if to strike her, caresses her face. She sobs for a long time; then, after threatening her, they set her free.

Misery had trailed her ever since he had brought her here . . . Leading her by the hand, he had brought her to Beirut, and she has never been back since. Her husband promised her she would go back for a visit, but he never kept his promise. He said life was nasty and disgusting over there, that it was better here. And so she lived here – where it was better . . .

She was just a child – she could not have been more than twelve – when her father took her to Mr Mitri Helou's house in Ashrafiyyeh. She had never seen such buildings before, nor lived anywhere else, nor met people who drank and danced with women! And such an abundance of food, and a mistress who slept till noon! At first she cried all the time and dreamed of running away, but then, she would forget for a while, she would watch T.V. and forget; she would see people, Mr Mitri, his beautiful wife, and their children, she loved them all, and she would forget.

On the very rare occasions her father came down from there, her eyes would cloud over as the tears welled up, and he would tell her that he would be back the following year to take her home. Slowly, however, she forgot. She forgot everything, even her father, so that next time he came, she stared at him vacantly and found nothing to say. He asked her if she was happy, she told him that she was, and she showed him her room and the toys and clothes they had given her. And then he left.

During all her time in this city, she never seriously thought of going back until she married Mahmud. She told him she wanted to go back there, and he promised she would. Every year he promised. And now where was she to go, with Mahmud dead, and her alone with the children? Where would she go, when she knew nobody? A first cousin on her father's side lives in a building nearby with her husband and children, but they don't pay much attention to her. They came to the funeral and helped out with the expenses and everything, but they still treat her like a stranger . . . and . . . they don't feel like family. She feels utterly alone in her predicament . . . And now there's this man, whom she hardly knows and who has brought her nothing but grief . . .

Her cousin told her that is what you get for marrying Mahmud Fakhro without consulting anyone! But who was she to consult? Her father had stopped coming, possibly he had passed away. Her cousin told her that he had died working in the fields and that her brothers had gone to Istanbul to find work. Her mother was long since dead – before she even came to work for Mr Mitri Helou in Beirut and her father's marriage to that wild-haired shrew! She did not have anyone to consult.

Mahmud had apparently approached Mr Mitri, and it was he who told her. The lady of the house came into the kitchen one day and told her that Mr Mitri wanted to see her in the living room.

She dried her hands, smoothed back her long, flowing hair, and went out to the living room. She remained standing, but Mr Mitri asked her to sit down in the armchair across from him. Fatimah was surprised: the *khawaja*, or master, had never asked her to sit, nor spoken to her in such a friendly way before.

"Fatimah, my dear, you're like my own daughter," he began. Then he cleared his throat and looked her straight in the eyes. Fatimah averted her gaze. "And . . . you know . . . well . . . such is the way of the world . . . you know Mahmud, the new caretaker of the building, Mahmud Fakhro. Well, he's come and asked me for your hand in marriage. He's a good boy, I've made enquiries about him – he's a Kurd, like you, and he wants to settle down. You'll remain close by, you know you're like a daughter to us, you'll live with him in the ground-floor quarters . . . and you'll go on working here, nothing will change. Mind you, I didn't make any promises. I said I'd ask you first. So, what do you think?"

Fatimah said nothing. The thing was, that whenever she thought of marriage, she imagined someone like Fadee – tall and fair and soft-spoken, with shy, doe-like eyes . . . But Mahmud . . . well . . . she didn't like him . . . no, it's not that she didn't like him, but he wasn't at all like Fadee . . . He was short and stocky and half-bald, and she could see the thick black hairs on his legs when he rolled up his trousers to wash the stairs . . . and the way he looked at her and intoned those *mashallahs* whenever she walked past him! She didn't feel the blood rushing to her ears when she saw him, the way she did when she thought of Fadee.

Fatimah said nothing. Then she burst into tears.

"Listen to me, girl: you're an orphan and this is for the best. You're not a child anymore, you're sixteen, a young woman already . . . And you'll remain right here with us." Fatimah was crying, and Mr Mitri got up and patted the shoulder of the weeping girl to comfort her.

After that, everything happened very quickly. Mahmud's sister came over and said Fatimah had to wear this white head-wrap from now on. Then they took her to his brother's house, which was full of people she did not know, and Mahmud sat next to her in the middle of the room. There was music, and everybody drank juice and ate sweets. Then everyone left and Fatimah returned to the building with him. When they entered the care-taker's quarters, Fatimah stood expectantly as Mahmud closed the door behind them.

"Take off your clothes," he ordered, and he turned out the lights and started to undress. Fatimah felt so scared her joints ached. He came up to her, clapped his hand over her mouth and started hitting her. Then he started circling around her, bobbing up and down on his feet and striking her. She tried to scream but his hand was still clamped over her mouth. She was ready to get down on her knees and kiss his hands, why was he hitting her so hard, and with that stick? Then he threw her to the ground, and began ripping off her clothes . . . she wanted to tell him not to tear them . . . she would undress by herself, she knew what a man and a woman did when they were married! But he just tore them off, raised her up towards him and, grunting and moaning, pushed in his thing. Despite the searing pain she felt, she didn't utter a cry – how could she, anyway, with his hand over her mouth – but she wanted to tell him to let go, so she could breathe. But he didn't. And that thing, oh God, the pain, the unbearable pain, it hurt so much . . . then slowly, gradually, his hand let go of her mouth, and he started stroking her, first her body, then her face. And the pain changed . . . she began to feel something similar to when Fadee held her hand once . . . except that it burst. The feeling she had had then was bursting in her now . . . and Mahmud seemed to be spinning around, it felt like everything was spinning around her. She closed her eyes at a sensation she had never experienced before, and when she opened them again she could make out his darkened face in the shadows. At that moment, she wanted to glue herself to him, to keep the thing inside her throbbing – she really wanted him now – but he pulled out.

Sitting up in bed beside her, he lit a cigarette and started to hum. Now she felt embarrassed, so she got up and asked him to get off the sheet. But when she tried to take a step, the soreness spread all the way down to her feet. Still, she took the sheet into the bathroom and came back to the bare bed.

He was still humming . . . But then he threw his cigarette to the floor, gathered her into his arms and started over again. This time she did not feel any pain: it was different, he was different. This man, Mahmud, was tender now, kissing her face and neck . . . she wanted to kiss him back, but she felt shy . . . afraid somehow . . . and so she lay in his arms, lips closed and teeth clenched . . . And when he climbed off her for the second time, he didn't light a cigarette, he just rolled over and went to sleep.

And that is how she became Mahmud's wife, and her name became Fatimah Fakhro. And even though he was no different than before the wedding, now she found him attractive – she

78

wanted him to come to her in bed, and longed for the darkness to fall.

Why then did she begin to dread the nights and loathe the man when he climbed off her? Why did the pain return – she did not dare tell anyone about it – and her belly start to swell? Children, that's why. Sitt Huda always said: "Why do you people have so many children?" And Fatimah would not know what to say. Sitt Huda had only two children, Fadee and Marie, who was studying in Paris, but she, Fatimah, had five of them, and she was pregnant again.

Mahmud would sit outside the entrance of the building all day, while she cooked both upstairs and downstairs. He just sat there, chatting to the shopkeepers, doing nothing – even washing the stairs was her job now, and she did not dare ask for his help. He only ever took care of her during her confinements. He spent all his time with little Ali – of course, Fatimah loved Ali, she loved all her children – but all Mahmud ever did was sit there playing with Ali in front of the building. All day. Every day.

And Fadee had stopped casting those sideways glances at her, maybe because she had aged. "I look older than Sitt Huda," she would say to Mahmud. But he would ignore her and keep humming. He would say the lady wasn't a real woman, anyway.

"Real women bear children . . . But this Sitt Huda, she does nothing all day, while her poor husband toils away."

Fadee would not even glance at her when he came into the kitchen. Perhaps it was because he was older now, but he was still fair-skinned and had those doe-like eyes that rekindled in her the memory of that strange sensation . . .

She had been sitting on the bed in her small room darning socks, and Fadee – who was the same age as her, as Sitt Huda liked to point out – had come in one day. He entered her little room just off the kitchen and asked her to make him a cup of coffee. She got to her feet.

79

"But you never drink coffee."

"I do now," he replied, as he puffed on an American cigarette.

She assumed that he was brazen enough to smoke and to drink coffee because no-one was home. In any case, she got up. As she filled the coffee pot with water from the tap at the kitchen sink, she felt his hand tremblingly reach for hers. How soft his fingers were under the water! . . . Fatimah felt the blood rushing to her eyes. He stood so close behind her that she could feel his warm breath on her neck, but she did not dare turn around. She felt him draw closer and the burning sensation in her eyes sharpened. Not even realizing how or why, she drew her hand away and spun round, dropping the coffee pot into the sink. A shudder ran through his body as he stepped back.

"With just a hint of sugar, please."

And he left the kitchen.

She refilled the coffee pot, lit the gas burner and stood watching over it: first, the bubbles rising to the surface as the water came to the boil, and then the coffee cascading down, mingling with the water, and finally dissolving. She stood there expectantly – with an almost liquid sensation of fear seeping from her belly – and waited for him, expecting him to come back. But he didn't.

She poured the coffee, set the cup on a brass tray, placed beside it a glass which she filled with water, and then carried the tray into the living room. He was sitting, one leg crossed over the other, reading the paper. He neither looked up nor turned to her. He did not say a word. She put the tray down on the table in front of him and stood there.

"Your coffee, Khawaja Fadee."

He set the paper down very slowly, tapped a cigarette out of the white box of Kents, stood up, and came towards her.

"Cigarette . . . ?"

He drew closer, placed the cigarette between her lips, his hand brushing against her face. He had stepped back and bent down to pick up the matches from the table when the telephone rang. Fadee dashed to answer. Fatimah put the cigarette down on the table and went back to her room to finish the darning.

He did not come back. He was on the telephone a long time: she could hear him, laughing and speaking in French. No, he didn't come back. Then everyone came home, the master, the mistress, and the house filled with the din of the T.V. . . .

And now he stood there, looking away, as though he had forgotten, or as if he were afraid of meeting her gaze.

Gradually, Fatimah forgot how that burning sensation felt. Even with Mahmud it had gone, and it never came back . . . and anyhow, by then she had become burdened with Ali. Fadee was always gone, Mr Mitri had become practically an invalid since falling out of bed and dislocating his hip, and Sitt Huda constantly went on about her cholesterol, as she grew fatter by the day.

It was Fadee who had escorted them out of the neighbourhood. He came in with Mahmud one day and told them they had to leave. He would take them as far as the Museum Crossing, he said, and there they would be able to make their way to West Beirut in a *servees* taxi. Fatimah was instantly overcome by the same feeling she had when Ali fell – a stabbing pain in her gut, and nausea. She was sure that Ali had not actually fallen off the roof, but her lips were paralysed and she cried soundlessly. Looking at him, you would think that nothing had happened – it was as if Ali were not his son. A monster, that's what Mahmud was: a monster who had killed Ali! That's what she said to herself whenever she looked over towards Ali's photograph sitting in its black frame on top of the T.V.

Anyhow, that day, the day they left, Fadee looked exactly the same as on that other fateful day: trembling from head to foot, his voice shaking as he told them they had to leave, while Mahmud stood by his side, blood gushing from the wounds on his face . . .

Mahmud had told her he was going up to the roof to repair the

T.V. antenna, and the boy had gone up with him. When Mahmud reappeared without him, she thought the boy was playing outside, but she felt uneasy nonetheless: she had worried about him ever since the day he had come home, blood dripping from his head, telling her he had fallen on the street and a nail had pierced his skull. And when she had taken him to the clinic, the doctor had ridiculed her. "A nail, you say? No, that's not possible . . . he does have some abrasions though." That's what the doctor had said.

But the boy was not the same. She could not pinpoint when exactly, but he had changed. His father had taken to hitting him over the head, and the shopkeeper for whom Ali worked got so exasperated he called Mahmud in to tell him about the boy's behaviour. The shopkeeper told Mahmud that, one day, when he had asked the boy to make him a cup of coffee, Ali made a brew of salt and pepper instead of coffee and sugar. And then Ali started eating pepper all the time and he stopped going over to the shop to work. He also hit his brothers and sisters, as well as other children from the neighbourhood.

Sitt Huda told her she should take him to the doctor because the boy wasn't normal. But Fatimah would not hear of it – it's just because of the nail, she thought. Even though one day, Ali had grabbed little George and fondled him. Mahmud told her all boys went through this, and there was no need to make such a fuss about it. Fatimah tried everything: she prayed for him, she gave him a talking to, she even dragged him with her when she went to the market. She would hold his hand like a small child, but he would break free and run wild in the street, beating up the local children and refusing to go to work . . .

She asked Mahmud where the boy was. He said Ali was still up there.

"Up where?"

"On the roof."

"And what's he doing there?"

"Playing."

"How could you leave him up there? The boy is not well!"

"He wouldn't come down with me, so I left him."

Fatimah ran; the lift was out of order, so she started up the stairs. And then she heard the screaming and the wailing. Stopping dead in her tracks, she didn't know whether to continue on up or go back down. Then, she heard Mahmud bellowing and a terrible commotion breaking out below, so she raced back down: the boy was like pulp, nothing but a mass of blood, broken limbs, and clothes. And when she glanced up, there was Fadee, looking like nothing she had ever seen before: screaming and crying simultaneously, his whole body shook and shuddered; then he bent down and picked up the boy and ran with him to the hospital.

Everyone said Ali had fallen. Mahmud said he had killed himself. "He's found his rest and so have we . . . you know, I saw him trying to rub up against his sister in bed." That's what Mahmud said, but Fatimah didn't believe him.

How could she? As far as she was concerned, it was all Mahmud's fault: he hit the poor child over the head until he got like that. How could a fifteen-year-old want to take his own life? . . . That was no suicide, Fatimah was sure, and she pounded her fists into her husband's chest, screaming at him and accusing him of being Ali's killer, as he, unmoved, stared at her silently through those narrow-slit eyes of his. Then he bellowed out a *hamdulillah*.

"God forbid, as if he weren't our own son!"

Fadee was there. And Sitt Huda was there. Everyone was there . . .

At first, Fatimah had not realized what was happening. It was Hussein, her second son, who had come up to Mr Mitri's apartment and told Sitt Huda. Then he told her.

"They came," he said. "Men in black hoods came asking for Father . . . then they saw him . . . they put a brown sack over his head and left . . . they bundled him into a black jeep and told us we had to leave . . ."

Fatimah raced downstairs wailing, but he was nowhere to be found. She ran out to the street, crying for help, and the neighbours looked on as if they didn't know her. In tears, she ran back into the building, and all the children gathered around her, crying. Then Fadee arrived: he seemed different somehow – she saw it in his eyes, the very same expression he had had when Ali died. He came into the room, asked the children some questions, and left.

Sitt Huda also came. She tried to reassure her: "Fadee can do whatever he wants, Fatimah. He knows all the militiamen in the neighbourhood; they look up to him, like a leader," she said. "Don't worry! Your husband will return." And so he did, with Fadee by his side, and his face bleeding.

"Pack your belongings," Fadee told them, "you've got to leave." They stood side by side, speaking in muffled voices, and Fadee gave Mahmud a key. Then he piled them into the huge American car – it was the first time they had ever ridden in the family car – and took them to the Museum.

"I'll never forget that car," Fatimah told her husband as they entered the building in Kantari. He told her this was their new house. A proper house it was too, with a T.V., a radio, a fridge, everything. "What a beautiful, comfortable car that was," Fatimah went on, as the children played in the courtyard and her husband puffed away on his cigarette, telling her they would all be dead if it had not been for Fadee . . .

"He's a good guy, you know . . . as soon as I heard his voice, I relaxed . . . it was as if I could see him from behind that brown sack they put over my head. You should have heard him swearing at them . . . he was the one who got me out of there . . . they wanted to kill me, you know, but he told them, 'Leave him alone, you sons of bitches, this one's mine, he's none of your business!' He grabbed me by the hand and said, 'Let's go.' As we walked out together, he took the sack off my head. The sons of bitches, you know what they did, they hit me again! And instead of bandaging me up, they put the brown sack back over my head. And even though Fadee was right there beside me, saying let's go, they had the nerve to stick the muzzles of their guns into the back of my head! I tried to look back, but Fadee said not to turn round, and I listened to him because he knows best."

As she looked at Mahmud, Fatimah could not help thinking that it was all over – with Fadee on the other side now and Ali dead. And him, here, in her face grumbling all day, and this building full of Armenians and rich *khawajas*, all of them trying to leave the country . . . she would have to stay at home now, nobody would be asking her to clean for them . . . life was better over there. She didn't know anybody here, what kind of a life was that?

And then all hell broke loose.

Mahmud told her the war had started again, and he was worried about them. He said he had found another building for them to live in and that they had to leave Kantari, as it was now overrun with militiamen. They gathered up their belongings once again and left. Only this time, Mahmud would not live in the new building with them. He would stay in Kantari by himself. When she questioned him, he said he knew best.

"Men know best," he said, "and it is proper that they leave." And he left.

All their stuff, and the children screaming, and the new building, and the man who comes out in his pyjamas every morning cursing the war, and Basheer al-Harati, the fat landlord, who looks down on Mahmud and loathes the children, and is constantly fussing about keeping the stairwell clean . . .

And me, Fatimah Fakhro, here with seven children . . . my eldest, only seventeen, working at Hajj Saleh's, the dry cleaner, and my youngest still nursing at my breast . . . Standing here alone before these

men asking about Khalil Ahmad Jaber. I told them he died. Everyone
dies, I said . . . Just the same as that time when I stood there all alone,
calling Sitt Huda to tell her that Mahmud was dead and the building
in Kantari was destroyed. When Fadee answered, his voice sounded
listless and rasping, like creaking bones. He talked to me as if I were a
stranger. He said Sitt Huda had gone to Paris, Khawaja Mitri had
passed away, and he hadn't much time now . . . why didn't I call back
some other time . . .

I stood all alone before these men, bristling with wrath and indig-
nation, and told them I didn't know anything. They wouldn't believe
me. What was I supposed to tell them? I didn't know what they wanted,
I just wept. We know everything, they said, but it wasn't true, because
after I talked to them, they took me back home. I'm all by myself now,
and if it hadn't been for Professor Nabeel, the children and I would have
been thrown out into the street, plain and simple! Everything's been
such a disaster! Why, oh why, did Mahmud have to bring us here . . . ?

Fatimah was always alone with the kids. Mahmud disappeared
for days at a time, and then he would reappear, hand her some
money – God only knows where he got it from – and vanish again.
When she asked where he was going, he would tell her he was
still in Kantari.

"I'm the building watchman. The war will end and Khawaja
Fadee will be back. He asked me to be the watchman. How can I
leave the building in Kantari?"

And Fatimah would tell him please don't go. "There's fighting
over there, why can't Mr Fadee come and guard his own building?
There's fighting over there . . ." she would cry, frightened.

And where was Mahmud now, when she needed him, with
this man sprawled out on the pavement, staring vacantly into
space? She had found him one winter night – it was cold and
raining, and there he was, bundled up in his coat on the pavement,
with his straggly beard, a pith helmet on his head, and a bucketful

of quicklime at his side. He asked her for some bread, so Fatimah went in and fetched him bread, some olives, and an onion. She asked him his name.

Spitting out an olive pit, he coughed and told her she was a wonderful woman. Then he started talking about his mother.

"My mother, Hajjeh Sobhiyyeh, went on the *hajj* and she never came back. They said she got some disease and died over there, and they buried her by the Prophet's grave. Hajjeh Sobhiyyeh, my mother, was a beautiful woman, she was fair and sweet! Whenever my father used to hit her, I'd run and hide under her skirts, and look up her long, milky-white legs as he pinned her against the wall. And though she cried from the insults and the blows, she would stay ever so still so as not to trample me. She'd slide her hand down to comfort me, even though he kept hitting her, over and over again.

"My mother died over there, beside the Prophet's grave. I bought her the plane ticket and she left. We put up all sorts of bunting and decoration for her return – I got a sheep that I tied up in front of the building for the ceremonial slaughter. But when she didn't come back, and the sheep was still there, everyone said I should slaughter it for the peace of her soul, that's what the sacrificial lamb of the feast is. So I went and got Abu Khaled, the butcher. Little Ahmad was just a child at the time. Abu Khaled grabbed the sheep, pinned it to the ground, and slit its throat with a knife . . . oh my, you should've seen the blood . . . I couldn't help but cry when the blood spurted out and spattered everything . . . then Abu Khaled bent down, blew into the sheep with the bellows and then set to skinning it. Me and my Ahmad, we were both crying, and Hajjeh Sobhiyyeh never came back."

Fatimah asked him his name once again; he tells her with his mouth full and carries on eating.

"Are you married?"

"I am, and my son Ahmad, the Lord be praised, has grown into a fine young man . . . he's an officer in the army now."

"In which army?"

"*The* army! The Lebanese army, he's the best officer they've got! As a matter of fact, I'm expecting him at this very moment . . . a military jeep should be here any minute now to take me to his office at the barracks . . . and there, the soldiers will line up on either side and salute as I review the troops, the way the president does, only better."

Fatimah went back inside and glanced over at Ali's picture. Mahmud still was not back. Then they came and told her the Kurds of Wadi Abu Jameel had killed him. But they hadn't, because he did come back, and they had not killed him. No-one could kill him, he told her. Then, after the war ended, they came and sprayed him with bullets and left his bloodied body riddled with holes, lying in a pool of shards from the shattered glass panes of the building lobby.

"Where oh where have you gone, Mahmud?"

Mahmud was always running. The streets of Kantari are long, and as Mahmud ran the streets with the young fighters, the very streets seemed to run. The building he watched over was completely abandoned; no-one ever came by but the Armenian doctor. He would sit on the building's front steps, with gunmen milling around, and run to meet the doctor whenever he saw him coming in the distance.

"Dr Harout, you mustn't . . ." he would say. The doctor, his frail body shaking, would look at Mahmud with those wilting eyes of his and commend the stone to Mahmud's care.

"Take good care of it, now, Mahmud . . . you know . . . the stone, in my apartment, it's a rare and antique piece, don't let them break it."

Mahmud would reassure the doctor and would not let on that he no longer dared go up to the sixth floor.

"The sixth floor is off limits," the comrade had said to him. "There are fighters up there, and it's exposed to shelling. There's no going up there." So Mahmud no longer ventured up . . . he wasn't about to die for the sake of a stone.

He spent all his time with the *shabab* – the young militiamen – and did as they did. Whenever he crossed the street, he would duck and weave fearlessly like them, even as he heard the bullets whizzing past his ears . . . the sky was interminable, the streets endless, but he stayed on with them as they shivered under the pouring rain, with their metal rifles and combat boots, and their hacking coughs mingled with fear, and cold. He was on their side. With them . . .

That is what Mahmud told the young man – twenty-five years old, handsome, with blonde hair and an assault rifle dangling off his left shoulder. He must want to die, thought Mahmud, as he stood explaining to him that he couldn't leave the building because he was the watchman.

"But it's dangerous here. Your life is in danger," replied the tall blonde youth who apparently coveted death. "Aren't you afraid?"

"Of course I am," Mahmud Fakhro told him, "but I've got to stay here. I have to, don't you see? I'm the watchman, and the landlord calls every day. He's the landlord. What would I tell him when he comes back?"

"Alright, O.K., stay here then – you'll find out for yourself that the landlords won't be back."

"Thanks, brother. I really appreciate it."

The blonde youth, a hand grenade dangling from his waist, turned on his heels and was about to leave the building when Mahmud stopped him.

"I have a question."

"Go ahead."

"And you, Comrade, aren't you afraid?"

"Of course I am, I'm only human; but I'm learning to be a fighter."

"But why fight?"

"We're fighting for the revolution, for the sake of change . . . for the sake of the poor . . . for people like you who have nothing and live in poverty and misery."

Mahmud agreed, he said they were right, but it looked as if it were going to be a long haul.

"And you, why don't you fight with us?" the blonde youth asked him.

"Me, brother, I can't, I have a family and children. And anyway, it has nothing to do with me. I don't understand politics. How about you? Why are you fighting?"

"I already told you, I'm fighting for . . . for the cause."

"But . . . don't you have a job or anything?"

"No, I'm a university student."

"That's really great, really . . . may the Good Lord protect you and keep you . . . But why are you hell-bent on dying? If you went home and they did the same, there wouldn't be any war. Why don't you just let it be, brother?"

As the blonde youth gazed at Mahmud, his eyes shone, both with love and contempt. He walked out of the building and onto the street, darting between the bullets that whistled all around him.

Whenever Mahmud talks about the war now, he recalls the image of the blonde youth darting across the street: how his body became airborne, with blood spurting everywhere, his limbs jerking and twitching, like a cockerel in a cockfight; how the blood streamed down his face and dripped onto the pavement; how his head dangled and his right shoulder slumped; how his rifle tumbled from his hand to the ground; how he continued to twitch, and his head hung lower and lower, as if he were looking for a coin that had rolled away; and then, the final spasm.

As Mahmud took off across the street to retrieve him, voices roared: "Stop! Don't move! There's a sniper! Nobody move! Leave him, nobody move! . . . A sniper, there's a sniper!"

The blonde youth reeled, like a dancer doing a jig. And even as his head came to rest on the ground, the hair already stiff and matted with dust, his body danced on, his feet twitching against the pavement . . . And then, finally, he slept . . . the blonde youth lay there asleep, all alone . . . no-one dared approach the peaceful supine figure, whose body seemed almost shrivelled now, khaki trousers shrunken, combat boots retracted into his legs, arms akimbo as though waving into the distance, the rifle by his side.

Mahmud wept. Squatting behind the sandbags, with three gunmen next to him, he sobbed: "Why don't you go and get him, he's my friend . . ."

But the air was thick with gunfire, the rain was heavy, and there were distant cries for help . . . and out of nowhere, women in white headwraps appeared, running for their lives down the endless street . . . still running, one of them scooped up a child that had tumbled from her arms and wiped his bloodied nose with her white wrap . . . Everywhere running . . . everything running . . . The gunmen shouted warnings at the women, admonishing them to stop . . . but the women just kept running.

"Stop crying, you're a man. And he's a martyr!"

"He's a martyr, and I'm a martyr," Mahmud said, bursting out laughing at the thought, with tears still streaming down his cheeks.

And then Dr Harout appears at the top of the street. He is about to cross, but seeing the corpse of the blonde youth, he steps back. Mahmud gestures to him not to try. One of the fighters trains his rifle on Dr Harout, and Mahmud grabs hold of the barrel.

"Leave the poor man alone!" he says, and yells to Dr Harout to run for his life.

The doctor scurries off, looking over his shoulder; the rain is flooding the streets, and he splashes through puddles.

"You'd think he wants to die," says the young man who had taken aim at him.

Now the doctor is running in circles, and the gunmen are firing, the rain is pouring down, and the corpse of the blonde youth begins to swell, water seeping into his clothes and his khaki shirt billowing out, but all Mahmud can see as he shivers are the red tracer bullets filling the sky. The gunmen fire, again and again. The doctor's dead, Mahmud is sure of it, the doctor's dead and he has left the stone.

But the doctor did not die. He just kept running, terrified by the bullets flying around him, not realizing they were shooting at him, with the beating rain and the women's shrieks reverberating all around the street. It only appeared that the doctor was running in circles because Mahmud caught glimpses of him every now and then. *If you all went away, then this war would stop*, Mahmud wants to say, but he does not, because the terror he feels has spread to his knees and he urgently needs to relieve himself. As the urge intensifies, his neck hangs limp, as though it were not his own, as if it were just dangling from his head and about to come unstuck, to fall off . . . he bends down to pick it up, or tries to, but as he tries, he slips and falls to the ground, and the hot liquid floods his trousers. He tells the gunmen it's nothing, he can hear them talking, and see their fingers . . . he sees nothing but fingers, fingers stretching endlessly, fingers dangling loose, fingers attached with string . . . he wants to tell the fingers to go away, but they approach his eyes, they are in his eyes . . . and then everything turns red, and all the colours of the rainbow appear behind his eyes, and he can see the rising sun . . . but then, the sun is setting . . . sleeping sun, dying sun . . . They're all laughing . . . he can hear them quite clearly, the laughter rises, it's turned into cackling, now all their teeth are exposed, white teeth, yellow teeth, teeth and more teeth, and a long red tongue dangling and falling to the ground . . . trucks going by, and cars, and the din of engines . . .

"Hey, you!" he hears them shouting as they shake him by the shoulders.

"You crazy or what? . . . running like that into the middle of the street . . . we told you there was a sniper . . ."

They prop him up, and, still dazed, Mahmud gets to his feet. The dank smell pervades his nostrils, and even his pores.

"I . . . don't . . . I . . . didn't . . ."

"Don't ever do that again. We'll let you off this time. Next time we'll kick you out of here."

"O.K, O.K."

He wants to ask them what they have done with the handsome blonde youth; he wants to ask if they need his help . . . I could make tea and coffee for everyone, this little place of mine is already practically a youth club . . . they come here, they have something to drink, and they never pay. Far be it from me to accept payment or anything . . . please come in, do come in . . . make yourselves at home . . . But why are the buildings burning?

And as the buildings burned, the watchman stood in front of his building and watched the gunmen cart away everything they could find: fridges, T.V.s, sofas . . . anything they could lay their hands on. They said he could go up too but he was scared; eventually, he did go up to the top floor and, when he saw them rifling through drawers, he did the same, and when he saw them take every last thing, he too took things. Then he started going upstairs by himself; he would take stuff he could sell; and he even bought stuff. Whenever he heard the sound of gunfire in the distance, or saw the fires breaking out, he would smile and bide his time for the gunmen to leave. And leave they did – all of them left. Now, the street is deserted, there is no more fighting in Kantari, and the war has moved on to the other side of town. That is what they told him. All that is left is a deserted street, faraway noises, and me by myself, thinks Mahmud Fakhro, standing all alone in the middle of a street, bereft of life. Just me, the stray cats and dogs, and the smell . . . Not a human being in sight . . . just a street.

He stayed on in the deserted neighbourhood, watching his building, and when Khawaja Fadee called, he reassured him. Things are fine, he told him, but everything has been looted. At that, Fadee's tone changed. He said he would be coming back, but it turned out that he didn't dare.

"And so here I am, all by myself, and the street is all alone too."

Fatimah said he had changed.

She was always waiting for him in the new building. She would be washing down the stairs and waiting, or helping Sitt Elham with the housework and waiting – but he never came by! And when he did, he was always in a hurry! He would give her a few lira and then sit on a chair in front of the building and smoke a cigarette.

And while Fatimah wondered why he did not sleep with her, she did not dare ask him. The fact is that he did not. Never mind, she would say, no matter, anyway that old shiver was long gone, even that discomfort she used to feel in the early days had disappeared. Still, Fatimah would wonder why he didn't come near her whenever he slept at home. Where was the Mahmud who lived only for the nights, so he could throw himself on her? It used to be that nothing could put him off, she would whisper in his ear, "The children will hear us," but he would not listen, and just like that, he would climb on top of her, thrusting and groaning, and she would close her eyes and worry about the children hearing.

But now he slept with his back turned to her and snored loudly. She did not dare question him. She told him – no, she begged him – not to go back there when he told her how dangerous it had become, how the Armenian doctor came by every day to check on his apartment without ever actually going up there, just stood hovering in the distance, and how the young men were always bouncing around with their guns and their boisterous talk and news of their martyrs.

Fatimah looks at him, incredulous, and feels frightened as she remembers him with the hood over his head being led off somewhere far away. She did not see the hood – she was upstairs in Mr Mitri's house when they kidnapped him. But now, whenever Mahmud appears in the distance, she pictures him with a brown bag over his head, his navy trousers rolled up, his calves thick with black hairs, his feet in plastic slippers, wearing that blue shirt of his, and them leading him away. But then, as she rushes out to meet him with the children, the brown sack recedes, and all that is left are his chipped and yellowed front teeth. Hussein is not with them. Mahmud asks where the boy is, as he gathers up the youngest girl into his muscular arms and throws her up in the air; then he settles into a chair to have his tea and a cigarette, hands her some money and tells her about Fadee's phone calls.

"The boy keeps calling . . . what can I say to him? Shall I tell him that they looted the building?"

"No, don't. Poor thing, he's so young still, and he's got a heart of gold."

Recounting her story, Fatimah remembers the hood, and Fadee's face, how different he had looked in the car that time: with his bloodshot eyes, he resembled the gunmen who stood to attention as he drove them through Ashrafiyyeh, his hand raised in salute. He was not Fadee anymore, she thought. Mahmud was sitting beside him in the front, his face in his hands, as though he did not want to look . . . The children were crying . . . And all the stuff we had to leave behind . . .

Now Fatimah is washing down the stairs and waiting for Mahmud to come by. Hurtling down to the shelter for cover, the residents scream and tell her the place is filthy. Mahmud walks in and the landlord, Basheer al-Harati, starts wagging his finger menacingly at him, but when he sees the gun nestled against

Mahmud's right hip, his voice trails off and his finger sags.

"We're all brothers," the landlord says.

"Yeah, brothers," Mahmud answers him.

"I know we're all brothers, but my dear Abu Hussein . . ."

"It's Abu Ali, if you don't mind."

"O.K. brother, but Abu Ali, you're not taking care of the building . . . the rubbish is piling up and you're not doing a thing about it."

"There's a war on, Mr Basheer, a war . . . we all need to pull together. Put your rubbish into plastic bags and stop just tossing stuff down willy-nilly.

"Quite right." And Basheer al-Harati struts off with his pot belly and his spectacles, leaving Mahmud standing there, muttering.

"Dogs! The rich are nothing but dogs! Every last one of them! Even Fadee's a dog – a dog without a bark, a whimpering dog, but a dog all the same."

Fatimah takes the black plastic bag Mahmud has used to shield himself from the rain.

"It's raining a lot this year," she says, throwing the bag away. And she goes into their room and bursts into tears. Mahmud can hear her. He follows her in, cursing.

"Women! Yes, they're dogs too – the lot of them!"

He approaches her, laughing, then takes a seat on the floor; she sits down beside him. Fatimah tells him she wants to go back there, to the village. She tells him that the only thing she remembers is leaning over the edge of the stream and seeing the goat's horns reflected in the water, and that she wants to go back and visit her mother's grave.

"Come on, woman, there's nothing there, nothing but poverty and hunger and disease!"

"But there's a war here, and I'm scared," Fatimah says. "A war, in which we're all going to die . . ."

"But I can save money here. Look, once I've saved enough, we'll go back, I'll build a house, and we'll stay. In the meantime, I'm not prepared to work like a dog, do you hear? I'm not a dog and won't become one. Like them." And he walks out, hurrying off to the other place, leaving Fatimah sitting by herself on the floor.

Fatimah Fakhro stands before a man who looks furtively, first right, then left . . . he seems terrified, as if waiting for someone to stick a knife in his back. Then he turns to the wall and, reaching up with both hands, starts to rip down all the posters and film advertisements that have been pasted there. He peels the paper off in strips, crumples it up, and shreds it into tiny pieces that he tosses into the air. He splays his ten fingers against the wall and crouches, as if getting into the ready position to start a race, but instead of taking off, he remains motionless, as if glued to the wall. In his white-specked blue overcoat and pith helmet, he looks like someone about to break into song.

As Fatimah stands there, lingering, the man sinks down to the pavement, takes a piece of bread out of his pocket, and starts to eat. Turning to her, he says, "God bless you . . . let me have a drink of water." She steps inside and comes out with a bottle of water.

Even though the war was over, the streets were still deserted. At any rate, that's what everyone was saying, the war is over and the world's armies are here to stop the war. But Fatimah could not help feeling sad, because it truly was over for those who had died, the dead are gone forever. She thought the war would kill them all, that there would be no-one left to tell the tale. When Mahmud fell to the ground in front of her very eyes, blood gushing from every part of his body, she was sure they were all going to die – her, the children, all of them.

After Mahmud died, she would not go back to Kantari, she doesn't know anyone there, and he didn't tell her where he had hidden the money he had got from selling that woman's bracelets.

No money, no relatives, no war. In other words, everything just the same as before: Basheer al-Harati and his capricious ways; the protection of Professor Nabeel; the children, of course; and Hussein, who disappears for days at a time without coming back. She wonders where he goes . . . With Zeytouneh destroyed, there aren't any whores to be had these days! She really doesn't know where he goes and she dare not ask.

And now, here she is standing next to this strange man sitting on the pavement and talking to himself. Fatimah invites him in. His only response is to raise his eyebrows.

"What are you doing here, why are you ripping all the posters up?" she asks him. So he starts to tell her about the white sheets.

Fatimah saw him only a few times before he disappeared. Though she never asked, she heard that the *shabab* had taken him in for questioning. The fact is he disappeared, and anyhow, he never said very much.

"The white sheets," he says to her, "First, the bed has to be painted white, then we put a white sheet on it, cover ourselves with a white bedspread, and go to sleep. We must pull the covers right up over our eyes, so that all we can see are tiny white speckles of light." He tells her he is going to buy a sheet and sleep in it, with Ahmad by his side.

"Little Ahmad, chasing me chasing him, I hoist him up high and he flies . . . he flies through the air, and soars like a bird into the stratosphere . . . there . . . no higher than that . . . A man comes along, then two, then three, a thousand, a million men come . . . The man points his rifle skywards, he takes aim, he fires. The flames leap up towards him, but Ahmad soars, the flames licking all around him as he tries to escape, and he circles around and around, then crashes down and the fire devours him. The bird is on fire, its feathers are ablaze, it's nothing but a big fireball, and I will burn the sheet.

"I am white. I want a white sheet to sleep on, with a white

bedspread over the sheet, and a naked light bulb hanging in the middle of the room. Peering through the white fabric I can see the light refracting, nothing but little white specks. My teeth are white, and the walls . . . even the walls are white."

Propped up against the kerb, he goes on and on like this as Fatimah listens. He talks endlessly. The war is over, and this man is all alone, just like she is. And Hussein is never home, just like his father, forever leaving her by herself . . . she feels frightened, all by herself, standing before this man, staring at ravaged walls and ripped-up pictures. She turns on her heel and goes back inside. She is scared, but this man seems fearless, he does not seem afraid of anything. She feels as if she has somehow always known him.

Gradually, she begins waiting for him. One day, she goes and stands on the pavement across the street, but he doesn't come by, so she decides to go and do the day's shopping. After setting off, she realizes that she has left her money at home, so she hurries back to the room, tucks a little knotted handkerchief into her bosom, and goes out once again. She is still on the lookout for him, but no-one is there. And then, all of a sudden, there he is, plodding along slowly, hugging the walls, with his back stooped, in his lime-soaked shoes and his pith helmet, carrying his little bucket and his paintbrush, hugging the walls. Fatimah approaches him, but he just keeps going, so she falls into step beside him; he doesn't turn towards her but she knows he can see her . . . He halts, and then sets off again, going on his way without acknowledging her. Stopping in her tracks, she decides to head back home, but then out of the corner of her eye she catches him moving in her direction. People are rushing by, car horns are blaring, the city is humming with city noises. The man pauses, and then moves on again, while she heads home – she doesn't need anything today. She steps inside and waits.

That evening, he is back: he lies down on the pavement across the street and she takes a glass of tea out to him. Holding the glass

99

with a trembling grip, he takes a sip, and smacks his lips, as though chewing on something. Fatimah notices his dirt-encrusted fingers and his overgrown nails. She asks him whether he would like something to eat.

"No, but thank you for asking, my dear . . . No, my dear, I don't want anything. I'll just sit here." Then he starts telling her about boxing.

"I am a boxing and weightlifting champion. You know, like on television? You can ask them about me at the television station if you like, I'm the king of T.V." He falls silent, looks up at the sky, and then goes on. "But I don't like appearing on television anymore, the screen is so small and narrow I feel suffocated. I feel it pressing against my head. So I stopped. I gave up everything and decided to buy a white sheet, but sheets are expensive these days.

"The city's empty," he goes on. "The city's empty, all its citizens are under the sheet, you're under the sheet, and I am too . . . come and get in under the sheet."

Fatimah does not know what to say. *He must be delirious, but what if he is right? Maybe he is right . . . he doesn't seem like anyone I know, she thinks, no, not like Fadee or Mahmud or Ali, or anyone else for that matter, with that little beard of his – that little white goatee of his doesn't look like anything I know.*

"Come and get under the sheet with me. Go and fetch your children, and all of you come under the sheet. The city's all white, I'm painting it . . . Did you know that? That's work, real work."

"But you seem so poor . . . are they paying you?"

"Naturally I'm poor. No, they don't pay me. Of course not, because we won't take payment. I am the sole remaining volunteer in this country. I volunteer my services, it means I work and don't get paid because I have volunteered. All the walls will become white . . . And the hands . . . Hands are the most important thing in the world."

Fatimah looks down at her hands and fingers, while he stares into space.

"The most important things in the world are hands: every-one's hands will become white, fingers, fingernails, walls." And then he bursts out laughing. "I was a boxer once. No, no, I didn't get married. I can't stand women. I'm a boxer, and when I pull on my black boxing gloves and hit my opponent, the blood runs. But I gave up." He hoists himself up with both hands. "Even the sky's white, look."

Listening to him, Fatimah smiles. She feels just as she used to when she gazed at the little picture – the one Sitt Huda had given her long ago – of a woman with huge wide eyes, cradling an infant in her arms . . .

"That's our sacred Lady, the Virgin Mary, peace be with her. It's our Lady Mary with Jesus."

Fatimah loved looking at the picture of the woman with the Christ child, and those eyes of hers . . . she had hung it above her bed in the tiny room they had given her in that huge house, some-times she would talk to it, and when Sitt Huda caught her once, she smiled. Fatimah knew the little icon would not answer, but such a sweet little infant he was, she dreamed of having one like him and of cradling him in her arms like Our Lady Mary . . .

Except that Mahmud threw it away. It disappeared with him one day. He said there was no need for Our Lady Mary or for this picture anymore and started cursing. Fatimah was sure the Virgin was going to abandon her, she told him as much when he tried to snatch the picture from her hands.

Fatimah wept, she told him the Virgin was walking away, she was leaving the picture, walking out of it – still tiny like in the picture, a miniature Virgin in orange hues holding the sleeping infant in her arms, turning this way and that, with Fatimah walk-ing by her side. But Mahmud just swore and snatched the picture away. Fatimah felt sure they were all going to suffer some terrible misfortune. She thought of getting a new one but Sitt Huda was so far away. Mahmud said that Fadee had become like "them" – he wants us dead, he told her.

Fatimah knows neither how nor where, but somehow this man resembles the picture, even though he doesn't at all. She leaves him and goes back to her room while he sets off, slowly talking as he walks, addressing everyone that passes him, talking to people he doesn't know. No-one answers him and she wonders why the man is doing this to himself.

"What kind of a city is this?"

Mahmud Fakhro stands alone in front of the heavy metal door . . . The streets are deserted, they've simply emptied, there is nothing left but sandbags and distant gunfire . . . shattered glass of every colour is scattered across the asphalt, and the remains of gutted cars look like corpses strewn along the street. There's not a living soul around. Mahmud ponders what he's doing here, but thinks maybe he'd better stay on . . . true, the militiamen have taken a lot, but there's still so much left. He needs to make ends meet and how else to do it? He's got the gun, which provides some protection. They gave it to him finally, after he'd talked himself hoarse arguing with them. Yes, the building is quite empty now, but there's still a lot to be found in it.

So Mahmud Fakhro stays on over there, where there is nothing but the street, the remains of the shelling, and his solitude. When he goes up to the third floor, which he moved into after the gunmen left, and opens the fridge, it smells. There is no electricity. It is as though he is the only living being in a city of ghosts.

It was on that street that he met her. He wasn't looking or anything, she happened to walk by one day. When he first saw her, making her way alone down the street, he thought she was a pretty woman. Although she must have seen him squatting in the broken glass in front of the building, she didn't turn to look his way. She just kept going, while he followed her with his eyes.

No, she wasn't pretty, and she didn't take the slightest notice of him. And what was she doing there alone anyhow? On an impulse, Mahmud jumped to his feet and started to follow her. Her footsteps rang down the deserted street, and he walked behind her, but she didn't turn round. Then she veered off to the right, entering a narrow alley that stank of burnt paint. Or so he thought. She reached a metal gate, opened it, and was about to go in, when she turned and looked at him. He thought she was going to say something, at any rate that's what her lips suggested, so he smiled and said hello. The word slipped out so quietly that most likely the woman didn't hear it. At any rate, she didn't answer, and then slowly turned and entered the building.

Realizing he was alone again, Mahmud left. But the woman remained on his mind.

Sitting by himself in front of his building, fondling the pistol grip, he kept thinking about going back there and up those stairs . . . What could she do to him, a woman by herself? But he didn't go. He was afraid there would be other men in her household, or that she might have some disease. And he didn't see her again after that.

Alone on the deserted street, Mahmud occasionally sought the company of the fighters and went with them on forays to the old downtown souks. But mostly he spent his time sitting in front of the building.

"I'm not scared," he would tell the gunmen. "I'm on your side, honestly, but I can't leave the building."

The thing is he didn't want to die. Dying was serious business, as far as he was concerned. He did not understand how those young men went to their deaths so easily. Dying was no easy matter, he thought. So he sat there, alone.

And then he saw her again. He was sitting on the steps in front of the building, eating tinned beef, bread and a tomato, when he saw her coming down the street by herself. She was walking slowly.

"Please join me," Mahmud said.

She thanked him and continued on her way. No, not exactly – she slowed her pace, so he repeated his invitation. She halted and turned towards him, and leaned against the iron railing between the street and the steps where he sat.

She asked him what he was eating. "Meat," he said, his mouth full. And then again, "Please join me." Entering the perimeter of the building, she told him she didn't eat tinned meat, and stood there as he carried on chewing. Looking at her, Mahmud noted the tattoos, like rings, round her eyes. She's pretty, he thought, and asked her what her name was.

"Bahiyya," she replied. "Bahiyya Agha."

"Pleased to meet you . . . Mahmud Fakhro."

"*Ahlan wa sahlan.*"

He asked her what she was doing in this deserted neighbourhood. She told him she worked as a maid for Mr Ahmad Rustom.

"They went to France, and I am here by myself, watching the house for them."

"But it's dangerous here, it's a war zone."

She told him she placed her trust in God, and that her sons visited her from time to time. When he enquired further about them, she recounted that her husband had died of a heart attack three years earlier and that her sons worked as labourers on construction sites. She told him she felt scared living on this street all by herself and that she had better be on her way.

Mahmud was not sure what to do but he did not stop her. The days passed. She did not return, nor did Mahmud dare try to visit her.

One rainy morning, Mahmud Fakhro woke up early with a bitter taste in his throat. At first he thought he'd go home and visit Fatimah and the children. But then he quickly changed his mind.

He stretched, had something to drink, and ate an orange, singing some old tunes from his childhood. Then he shaved, dressed and went out.

He walked down the empty street, turned off to the right and stopped in front of her building. He pushed open the wrought-iron gate, noting its loud squeak, and slowly padded up the stairs. He wondered what floor she lived on. Reaching the first-floor landing, he found an open door. When he went in, there was nothing there – the apartment was completely empty, not a stick of furniture in it, nothing but the floors and graffiti on the walls. So he hurried up to the second floor, where he came to a closed door. He knocked, no-one answered, so he went on to the third floor. There, an acrid smell wafted out to the landing from an open door, so he continued on and reached a closed door. He knocked once, and then again. He heard a commotion inside and then a woman's voice: "Who's there?"

"It's me, Mahmud."

It was her voice, he was sure she would open the door. He stood there expectantly, but the voice disappeared and the door didn't open. He knocked again and again, but still the door didn't open. Mahmud felt humiliated . . . he had been rejected. She didn't want to let him in. But then the door opened a crack, framing her face. She asked him what he wanted.

"Nothing. I was just passing . . ."

"But . . ."

"But nothing . . ."

She opened the door all the way and he stepped in. He sat in the living room as she disappeared for a while and came back with a glass of tea. She settled down in a blue armchair across from him and Mahmud made conversation. He told her about the corpse that the "boys" had stumbled across in front of the clothing boutique down in the souks – they figured it was an impatient thief who had headed for the stores before the area had been secured.

Looking him in the eye, the woman bemoans the looting and the looters. Then, with her eyes still fixed on him, she falls silent, sips her tea, and clears her throat.

Mahmud does not quite know how to move closer. He feels that he's on fire, everything inside him is ablaze. He tries putting his arm around her but she won't let him.

"No," she says, "I have children, shame on you."

But from the tone of her voice and the glimmer in her eye, Mahmud senses that she too wants him. So he moves a little closer, and then, he takes her. He takes all of her, just like that. And oh, how different she feels! It has been so long since Mahmud tasted a "different" sort of woman. She is not exactly pretty, he thinks, as he watches her undress and cup her hands to her brown, slightly rounded shoulders, but she is something else . . . she moans and she screams, she says things and takes all of him, she kisses his neck and writhes with pleasure, this way and that way . . . as he lowers himself into her, he can hear her panting breaths, and feel the shiver in her body, as if she has not slept with a man for a hundred years. Making love to her, he feels as if he has known her forever, and he wants to cry; he feels a sob rising in his throat but it remains stifled, only the tears flow down his cheeks. Later, silently, he just listens to her moaning as she melts under his touch, like a piece of dough he is kneading, and wraps her body around his as he lies back in bed, smoking; then he rests his head against her belly, and listens to her telling him about the trouble with the children and her fear of living on this street.

And I, too, am afraid, he thinks, realising now that he dare not go with the *shabab* anymore because he is really afraid. But he says nothing. He listens to her, cradles her under him and takes her once more, while she surrenders and quivers with pleasure. Oh, what a woman, a woman who quivers! Mahmud wants to tell her about little Fatimah, how he used to watch her going down the stairs and call out *mashallah* after her, and how she has

changed . . . she is like a stone in his arms now and he no longer
desires her . . . how he still loves her, and loves Ali and, even though
Ali is dead, he is still Abu Ali, even though Ali did himself in and
seared everybody's heart.

But he says nothing. He just lets his body plunge into that
warmth, into that wetness that fills every crevice, like the water
from the spring over there, in the distant village. And then she
tells him that's where she's from too.

"I'm a servant, born a servant and I'll die a servant."

She gets up – no, she isn't pretty, but she is different – and pulls
on her dressing gown. She's older than me, Mahmud thinks, but
she's lovely and sweet.

She asks him to leave. "The children will be here soon. The
oldest one will be coming round and asking for money. He's not
working, and even though I have nothing to give him, he comes
by every day. I told him to find himself a job, any job, even with a
militia; but he won't, and he comes to me for money."

Mahmud gets up and dresses, wraps her in his arms, and plants
a kiss in her long curly hair, telling her he'll be back the following
day.

"No, no, don't. I'll come to your place, I'm afraid of the
children."

He leaves. Going downstairs slowly, his thighs and groin feel
pleasantly sore. When he reaches the street, the smell of the city
hits him – a mix of rubbish and rain and remains – but he feels
strangely energized. When he gets back to his building, he climbs
up to the third floor, where he now lives, turns on the radio and
listens to the same old news. Feeling hungry, he decides to go
and visit his wife and children – he'll see them and eat there.

He walks down the streets, long endless streets, and when he
arrives, he kisses Fatimah on both cheeks before entering the
house. He has something to eat, asks after the children, takes a
walk around the neighbourhood, and then goes back to Kantari.

There, he sits and waits.

He waits a long time.

Mahmud Fakhro, otherwise known as Abu Ali, sat in front of the building and waited, his heart leaping in his chest whenever he heard footsteps. He would swing round – no, it wasn't her – then he would forget that he was waiting for her, and wait again . . . as though he were young all over again, in love and waiting. But she never came. Ten whole days he waited, but she did not come.

He resolved to visit her again: when he went and knocked on her door, no-one opened . . . so he stood in front of her building and waited on the street. And along she came, with a young man by her side. For a moment, Mahmud was fearful that it was her son, but she stopped and greeted him, and introduced him to the young man. Then, she invited him up for a glass of tea.

They went upstairs together. As she busied herself in the kitchen, Mahmud sat in the living room, opposite the young man, who looked him over and asked after his health and spoke of the weather. Then she came in carrying glasses of tea and smiling. He drank his tea hurriedly and left.

He expected her visit, and sure enough she came past the next morning, but she would not go upstairs with him. "No," she said, "it won't do, it won't do at all. I've spoken to my son and he's O.K. with it if we get married . . . but not like this. I'm not a fallen woman, I have children, I'm a widow, and I don't want my name dragged through the mud." And she left.

What to do, thought Mahmud. Should he marry her? No, he'd just go back to her place and make love to her again and that would be that! But what if the son was at home with her? He decided to forget about it, and for the most part he did – except for that liquid fire blazing inside his groin.

He sat and thought. He couldn't go home anymore, he did not want to stay here guarding the building, and he did not have what it took to join the ranks of the *shabab*. He told her he was lonely.

She merely repeated what she had said before.

"But I'm already married."

"That's no problem."

True, where was the problem?

Still, he sat alone and waited.

Out and about one day, he saw the *shabab* and decided to join them around a fire they had lit in the Capuchin Church. And, suddenly, he saw it, the painting of Our Lady Mary: it was the same one, the very same Our Lady Mary that he had taken from Fatimah and thrown away. There she was before him now, but bigger. He aimed his gun and fired. Then, he had a glass of arrack with the boys and fell asleep under the ruined image.

When Fatimah saw him coming with that old woman by his side, she could not believe her eyes. She had heard – of course she had – but how dare he come to the house with her? Hussein had told her. He had gone to visit his father and found an old woman there, with a white headwrap and tattoos around her eyes and across her face, acting like the mistress of the house.

And here she was now, walking by his side . . . Fatimah was stupefied – she stood there, transfixed, speechless, when all she felt like doing was running away and screaming . . . Yes, there he was, with his stocky little body, getting closer, turning this way and that, as though answering the greetings of passers-by, his stride self-assured, with that woman at his side!

Entering, the woman extended her fingers to shake hands and Fatimah did likewise. They sat down, the children gathered around, and Fatimah went to the tiny kitchen to make coffee. She sensed him coming in behind her, and swung around angrily.

"I've married her, she's my wife now," he said, patting her on the shoulder.

Standing before the sink, coffee pot in hand, a great burning sensation spread between Fatimah's shoulders and down her spine, but she said nothing. Mahmud wiped the tears from her eyes, then left her to it and went back to the other room.

The two of them drank their coffee as Fatimah sat with the children clustered around her. That woman's manner was so different! She did all the talking and Mahmud went along with everything she said – it was as if he had turned into a woman! Every time he tried to say something, she would interrupt him, and he would fall silent! She looked the children over and asked imperiously why little Hassan's shirt was not clean, as Mahmud concealed his embarrassment with forced smiles.

Fatimah was stunned. This man was not the husband she knew! She was aware that men did this sort of thing, Sitt Huda had warned her. "A man is a man," she had said, "he's free to do as he pleases." But how could Mahmud go and marry this hag when they didn't have enough to eat – and then play wife to her!

With nowhere to go, Fatimah, who had waited and waited for him, now felt like a stranger in her own home, as this Bahiyya woman sat there one leg crossed over the other, brazenly smoking in front of everybody, flicking the ash from her cigarette with such an air of superiority, you'd think she was Sitt Huda . . . and gesturing showily, making sure everyone saw those gold bracelets coiled around her wrist . . . Fatimah counted, there were six of them.

Why, oh why, did this have to happen? And look at him, smiling beatifically at her . . . this was not the same man, not the Mahmud who beat her, the Mahmud who made her quake and beg for mercy. How he had changed! Damn, how this cursed life could bring a man down!

Fatimah does not know how she plucked up the courage to ask her husband where the two of them would live. The woman replied that they would stay in Kantari, in Khawaja Fadee's building, on the third floor. And she invited the children to come over and visit.

"We've redone the apartment, it's a proper home now, with

110

three bedrooms, a living room, a dining room, three bathrooms, a small room for the maid, wall-to-wall carpeting – you know, the works! And if it weren't for the water and the electricity being cut off, we would have hot running water and central heating!"

Then the two of them rose to leave, and Mahmud said he would be back the next day.

But he never did come back – at least not until the day they pumped all those bullets into his body. Actually, that's not true, he came back once before that, to tell her he'd divorced Bahiyya and thrown her out. But Fatimah didn't believe him. "You're lying," she told him, "I don't believe anything you say anymore!"

And when he did come back, his body was bloody and riddled with holes.

Everyone said he was a thief. Even at the funeral, she heard people say he had stolen that woman's bracelets and then turned her out. But she never saw him with any bracelets, and he never said anything about them . . . No, he didn't steal . . . But then why did they kill him? Fatimah doesn't know, she is all alone now, and this Hussein of hers has become like his father, always gone from the house. Whenever he shows up, he asks for money, and when she tells him she has nothing to give him, he starts yelling that he wants his father's bracelets.

"But your father didn't have any bracelets, and anyway I don't know anything about it!"

So he hit her – the dog, hitting his own mother!

And then he disappears again, and Fatimah remains alone, with that damned landlord Basheer al-Harati – all by herself, her work is never finished, and they threaten to kick her out. Were it not for Professor Nabeel Assi, she doesn't know what would have become of them. You'd think they wanted her and the children to starve to death.

I was frightened, says Fatimah. *No, no-one else died. The war was over, but why was there still shelling? The fighting had stopped, but not the shelling . . . the war's finished, they said, and nobody's dying anymore. Everyone was carrying on as if nothing had ever happened, as if those who had died weren't gone forever, as if Mahmud . . . oh, poor Mahmud . . . how they killed you! And now there was this man, standing on the pavement, eating silently, and nodding his head whenever I asked a question.*

"Why are you whitewashing the walls?"

Looking into her eyes, he tells her that it's on the way.

"Listen," he says, "it's coming . . . things are coming. Death is on the way." Pulling the navy-blue coat tight around his thin body, he drops his head. "The things that are coming, you don't know, no-one knows . . . but these walls . . . we must erase everything . . . everything must be whitewashed, every single solitary thing."

Pulling out a little rubber from his pocket, he goes on. "You see this rubber? They're going to give me a bigger one." Then he spreads his arms their full span and says. "It'll be this big."

"And who will give you the rubber?"

"They will. You don't know, none of you does . . . it's a huge rubber, and it doesn't just erase what's written on the walls, it'll wipe everything out . . . all I'll have to do is put it, like this, against the wall, and boom, the wall itself will disappear. No, it won't blow up: there'll be no noise, no explosion, no dust or debris, no rubble! I'll put it against the wall and the wall will vanish, it'll disappear just like that! Now you see it, now you don't . . . There'll be a thousand men and a thousand women, we'll all go out, each with a huge rubber, and we will erase everything . . . wipe out walls . . . houses . . . faces . . . everything. There'll be nothing left, everything will vanish, you will vanish and I will vanish, the city will vanish, and the posters too, everything will vanish into white, white-as-an-egg white, white as the whites of your eyes, white as white. Everything will be erased . . . things will fall apart, just like that, as if they weren't already falling apart. Like the officers. I used to be an officer too, but I quit . . . I was the greatest officer, I'm sure you've heard about my exploits, how I used to kill . . . how I would ambush them at the crossroads and kill them. And now I carry around the rubber . . . Look! You're not really looking, your eyes aren't focusing . . . but me, I can see, I can see it all, as clearly as the palm of my hand . . . my palm is white, I painted it with whitewash . . . Everything is like my palm, but you don't see my palm, no-one can see it, because it's different. And here I am, the officer, my men all around me, soldiers standing to attention in silence. I march ahead of them, they dare not breathe, and then I strike one of them with the cane I carry in my hand. But you don't see my hand. The soldiers run away, and I laugh at them, poor wretches! They don't know and you don't know, no-one knows the truth. And I don't know what the truth is. But they will give it to me, and we will be a thousand men and a thousand women, can you imagine how many we'll be? We will erase everything and die. Everything dies . . . it's as if we died, as if everything died, as if everything . . . No, marriage and women aren't for me . . . I don't go near women, but you're different . . . your cooking tastes good . . . your *hindbeh* is delicious . . . I hate food . . . why don't you drink *laban*? *Laban* is the best thing in the world. I get by on nothing but *laban*."

And he leaves.

Standing there alone, Fatimah sees Mahmud going into the house, looking scared.

"Now what?"

"Nothing," Mahmud answers. "Just this damned woman."

"Bahiyya . . . ?"

"I've divorced her, woman, I've divorced her. But she's following me around."

"What do you mean?"

"I don't know, but her children . . . ."

"What children?"

"She has three boys."

"And what do they want? Goddamn her and her children!"

"They want the money, the *mu'akhar* – the compensation."

"And you, you promised her the *mu'akhar*, you wretched man! . . . Lord, protect us from your sort! A decrepit old hag like her, and you signed over a *mu'akhar*!"

"No, I didn't sign . . . but they still want it."

"Lord, have mercy . . . and how did this come to pass?"

"They came and threatened me. I told them to take the apartment, take the whole building, take everything in the building. But they rejected my offer. They threatened me, so I ran away."

Mahmud was really scared. Only twice before had Fatimah seen him like this: the first time was over there, when they put the bag over his head; the second time was when he and that Bahiyya came to visit together; and now, because of those children of hers.

He stayed at home all that day, reading the papers and smoking. He went to bed early that evening, long before the children did. And when Fatimah lay down next to him and tried to cuddle up to him – he had not slept with her in such a long time – he pushed her away roughly and sat up in bed smoking. He chain-smoked all night. He did not sleep, just smoked one cigarette after another. She didn't dare go near him again, and fell asleep.

She woke up early to a strange noise. When she got up, he was making tea, so she sat with him in the kitchen and tried to talk to him. But he would not say anything. He just smoked, looking into the distance while she sat beside him, feeling scared. She felt paralysed with fear, as if her limbs were frozen.

But no-one came.

He hunkered down inside, while she was in the lobby of the building sweeping as usual, and the children played outside by the pavement. No, they won't come, she thought, what was all this fuss about the *mu'akhar* anyway, they were just being bullies.

She told him she thought they were just bullying him, just so they could fleece him.

"They won't do anything," Fatimah said. "She should feel grateful to be married . . . who'd marry her, the ugly old hag . . ."

But why had he divorced her?

Fatimah asked him why, but he hemmed and hawed. She screamed the question at him, but when he looked at her with that old look of his, she gave it up.

Why did he divorce her? Was it because he realized she was ugly? Or was it maybe because he loved his own wife? But why was he staring at her like that? He must have divorced her because he loved his family. How could he leave his family, his own children?

Fatimah was standing in front of the building, broom in hand, when she saw them. All she saw were faces, dark faces, and guns. There were at least three of them. They spilled out of a black Chevrolet and came towards her, their guns cocked, their faces blackened. Fatimah stepped back, she wanted to run and gather the children together, but they were closing in on her.

"Where is he?" one of them asked.

She retreated further and reached the door to their quarters; she opened it and ran in, locking the door behind her. Where was he? She could not see him anywhere.

"They've come," she said. "Mahmud! They're here!"

She expected him to leap out, gun in hand, but he had vanished. When she looked, she found him standing in the corner of the kitchen, shaking. As she opened her mouth to speak, he put a finger to his lips to silence her. It looked like he was crying. She ran to go back outside and get the children and saw him edging out of the kitchen. As he reached the door to their room the wooden panels were blown off the hinges, splitting, and Mahmud stood there bleeding.

"They got me!"

She took a step in his direction, but bullets were whizzing through the air; she crouched down in the opposite corner. Mahmud, still standing, fell to his knees, and there was blood everywhere. Now she saw that he wasn't carrying his gun after all. There was more blood, and then Mahmud keeled over and collapsed onto his left side. One of the gunmen kicked the door down, Mahmud's body shifted slightly, shuddering, as if a remnant of life still coursed through him. Then this black face appeared, smeared with soot, its white teeth glistening. His machine gun was pointed at her, but he didn't fire.

Slowly, the gunmen retreated.

As she rushed to Mahmud's side, Fatimah began to wail. She grabbed hold of her husband, trying to drag him away from the door, but she couldn't. She stepped over him and ran outside to find the children huddling against the wall like terrified chicks. She grabbed them, all of them, including the neighbours' children, and herded them into the room. Her dress was soaked with blood. People gathered around her but no-one offered to take him to the hospital, until Professor Nabeel Assi arrived and took him in his car, leaving her alone in the house. When he returned two hours later, he told her Mahmud was dead.

She wept, everyone wept, even strangers wept with her. After the burial, Professor Nabeel took her aside – he too believed the bracelet story – and told her not to tell anyone about the bracelets.

"Keep them," he said, "you may need them one day."

When Fatimah told him she knew nothing about them, his smile was full of derision.

"You're free to do as you please, but I'm telling you, don't breathe a word about them to anyone. You may need them yet."

What good were the bracelets anyway with Mahmud gone? And now even Hussein didn't believe me. He was convinced I was hiding them somewhere, and was determined to get hold of them. What kind of child does that? At least his father used to give me money, but all he ever does is hit me. No-one has ever raised a hand against me . . . Mahmud did, of course, but that was different. The wretch, how dare he! . . . Well, no matter, God is great, and yes, as God is my witness,

I stand here alone with the children, the building, and me all on my own . . .

But now there's this Khalil Ahmad Jaber, or the man they call Khalil Jaber, and that's another calamity. And what a calamity! Men! The cause of all my problems! All the men I've ever known have been a problem – and now there's Khalil.

"*Ya akhi*, I tell you I don't know him, I swear to God, I don't know a thing."

Fatimah Fakhro is standing in the local party office, surrounded by militiamen. Sobbing, she repeats over and over again that she knows nothing. But this one man, the one with the shades, is not paying the slightest bit of attention to anything she's saying – it is as if she were talking to the walls . . . Her, talking, and them not hearing anything . . . She is frightened, she feels the same fear as when she saw that other face – the very same fear she felt when he pointed the machine gun at her and didn't fire.

"I swear to God, I know nothing. Yes, I did see him, I saw him several times. Yes, I spoke to him and he told me, he told me that he would erase the walls, and I believed him, I swear I did. I'm not sure how, but I believed him. What have I got to do with anything? I didn't kill him . . . you're not serious . . . yes, yes, he said all those things and more. I wanted to give him something to eat . . . he reminded me of Mahmud . . . I got to thinking of how he was all alone in Kantari, Hussein had told me how spooky it was on that street and I thought of Mahmud, sitting there out on the pavement, all by himself, guarding the building. And I said to myself this man is just like him, and I took pity on him. No, no, he didn't say much . . . well, yes, he used to say that . . . but I didn't believe him. The fact is, I didn't believe his story about the thousand men and the thousand women – they aren't stories you can believe. But then, I thought, maybe he's right . . . everything's possible these days . . . who would have ever believed that all that has happened

117

to us would happen? But it did. No-one would have believed it possible, and yet these things happened, and he died. So I thought, well, maybe . . . And he looked so poor, flapping his arms in the air like a pigeon fancier, yes, just like a pigeon fancier who couldn't find his pigeons. I used to bring him bread and cheese, and he'd say he liked *laban*. No, no, he had nothing to do with it, he didn't talk to me about anyone, only about the thousand men . . . I don't know, I really don't. He said a thousand men and a thousand women, but I don't know any more than that, honestly, I don't. He only spoke to me once, just once, and he asked me to make him a dish of stuffed grape leaves; so I made him some, and I waited for him, he told me he would come to visit me, he said he would eat it sitting on the pavement . . . yes, that's right, he told me to bring it out to him, over by the white wall. I waited for him, but he never came. And when I went out to look, there weren't any white walls – all the walls were covered in pictures and posters. None of them were white. I did see a yellowish wall, so I waited there. It was my fault – he said he'd wait for me next to the white wall, but I couldn't find it. So then I waited for him at home, but of course he didn't come. Then the mistress told me he'd been found murdered . . . I really don't know anything, sir . . . Yes, of course, you're right, sir . . . "

With a look of utter scorn, "Sir" got up and struck her. Fatimah wept and wailed, but "Sir" just slapped her face again. And then, they let her go.

"They let me go, I didn't say anything and I don't know why, I swear to God I don't. What I know, I told them. I told them everything I know. *Ya akhi*, it's nothing to do with me, I'm not the one going around killing people; we're not the ones doing the murdering, are we? They're the ones killing us! We don't kill people. Don't you see how Mahmud died? And, to add insult to injury, they demanded that I repair the lobby of the building. Instead of feeling sorry for me, Sitt Elham told me her husband, Basheer al-Harati, had agreed to let me stay on in the building only if I paid for the repairs."

"But I have no money."

"You have the bracelets, sell the bracelets."

"Even her! Poor Mahmud, you died like a thief! Everyone thought you stole the bracelets! But if you did, I'd like to know where they are! . . ."

Fatimah searched high and low but did not find anything. She went so far as to rip the tiles up from the floor of their room. Then she thought she would ask Hussein to help her look for them. When she did, he stared at her witheringly, as if he suspected her. She asked him to go to the house in Kantari and look there.

"I can't. Her children have taken over the apartment," Hussein replied.

"Alright then, let's phone Khawaja Fadee and tell him. Maybe he can help us evict them."

"How would he do that?"

"Well, it's his house, isn't it? He'll find a way . . ."

"No, he can't. It's no longer his. He no longer owns anything here, don't you realize? No, he can't help us."

Fatimah is sure that Hussein does not believe her and that he is convinced she is hiding the treasure. And now that he has found out about her thing with Khalil Ahmad Jaber, he has started to look at her in that strange way that he has – he does not have to shout or lift a finger against her anymore, all he has to do is give her that look, and she hands over whatever money she has. Regardless of what she pulls out of the handkerchief tucked in her bosom, he asks for more.

Still, she had to find those bracelets . . . but how? She thought of getting Professor Nabeel to intervene on her behalf about the Kantari house, but he did not believe her either. He thought she was lying. Even him, her sole advocate, her benefactor . . . So she decided to stop speaking. The best thing was to say nothing and do nothing. They were all going to die anyway, she thought, just like Mahmud, every single one of them.

As she sleeps, Fatimah dreams of Basheer al-Harati, dead; he is coming towards her, a white stick in his right hand, and everything is white. The walls are white, his face is white, his hair, everything. Holding on to the white stick, he advances slowly, and when he reaches her house, he falls to the ground. He falls on his knees, then keels over to the left and rolls away further and further into the distance like a barrel rolling off into the void, and she hears crying and wailing, the very same sounds she hears when the shells rain down on the neighbourhood.

Fatimah wakes up shaking with terror. She feels around for the children sleeping beside her, and tries to go back to sleep, but she can't. It's the first time it has ever happened to her. Khalil used to tell her that he couldn't sleep either.

"Why sleep? Half of life is wasted in sleep. Why do we have to sleep? I can't sleep, and soon no-one else will be able to either."

But he did. She saw him, with her own eyes, asleep on the pavement at about eight o'clock one evening. She walked right by without him noticing her. Fearing him dead, she went up to him and, after looking around furtively, leaned down close: his chest was rising and falling and this smell – an incredible stench – emanated from him, it was like . . . like what? She didn't know how to describe it – it was unlike anything she had ever smelled before . . . this smell of his, it remains in her nostrils to this day. Every time she wakes up at night and sits up in bed, the smell is there, as though he were asleep by her side – even though he died.

She gets up and washes her face, rinses out her nostrils and goes back to bed. But the smell will not go away, it is stuck to her. And so she has come to loathe the man – that's all she needed now, this man!

"I swear to God I don't know him," she told them, "I don't know anything."

Even though they didn't believe her, they let her go.

Professor Nabeel told her it was a bad idea to get mixed up in that sort of thing. She tried to tell him she had nothing to do with it. He said he believed her, but that other people didn't, and that there was talk of a relationship.

"God forbid, sir! Not me! God is my witness."

Professor Nabeel told her not to cry, and tried to comfort her.

As for this man, have any of you seen a frail man, with a navy coat glued to his body and his scrawny salt and pepper beard, shuffling up and down the streets like a sleepwalker, with a little bucket in his hand? Turning this way and that, tearing down what he has pasted up on the walls, chewing the shreds of paper, then bursting out laughing? Standing alone and chuckling loudly, he appears unseeing, as if he were the only person around . . . people going and coming around him – children throwing stones at him, old men indifferent, young people tossing a few coins into the bucket, assuming he's a beggar – and him, chewing away, his jaw moving up and down, up and down, then spitting something to the ground, and walking on . . . He jumps across the rubbish piles, throwing scraps at the cats, and leans against the wall, not speaking to anyone . . . he doesn't respond when spoken to and darts between the cars halted in traffic, not looking at the drivers or their passengers, just hurrying on, oblivious to the mockery directed at the pith helmet on his head.

He walks on and on, tirelessly. And when he stops before the wall, he looks right and then left, and, after making sure no-one's watching him, he starts tearing at the paper, slipping the shreds into his mouth and chewing. Every so often, he dips a tiny paintbrush into the bucket he carries around with him and tries to paint the wall white, leaving nothing but barely visible white squiggles. He stands back and looks at the wall, as though admiring his handiwork, and then goes on his way.

This is Khalil Ahmad Jaber. Has anyone seen him?

Fatimah says she has, but that she didn't believe what he was saying.

Ali Kalakesh saw him, and so did Musa Kanj. Mahmud Fakhro didn't see him, and neither did Sitt Huda, Khawaja Mitri or Khawaja Fadee.

But he was here. Before he died, that is. Fatimah told them it could have been suicide.

"Maybe he killed himself," she said.

The one in the dark sunglasses slapped her, and then asked about the bracelets.

"Where are you hiding the bracelets?"

"I swear, I'm not hiding them, sir. God is my witness! I don't know where they are. I swear Mahmud didn't steal them, that woman's lying . . . she killed him because he divorced her, *Effendi*‡."

He told her he was not an *effendi*.

"As you wish, sir . . . But she's the criminal."

"And this Khalil Ahmad Jaber, what were you doing with him?"

"Nothing, I swear, we didn't do anything. He didn't even eat the food I made. I cooked him some *warak 'inab* – Mahmud, may he rest in peace, loved stuffed grape leaves, and so did this man – he said he wanted them with *laban*. So I made him some, but he never ate them."

And although he wandered around looking petrified, as though he'd been terror-struck, he laughed at the same time – a frightened, laughing, wandering man, with bits of paper dropping out of his pockets! Not speaking to anyone, answering no-one, and little pieces of coloured paper cascading from his coat . . . that was Khalil Ahmad Jaber! Everyone saw him, lying on the yellow paving stones, propped up against the wall, dreaming.

‡A term of respect, from Ottoman times, similar to the English "sir".

No-one knew for sure whether he dreamed, but he was there alright, lying back, asleep, with his head buried in his coat.

Except that when they found him, there was no coat. He was naked from the waist up and riddled with bullets – his face torn up, his mouth open, his teeth smashed, and the coat gone. No-one asked about the coat.

And Fatimah remained alone, with her seven children, the eldest always gone, every morning going up to Mr Basheer al-Harati's apartment and coming back down in the evening, sweeping the lobby, cooking for the children, and saying very little.

Sitt Elham asked her once why she said nothing. Fatimah did not know what to answer, she just shook her head, which made her hair fall across her face. "And why haven't you got your white wrap on?"

So Fatimah smoothed her hair back and went downstairs to get her white headwrap.

"But you never say anything." Fatimah just smiled, baring her glistening white teeth.

No-one notices anymore that she hardly ever speaks – even Sitt Elham has stopped mentioning it.

Her work done, and the children asleep, Fatimah stands in the doorway of her little room – having repaired both the door and the lobby – and gazes into the distance. Gazing out in silence, she sees a white man, holding a white stick, coming towards her.

CHAPTER IV

The Dog

The clatter of the ancient truck lumbering through the hazy Beirut morning. The sea, the mingled smells of saltwater and fish . . . Sky, grey clouds, waves . . . Engine clacking, wheels pitching the ruts, the truck rumbles along. Zayn 'Alloul is sitting next to the driver in the front. Mohammad al-Kharoobi and Saleh Ahmad are crouched on two small fenders at the back-end of the vehicle. The aroma of Virginia blend suffuses the front cabin: the driver, known as Nabeel al-Hallaq – Nabeel-the-barber – is smoking. Finding this unpleasant, Zayn fans his face with his hand to try and disperse the smoke, but it still penetrates his nostrils. When he coughs and opens his window, the chill air is like a slap on the face. Rolling the window shut, he turns to the driver:

"Now, really, tell me, is this normal – to be smoking at four in the morning?"

The driver looks at him unperturbed, inhales deeply, and carries on driving. Zayn 'Alloul opens the window once more and breathes in the sea air while the vehicle rumbles on its way.

Thank goodness, things are back to normal: a big city like Beirut with no rubbish collection and rats practically eating people alive does not bear thinking about! Zayn's neighbour, in Hamra, reported seeing a rat as large as a cat once. Zayn told him it was because of the rubbish everywhere. The neighbour, an old Beiruti who runs a juice shop on Hamra Street, claimed that he had seen rats crawling out of the sea!

"I tell you, I saw them with my own eyes! Can you believe it, rats actually swimming in the sea and then coming ashore? No way to eat fish these days, it's out of the question! No wonder people get sick after eating fish . . . The fish are being bitten by disease-infested rats!" Zayn himself does not believe that matters have come to quite such a critical pass; at any rate, he is not all that bothered about it. Grumbling comes naturally to most people but, as he likes to say, the poor too have to live, and dirt is like a vaccine.

The thought brings to mind the paediatrician at the American University Hospital who found it difficult to believe that Zayn had not had his son vaccinated against polio – though he found it easy enough to pocket his fifty-lira note! Holding the baby in his arms, Zayn tried to explain to the doctor that he had seven children – and none of them was immunized. The doctor, appalled, spoke to Zayn curtly.

"But dirt is a natural vaccine, doctor," the nurse butted in. "It strengthens one's immune system."

"We are not dirty, ma'am," Zayn told her. "We're cleaner than you are."

It is true though, and the nurse was right, dirt acts like a vaccine. His mother was always telling him to let the children play in the sand. "But they'll put it in their mouth, Mother . . . Think of it, all that dirt!"

"It's pure penicillin, son. Let them be. Penicillin is a kind of mould, and dirt is pretty mouldy. Leave them alone."

"Mother, that makes no sense."

"It's true though. The nurse told me all about penicillin."

So he lets the children be, and his mother prattles on about the olives up in the village. Zayn does his best to comfort her. He tells her it is very dangerous to go up there at the moment, because of the shelling everywhere.

"You can't possibly tend the olive trees under these circum-stances."

But she simply doesn't understand.

"I'm going anyway, my dear," she tells him, reclining in bed.

A partial stroke has left her bedridden, with a strangely lop-sided face, a twisted mouth and a semi-paralysed arm. And then there is Husniyyah, his wife, constantly complaining that it's becoming intolerable to live like this, and him trying to calm things down.

Honestly, all this talk about life being intolerable! Zayn thanks the good Lord that they all managed to escape Naba'a[‡] alive during the fighting – before it was overrun, and all those atrocities took place. Initially, they fled to the village, and when they returned to Beirut, they found a place to stay in Hamra. Now, honestly speaking, how could Naba'a possibly be better than Hamra? True, there they had their own house, even though it was a rental, and here they're only refugees . . . But at least now there's no rent to pay, and what's more, here it's a building, a high-rise – even though there is the landlord, damn him and his petty ways, . . . always coming around to "inspect" the building, casting sideways glances at everybody, as if we had the plague, and disapproving of the laundry hanging from the balconies! What does he expect, that the clothes should remain unwashed? He says it mars the beauty of the building! I suppose he thinks we should be dirty so the view can remain unspoiled! Still, when all's said and done, Hamra's better than Naba'a: there the house was small, just one room and a poky kitchen; here it's large and airy. There are three rooms – two bedrooms and a living room – plus it's furnished . . . fridge, oven, armchairs, all the modern conveniences you could want . . . All of that, and still Husniyyah says that life in Naba'a was better!

"There, people were human beings at least!"

Well, what to do? They can't return to Naba'a, and living in the village is out of the question.

‡ Naba'a was a northeastern suburb of Beirut which grew into a slum settlement during Lebanon's boom years in the 1970s. Largely populated by Muslims, it was "ethnically cleansed" in the initial phase of the civil war by Christian militias trying to consolidate homogeneously populated territory.

The only thing that bothers Zayn 'Alloul about their new home is the cinema on the first floor of the building: its lurid posters of naked women, and the laughter and raucousness into the early hours, they are truly a thorn in his side. "We're decent people, we are, with young daughters!"

The smoke from the American cigarettes envelops the front cabin, as the truck crawls along the blue-grey and seemingly endless shore. Joggers, in navy tracksuits or shorts, gradually emerge, some running, others walking briskly, with their heads held high and their arms swinging vigorously back and forth. The early-morning stillness is broken only by the noise of the passing truck and the rolling sea.

"What do they do out here every morning?" the driver asks.

"Exercise, man, exercise," Zayn tells him. "I'm no expert, but doctors say people should jog so they won't get fat . . . It's just another fad of these cursed times!"

"You know Jameel? The son of Imm Mohammad as-Saqa – he was big as a bull, they thought it was his glands, but the doctor told him the only solution was jogging . . . So out he went out and bought one of those navy tracksuits . . . What a wimp he turned out to be: he did it a few times then stopped, because he couldn't face getting up that early – at any rate, that's what people said!"

The truck comes to a halt beside a mound of rubbish. Moham-mad al-Kharroubi and Saleh Ahmad jump down and start shovel-ing the rubbish into the back of the truck. Zayn remains seated next to the driver – he does not like working this strip of the Manara Corniche: it's littered with empty beer cans that make him feel nauseous so early in the morning; and anyway, he is the most senior man among them, he has been a rubbish collector for twenty years, and he is entitled to a rest.Glancing out of the window, he sees al-Kharroubi ogling a young girl wearing blue jogging shorts. She is blonde and fair-skinned, clearly a foreigner.

Strange creatures they are, these foreigners . . . Fancy getting up at the crack of dawn to jog!

The girl is alone. There is no-one else around. Mohammad al-Kharroubi goes up to her.

"Mmmm . . . hot stuff!" Then he wolf-whistles, and intones "*Allah-uakbar*! God is great who bestowed this morning on us!"

The girl steps back as al-Kharroubi draws closer and leans nonchalantly against the front of the truck, baring all his teeth. Then he edges closer and makes an obscene gesture. All of a sudden, seemingly out of nowhere, a young man appears and grabs the girl by the wrist. He glances menacingly at al-Kharroubi, who continues his approach undeterred until the young man releases the girl's wrist and comes right up to him.

"Looks like we're in for a bit of trouble," the driver says, watching the scene impassively and puffing on his cigarette.

Zayn hops out of the vehicle and tries to pull al-Kharroubi back.

"Leave them alone, man." And looking at the young man, he adds: "Really sorry about this, my apologies, brother."

The young man turns towards the sea and goes on his way with the girl.

The truck rumbles on. Zayn 'Alloul does not like trouble, he is sure the young man escorting the foreign girl must be in some position of responsibility or else he wouldn't dare to be out with her so early in the morning; what is more, he was armed. If this Mohammad al-Kharroubi had persisted, the man would surely have fired the gun and al-Kharroubi would have died like a dog, without anyone even bothering to ask after him!

He has got to be someone important, Zayn is sure of that. A neighbour of his in Hamra, a young man about the same age as this one, with a senior position on a newspaper, told him once that the best thing about his job was the foreign women. "They come as reporters to witness the revolution, the toiling masses, and the armed struggle," he said, "and when we take them to the training camps and the military outposts, they go nuts – they start feeling the guns and firing them. God only knows what gets into them, all they seem to want is to bed the boys . . . Maybe it's so they can feel proud that they've slept with a revolutionary, or that they can tell everyone back home how they've participated in the national struggle, or that they . . . this or that."

"We only just averted trouble there," says Zayn 'Alloul out loud. Not that he was scared. Not him. Even at the height of the Israeli shelling of Sharqiyyeh, when everyone in the village was running helter-skelter, screaming and shouting for dear life, his heart was like granite . . . he absolutely refused to leave the house with the rest of his family that day, despite his wife's entreaties.

Still, though, Zayn hates trouble: meddle in something that doesn't concern you, trouble is bound to follow – and you end up with a bruised face. Zayn 'Alloul feels his face gingerly.

Like that day when he got back home – they were still in Naba'a then – and instead of jumping for joy that he was safe, his wife started wailing, "*Ya msibati, ya sh'haari!* Oh, that such a fate has befallen me!" He tried to calm her down but she went on and on about his face. He knew how it looked, even though he wouldn't look in the mirror, he knew his face was swollen and black and blue all over. That was his mistake. He should have kept his big mouth shut . . .

Zayn 'Alloul had not done anything. The air battles were raging and people were huddled around their radios listening to the Cairo broadcast. Everyone was incredulous that the Egyptian army had managed to cross the Suez Canal and that the Arabs were now poised to defeat Israel. Zayn and a few other men were standing outside Abu Khalil's shop, drinking tea and talking, when the conversation shifted to the Bank of America incident. A unit of the Lebanese police had launched an assault on the bank after an armed group had taken some hostages, demanding that the bank contribute to the Arab war effort. As a result of the operation, two gunmen had been killed, two others arrested, and the hostages released.

"It was wrong to do that," Abu Khalil was saying. "The war is with Israel. Why attack the bank?"

"It's an American bank, isn't it? And America is Israel. Whether it's over there or over here, it's the same war, can't you see?" one of the young men gathered around the shop said.

Newspaper in hand, Abu Khalil edged towards the shaft of light pouring out of the shop.

"Listen up, you young ones, Ali Shuayb took an American man hostage – an innocent man – and killed him. That's not right." Then he read from the paper:

"It was Ali Shuayb who killed the American, John Conrad Maxwell, after explaining to him – with a bit of help from one of the other hostages, as Ali knew no English – that he was going to die because the deadline he'd given the authorities had expired. The American begged for his life to be spared but Ali Shuayb shot him in the back. The American fell to the ground screaming and pleading for his life, while Ali Shuayb and another gunman, thought to be Jihad Assad, kicked him as he lay on the floor. Then Ali aimed at his chest, fired the gun, and the American breathed his last."

"Tell me now, how can that be right? It's outrageous," Abu Khalil added. "We are fighting Israel, aren't we? So the war's over there. This isn't right."

"Lies, nothing but lies!" Zayn 'Alloul retorted. "Ali Shuayb didn't shoot the American in the back! He shot him in the chest. We don't shoot people in the back. It's nothing but a lie, the government is lying."

"Ali Shuayb! By God, now there's a man for you!"

"A man to feel sorry for nonetheless . . . He was poor, and it's always the poor that die!"

And thus it was that Zayn 'Alloul began to recount stories about Ali Shuayb, about guns and weapons, answering this question and that, as if he knew it all. He'd known Ali Shuayb as a child playing in the dirt, and then as a young man, when he and Ali discussed politics. Ali always said that without the armed struggle, there would be no solution. But Zayn hadn't known that Ali was involved with the *feda'iyeen*,‡ that he was the leader of an armed group, and that he could occupy a bank in the commercial centre and kill one of the hostages, and then die like that. Zayn was getting quite carried away.

"I swear to God, tomorrow I'm going down to the village to attend Ali's funeral. And everyone else should do the same. Ali's a martyr: a martyr who carried arms, fought, and died for the cause."

As he answered everyone's questions, Zayn 'Alloul felt swollen with pride: Ali Shuayb was from his village after all and he knew him very well. Now they would no longer look on him as a mere rubbish collector, as someone with a despicable job.

Then the conversation shifted to questions relating to municipal services, and Zayn told them that though work was proceeding normally they needed more trucks, as the city was growing rapidly. He also said that they really should be armed – well, he didn't say that exactly, but he said things that were understood to mean that he was calling for an armed uprising against the government.

That night there was a police raid.

A military jeep drew up outside his house, policemen, with rifles cocked, banged violently on the door. Sleepy-faced, Zayn opened the door in his pyjamas. They grabbed him and dragged

‡ The plural of *feda'i*, the popular term used to refer to Palestinian fighters. Literally, it means one who sacrifices himself, especially for his country.

him out by the arms and legs. His wife got up, frightened, and then his children all woke up, just in time to see him being led away. He did not know what was going on; he asked the officer, but they shoved him into the jeep under a torrent of blows, punches and curses, and took him straight to Internal Security in Badaro.

"But I haven't done anything . . . I don't know anything!"

They hustled him out of the jeep and pushed him into a dark cell, slamming the metal door shut behind him. Zayn began to wail, he had done nothing, nothing at all, he had no links to anyone suspect, why had they thrown him in here? He fell into a fitful sleep, dozing and then waking with a start, as if someone had punched him in the stomach. He tried to doze off again but he was desperate for a cigarette, so he began pretending to smoke, bringing up to his mouth the two fingers that usually held the cigarette, drawing them close to his lips and inhaling deeply. Then he tried to go back to sleep again. It was a night he would not easily forget. That's what he had told his wife when they brought him home three days later: the three nights in that cell were unforgettable. He didn't have words to describe it, he told her. "It was revolting. I had to urinate in the same room I was held in – into a little tin can which stayed there for the whole three days."

Then they took him off for questioning. But there was no questioning, just beating and kicking. There were four of them in the room, with him in the middle, like a football; first, one would punch him, then the next one would catch him, and so on. After that they gave him a taste of the "chicken",[‡] and one of them told him they'd make "mincemeat" out of him.

"Godless wretches! Atheists, Communists, sons of bitches, the lot of you! . . ."

"I'm not an atheist . . ." He could hear the blows but could not go on.

‡ A well-known method of torture whereby the victim is hung upside down by his feet, like a plucked chicken.

"Don't talk back, you son of a bitch."

He was more than willing to talk, but they weren't asking him anything. Not one question! All they did was beat him, and then they took him to see the officer. Standing behind his desk, he looked like he too was ready to start thrashing him.

"My respects, sir."

"Out with it now! And quickly! Tell us everything you know about the organization."

"What organization?"

"Ali Shuayb's."

"I swear I don't know anything."

"What do you mean you don't know?"

The officer told him they knew everything there was to know about him. They knew that he had been standing outside Abu Khalil's shop talking about his acquaintance with Ali Shuayb; they knew he was married to Husniyyah and that he worked for the municipal authority; they knew that he was thinking of selling a piece of land he had inherited from his father; and they also knew he was involved in smuggling arms from the South to Beirut, and that he kept the weapons hidden somewhere outside his home.

"Where are they, you dog?"

"Sir, there are no weapons."

It was then that the officer went for him. Zayn stood absolutely still as the officer struck him, shouting and cursing, and spraying his face with spittle. The officer then dragged Zayn back to his cell with a bloody nose.

Oh God, now he'd lose his job with the municipality. In that dark cell of his, Zayn felt very sorry for himself. "If I lose my job, what will I do? Nothing! There's nothing I know how to do aside from being a rubbish collector. And the municipal corporation is a state agency. But I haven't done anything against the state, I'm not against it, on the contrary, I'm all for it. And I don't know any

Ali Shuayb. Poor Ali, calling him a dog when he's a martyr . . . they're the dogs . . . and even if he weren't a martyr, he's dead, and they killed him . . . and the dead may suffer only mercy! Some God-fearing officer he was! . . . Oh, but why won't they let me smoke?"

In the evening, a man in civilian clothes came and unlocked the cell and told him to come out. Zayn was sure he was in for another beating.

"Sir, honestly, I know nothing."

The officer in charge of the so-called interrogation had told him that if he confessed and told the truth, the beating would stop. So he made up his mind then and there to confess. He would tell them that he was a member of Ali Shuayb's organization. And then surely the beating would stop.

"I have something to say," Zayn said.

"Shut up," the man said.

"But sir, it's something really important."

"Shut up, will you! And listen. A jeep is on its way here now, and there'll be a First Lieutenant Nujaym asking for you. You are to go with him, understood?"

"But sir, I have something to tell you, I want to talk to the officer who interrogated me."

"It won't be necessary. Not necessary, you hear. First Lieutenant Nujaym will be coming here to take you to the Military Tribunal. There you'll sign some papers and then you can go."

"What do you mean, go?"

"Go home."

Zayn 'Alloul could not believe his ears. They were lying to him! They were going to take him off for more questioning and another beating. "But sir . . ." The man in civilian dress walked off and Zayn 'Alloul waited, sitting on a wooden bench in the empty hall. His mind was made up, as soon as he saw Lieutenant Nujaym, he would confess. A knot in the pit of his stomach.

Night fell, and still no-one came for him.

Then there were footsteps outside and, craning his neck, Zayn saw an officer running in and shouting.

"Zayn 'Alloul!"

"Yes, sir!"

"Get up and walk."

Zayn did as he was told.

"Where are your clothes?" the officer asked, surprised.

"They took me from the house in my pyjamas."

"O.K. Let's go."

He was bundled into a big estate car. The officer sat in the front, Zayn in the back, next to a soldier holding a rifle between his legs. The officer said something to the driver, which Zayn strained to hear. The officer was saying that the question of Ali Shuayb and his extremist Communist group was really getting to him.

"We've arrested a hundred people, and not one of them is linked to the organization. So where is this organization, then? All our information seems to be false. The organization has disappeared, vanished into thin air. Yet they're still out there killing people. It'll be our turn next."

Clearing his throat, the driver ventured that it had nothing to do with them whatsoever.

"It's between them and the authorities."

"What do you mean? We are the authorities. You want the country to fall apart? We are the country, and it is our duty to eliminate every single one of them."

The car reached the Military Tribunal.

"Get out!" the officer barked.

Zayn 'Alloul climbed out of the vehicle and followed the lieutenant. They entered a luxurious office. The officer saluted and stood to attention. The man sitting behind the desk was in civilian clothes; he yawned ostentatiously as he asked:

"Where is he then?"

"Right here," replied First Lieutenant Nujaym.

Zayn stepped forward; he could see there were papers on the desk.

"Sign here."

"What are these?"

"Hurry up, will you . . . you don't need to know everything! They're papers, just papers. Sign."

Zayn 'Alloul took the ballpoint pen from the man in civilian dress and signed.

"You can go home now."

Joy slowly enveloped Zayn 'Alloul. He had never felt so happy, not even on his wedding day. Of course he was happy the day he got married to Husniyyah, but he was also consumed with embarrassment. The young men from his village were being bold, slapping him around the neck and shoulders as he cringed with shame. He knew they were all thinking about how he was going to sleep with her that night. But his happiness now was different: it was pure.

Zayn took a step towards the officer, who held his hand extended. He felt so grateful that he bent down to kiss it, but the officer withdrew his hand.

"Go on, man. Get out."

Zayn stepped out of the large hall into the street, in filthy blue striped pyjamas and a pair of old, holey slippers. He felt like dancing for joy at the thought of his home, his job, even the truck. He stood waiting for a taxi to pass, but then realized he wasn't carrying any money. So he walked, past the Museum, past Sinn al-Feel, finally reaching Naba'a. He was exhausted, walking all the way home in his pyjamas, in the dead of night, like a beggar. Ignominy, that's what it was. And then when he arrived, instead of being happy, she started to wail – she didn't know how to be happy, that was her trouble, he always told her so. After having a wash, a proper one with soap and water, he had something to eat and went to bed. He ate without appetite though, as if he had not felt hungry during those three long, dark days. He went to bed, but instead of waking early as was his habit, he slept until seven.

"Why didn't you wake me up?" he asked her, irate.

She said she wanted to let him rest. But he wanted to go to work, he was afraid they would fire him because he had been absent for three days without a valid excuse. But when he went down to the municipality building, everything was quickly settled. His boss said they would just deduct the three days from his leave and then advised him not to get mixed up in politics.

Zayn was not upset about losing the days. He was happy just being back at work; actually, he was glad about the deduction, as it meant that the whole nightmarish episode was over. So there he was now, back at work, making the rounds with the truck, as usual.

Except that things had changed, they were different now. You needed special favours from friends in high places just to stay out of trouble. The biggest problem nowadays was that they fired at you if you so much as blinked. They neither heard you nor understood when you spoke to them. Where had these goons come from? It was as if the earth had suddenly spawned them out of nowhere! There were bullies everywhere, nothing but bullies in this city. Zayn 'Alloul certainly was no bully, he hated that kind of stuff, which led to all kinds of atrocities . . .

As he told his friend the juice-seller, the best thing to do was to steer clear of trouble. Even the question of Ali Shuayb did not mean much to him anymore – true, Ali Shuayb had been different from the others, and ever since his release from jail, Zayn had realized how important Ali must have been. He obviously knew political players well enough to compromise them. But nowadays, everything was up for grabs, daylight robbery was the order of the day, and it was all done "in the name of the people" and "for the just cause of the nation." What cause? What bullshit!

The thing is, why isn't the city buying them those handsome red trucks anymore? The ones where you pile the rubbish in at the back; then, when the driver switches on the engine, great big rolling blades churn all the rubbish into the belly of the truck? With those trucks, the vehicle stays pretty clean and there is no smell – or at least it's bearable. They've set them back a couple of decades with the open dump trucks they have now, and it makes the job so much harder, there's no pleasure in it anymore. And then there are the new workers, who take no pride in the job whatsoever! They assume, like everyone else, that a rubbish collector is just someone who doesn't know how to do anything else. That's not at all the case! It's an occupation like any other, requiring both skill and experience. The Lord alone knows where they got these new recruits from: ignoramuses who mix everything up together – tin cans with tomatoes, bottles with shoes. That's no way to work!

And then, when you get this old, battered truck to the actual dump, in Shuwayfat, they go and set the rubbish on fire! That's no way to work, there's no comparison, no comparison at all, between Shuwayfat and Qarantina! Now that was a proper rubbish dump: a clearly defined area, with a name, where the rubbish was dumped and then sorted, at least to some extent anyway. Even though the rubbish was piled everywhere, it wasn't harmful, because there were people who sorted it. They sorted it out well, putting each thing in its place.

Nothing gladdened our hearts more than seeing the street kids jumping up and down in excitement when they spotted the rubbish truck. As if it were laden with presents! As soon as we'd emptied the trucks, the hills would swarm with them: children of all ages, girls and boys, squatting over the piles of rubbish and working quietly, without fighting. It was like watching a silent game being played – hundreds of children on the rubbish mountain fashioned by our labour, sorting rubbish and making an income, thanks to our work. They'd take things and resell them, that way we earned a living and they earned a living. We learned to set special things aside, like shoes and bottles, before shoveling the rubbish into the truck. And however much we took, there was always plenty left to go round. We filled our bellies and they theirs. The children, the men and the women of Qarantina scattered across the hills we created, and all of us made a living.

Some said the stench was foul, but it wasn't: yes, it smelled bad, but it wasn't foul. It was quite bearable, and the children could play. I'd watch them sometimes playing house, perched on the top of the rubbish hills; they'd visit and take presents to each other, eyeglasses, combs, any little thing, all valuable things the rich threw out because they're godless and ungrateful for their lot. For our part, we counted our blessings . . . we'd kiss the ground in gratitude for the bounty we enjoyed. But the only thing people ever talked about was the smell. The men in Naba'a were always wondering how I put up with it. As if their jobs were any better, what did they think they were doing down at the docks as long-shoremen? They were mere beasts of burden – yapping on about the smell! I don't think the smell was foul then, but it is now, it's disgusting. We dump the rubbish in Shuwayfat, right by the seashore, and people come and burn it. Then they douse the fires with water and that's what stinks and causes all manner of disease – not to mention rats!

I don't like to work on the Corniche by the sea. The sea's gone, there's no more sea . . . they've blocked it off with all those road-side stalls. A scourge on those shopkeepers! And what's worse, they parade themselves on T.V. as refugees. Some refugees! Their shops in the centre of town were burnt to cinders! They've opened new ones, where the prices are sky high, which means that they're making profits many times over what they were used to in old Souq Sursock – and then they go on T.V., and bemoan their fate, and claim to be poor. They're the rich, not the poor, and they're the ones complaining about poverty, while we keep our mouths shut and our heads down and thank the Good Lord for what we've got. What kind of people are they? Nothing but unscrupulous mercenaries, shamelessly money-grubbing and greedy – and living in filth too! It's unbelievable! Imagine this high and mighty fabric merchant who's not even capable of sweeping up in front of his shop: he wants us to do it! He doesn't even ask himself how it's possible to live in such filth! It's disgusting, I told them it was filthy, and that I refused to work on the Manara strip of the Corniche. Oh, they replied sarcastically, you expect us to do your bidding, who do you think you are, the president of the republic? Even the president doesn't talk to us like that! So I kept quiet. But these new guys, they know nothing about this job, that's why they agreed to do it. Not me. The boss said we had to sweep the litter off the Corniche and take it to the truck. No way, I told him, we're not street sweepers. Sweepers are one thing and we're another.

I flatly refused – I take pride in my work. But those two at the back, they agreed. Of course things won't be like this forever; everything comes to an end. The war will end and, in the fullness of time, good will prevail over evil. And when our occupation recovers the respect it deserves, they will appreciate my integrity, and they might even promote me to supervisor. And I'll sit behind a desk without lifting a finger all day, answering the telephone, registering people's complaints and settling their problems. Still, we must bide our time and wait: everything in its own good time.

But these new fellows, especially that devil Mohammad al-Kharroubi. Who does he think he is? . . . Just yesterday, he asked to sit beside the driver, leaving me to hang off the back of the truck! What complete disregard for age or seniority! Me, a rubbish collector of twenty years' standing, and him scarcely out of his teens . . . if I'd married a little earlier, he'd be the age of my children!

I regret not having listened to my mother's advice now. She always told me to marry early, but I wouldn't. I wanted to have some security before getting married. How could I marry with nothing more to my name than fifty lira? I said no, my mother said I'd get too old, but I still said no.

Then, may he rest in peace, my uncle Hajj Mahmud 'Alloul came to visit. After we all sat down, he spoke to me and my mother and then put his arm around my shoulder.

"Zayn, you're not married, and Husniyyah is your cousin. I kept her for you. (I never asked him to!) Your late father, before he died, made his wish known to me. 'Mahmud, Husniyyah is for Zayn,' that's what he said."

"When shall we sign the contract, my dear?" he asked, turning to my mother.

"Tomorrow, with the blessing of the Almighty," she replied.
So they signed the contract, and I married Husniyyah. She's a good woman, Husniyyah. Cooks and cleans and looks after the children. But she's come to hate my mother. "Don't you fear the Lord, woman?" I ask her. "Were it not for her, I wouldn't have married you!" But Husniyyah just grumbles on. And what can I do? Throw my mother out on the street? I can't do that, a woman of her age, and paralysed – from her stroke. The doctor said there was no hope, so we brought her back home. But she can't walk, and every time she has to urinate, Husniyyah complains. No, bless her, she doesn't complain, she's tired though. An invalid is a burden. My mother doesn't complain either, she spends all her time reading the Qur'an and praying . . . And now this al-Kharroubi fellow here wants to take my place in the truck, he does, as if there were no levels or seniority! I'm the boss around here; Mr Kabbani said so, he said it in so many words: "You're like the captain of a ship," he said. I'm responsible for the entire area's rubbish collection, and he expects me to stand on the fender at the back of the truck! He insisted, you know, and if it weren't for the driver's intervention, we would have come to blows. A fine man that driver is, and he's fond of me too, he knows I'm conscientious and that I always look out for them so they don't work too hard.

Anyhow, the driver stepped in and al-Kharroubi went back to his place, behind. I sit beside the driver and ask him to stop whenever there's a proper pile of rubbish to collect, then the two at the back hop off and shovel it onto the truck. I don't always get down . . . I used to before, but I'm tired now and I'm entitled to a rest. When the pile is really huge, then I get down and help: I take the shovel and let one of them rest while I work in his place.

"What are all these people doing here, sitting in front of their cars sipping coffee?" the driver asks, puffing on his cigarette in the front cabin.

Yes, thinks Zayn 'Alloul, what are they doing there? People have become so . . . Oh, well . . . may the Lord preserve us from people!

As the truck rumbles on its way in the early morning haze, it passes a group of fishermen and fishmongers. Zayn asks the driver to stop and gets down to ask about the price of a kilo of fish.

"Forty lira," the fishmonger replies, as he lifts up the large wooden crates and pushes the ice aside for Zayn to see.

Zayn does not buy any fish. How is he supposed to come up with forty lira just like that? So he walks away. He sees a child crouched next to a crate full of fish, selecting a piece and dipping it in a bucket of water.

"What's this?" he asks.

"Frozen fish."

"Why the water?"

"So the fish defrosts and we can sell it as fresh."

White, dead fish . . . Zayn picks one up but it slips from his grasp and he hears al-Kharroubi yelling: "We've got to get a move on! We're late!"

Zayn is tempted but the feel of the fish makes his flesh creep, like that time when he kissed his dead father's hand before the burial. He gets back into the truck. It continues on its way. The driver says he thinks frozen fish is alright, it's cheap. The truck rumbles on, now it is almost at the last stop, at the U.N.E.S.C.O. roundabout. There's always a big pile of rubbish here, so they all get down and shovel, and after they are done, they head for Shuwayfat. Zayn sighs with relief: soon, he will be home, having a glass of tea and a cigarette. He does not like to smoke on the job. A cigarette doesn't taste the same when you're working. At home, with a glass of tea, then it's a cigarette.

The vehicle brakes, everyone jumps out, and the clanging of the shovels begins. Zayn too hops out of the truck.

"It's an even bigger lot than usual."

Mohammad al-Kharroubi and Saleh Ahmad grab their shovels, and the rubbish starts cascading into the truck.

"Boy, what's that smell?" Saleh Ahmad asks.

"Burning," replies Zayn as he bends down and gestures to the charred contents of the rubbish.

"No," the driver says. "It smells like . . . a dog . . . a dead dog."

Zayn steps closer to the statue of Habib Abi Shahla. Yes, it really does smell like there's a decomposing dog.

"That's not part of our job," Saleh Ahmad says, tossing his shovel aside.

"Take it easy, man."

"No! Let them bring in the bulldozer! I'm not about to pick up a contaminated dead dog."

Mohammad al-Kharroubi hops gingerly across the rubbish towards the statue.

"Uh-oh!" the driver says. "He's going back to his filthy old habits. Last time, he picked up a rat by the tail and dangled it under our noses. It was disgusting!" The driver climbs into the truck and rolls up the window.

Al-Kharroubi steps forward and, with his bare hands, pushes the rubbish to one side and chuckles loudly. Pushing and toiling, his clothes gradually blacken as the soot from the burnt and charred refuse rubs off onto them.

Then, an almighty exclamation as the man's voice shudders and his face freezes.

"It's a man!"

"What do you mean, a man?"

"The corpse of a man. A man's corpse."

Mohammad al-Kharroubi lurches back and is violently sick. Hands on his belly, vomiting yellow-green liquid, he backs away towards Zayn 'Alloul.

"I tell you, it's a man . . . the corpse of a man. Dear God in heaven!"

The driver gets out of the truck and stands next to Zayn 'Alloul. Saleh Ahmad approaches cautiously, reaches al-Kharroubi, and then backs away, spitting and cursing. Zayn advances. He can see the corpse: a man lying on his back, his chest completely bare, with traces of burns on the hands, his body pierced with bullets.

"What are we going to do?"

"Listen, guys," the driver says, "we should notify the police, or else they'll frame us for it."

"No, we should just leave; we haven't seen or heard anything, and that's all there is to it," al-Kharroubi says.

To al-Kharroubi and Ahmad Saleh, Zayn says: "You two stay here. Me and the driver are going to Hobeysh police station." Zayn's head is spinning. "Goddamn, goddamn this shitty job! Fucking country falling apart . . . look at that! Dumping bloody human beings in the rubbish! I swear to God, a dog's life is worth more than a human's." The driver is mumbling under his breath, presumably in prayer. Finally, the truck reaches the police station.

Zayn jumps down, the driver follows. They enter the police station, where the guard on duty questions them.

"We want to see the officer on duty."

"There's nobody here," the guard tells them.

"Well, we've got to see someone; we have a crime to report."

"What crime?"

"A murder."

The policeman pouts indifferently and gestures them towards a room inside. They go in. A man in military fatigues is sitting at a desk. After exchanging greetings, Zayn speaks.

"We've come about a murder."

"Sergeant Hassan Fakhreddin," the man replies, looking from one to the other. He reaches for pen and paper, notes down their names and asks about the circumstances of the crime. Zayn does all the talking as the policeman takes down his statement.

"You are both rubbish collectors?"

"Yes, sir."

"And what does the corpse look like?"

"It's decomposed, sir. We couldn't see much, but we think it's likely that the death occurred a while ago."

"Do you know the victim?"

"No, not at all."

"Had either of you ever seen him before?"

"No, never."

"O.K. then. Alright."

The policeman closes the register in front of him and asks them to sit down.

"But why, sir?"

"You'll have to stay here until the officer arrives."

"We can't," Zayn replies. "We've left Mohammad al-Kharroubi and Saleh Ahmad at the rubbish site, we've got to let them know. We'll go get them and come back."

"No, you'll both stay here. The officer will have to question you."

"But it has nothing to do with us."

The police sergeant picks up the telephone and dials a number.

"Yes, yes . . . In an hour . . . O.K. As you like, sir . . . At your service . . ."

The two men wait a long time.

"But the corpse should be removed," Zayn says.

"Everything in its own good time," the sergeant replies.

Some two hours later, the officer strolls in, yawning. He asks them a few questions, and then tells them to follow behind him in the truck. Accompanied by several policemen, he gets into a jeep parked behind the truck. When they reach the rubbish mound, they find al-Kharroubi and Ahmad sitting on the pavement across the street, smoking. The officer approaches the corpse; he bends down, chalk-marks the road beside the statue, and asks Zayn to remove the rubbish covering the corpse. Zayn works alone, without anyone's help. The officer marks out the contours of the corpse.

And then, all of a sudden, the place is swarming with cameras. Journalists and photographers are everywhere. One of them takes a picture of the corpse and then of Zayn, as a man stands nearby taking notes. He asks Zayn how they discovered the corpse. Zayn repeats what he told the officer, but adds the part about the dog – how they had all assumed that the putrid smell was because of a dead dog. Then it's another journalist's turn, and Zayn goes over his story once again, but includes the detail about al-Kharroubi hopping across the rubbish, how he wanted to grab the dog by the tail and frighten the driver.

Then, an ambulance arrives, and three men in white spill out. They cover the corpse with a white sheet and stand there while the photographers click their cameras furiously at the white sheet.

"Why don't you remove the corpse?" Zayn asks.

"We're waiting for the forensic expert," the fat one replies. "He has to examine the corpse before we remove it."

"To the graveyard?"

"No, to the hospital, for the autopsy . . . Then we'll hand it over to the relatives, if there are any."

The officer asks the crowd of bystanders to disperse. Then he turns to Zayn and his colleagues and tells them irately that they need to leave. Zayn is puzzled by the officer's behaviour, but they all get into the truck and drive off.

"But we're the ones who found the corpse," Zayn says to the driver. "It's ours. And he won't let us watch? He's watching alright. Despicable, that's what he is. I can't stand police officers."

The truck reaches Shuwayfat. With the engine running, it tips its load onto the rubbish mound and continues on its way.

Dr Marwan Bitar, a sixty-five-year-old surgeon, was Head of Surgery at the German Hospital in Beirut for many years. He stopped practising in 1973 after his hands grew unsteady, and now he is a forensic pathologist – a semi-retirement of sorts, and a lucrative one. He does not like this work: handling corpses and conducting autopsies, and then having to write up his findings. Still, Dr Bitar has convinced himself that it makes no difference whether it's a corpse or not, it's just the same as performing a surgical operation. After all, a patient under general anaesthesia is like a corpse, he feels nothing. The difference though is the blood. In an operation, the scalpel is real, but here, it's like nothing; there's no blood, no responsibility, you can cut a corpse up any which way you like, and mistakes are not an issue.

"I have a fail-safe job," Dr Bitar tells his son, Ghassan, who became a gynaecologist. Dr Bitar advised him against that specialization, but the boy went ahead and did as he pleased.

"Son, how can you sleep with a woman after that?"

"I manage. Work is one thing and sex is another."

The boy has become well known and wealthy. After only eight years in practice, he owns an entire apartment block in Ramlet al-Bayda, while he, Dr Bitar, who has been working for more than thirty years now, has no more to show for it than that lousy old building in Kantari, which is full of refugees. There are rumours that Ghassan has come by all that wealth in a rather unsavoury manner, doing abortions. They say he does them on request: the woman comes to the clinic, asks him to do it, and he goes right ahead without the slightest hesitation – nor the slightest bit of shame or fear of the Good Lord! Of course, Dr Bitar has not ascertained any of this for himself, he would rather not know whether his son is an abortionist or not – as far as he is concerned, Ghassan's free to do as he pleases and may God forgive him. Still, the boy hasn't married. And it's got to be due to his line of work.

"You haven't married because you feel nothing but disgust for women," the old man tells his son, reminding him that he had warned him, but Ghassan just laughs.

"I sleep with the whole of womankind! After I give her the anaesthetic, I have sex with the woman before carrying out the operation. Medically speaking, it's helpful – having sex with a pregnant woman before an abortion is helpful. I sleep with her and she feels nothing, I operate and she pays. Instead of having to pay for it, I do what I feel like and get paid for it. So why get married?"

"God forbid!" Dr Marwan Bitar can't believe his ears. "You're not serious?"

"Sure I am. Why not? Look at it this way: she's asleep and feels nothing, so it's not like she's being unfaithful to her husband. And anyhow, most of them aren't married. Sex is like food, Father, it's of little consequence!"

"God forbid!" Dr Bitar exclaims once more. "You're making it all up."

But Ghassan just laughs.

He has got to be lying, though. It's just not possible. Medicine is a sacred calling; a medical practitioner takes an oath to honour his profession. In ancient times, priests were the medical practitioners, treating both the body and the spirit. And that is the way it should be. Medicine wasn't debased until it became just another job. But it's a sacred mission, and Dr Bitar simply can't believe that his son does those things. No, no, it cannot be possible. He must be making it up, look how he just laughs. But why hasn't he married?

I'll find you a girl, Dr Bitar tells him, time and again. But Ghassan just makes fun of him.

"Those days are over, Dad," he says.

He is right, of course. But why doesn't he marry the way people do now, for love? Go out with a girl and then marry her. He doesn't have a girlfriend and he's never brought a girl home with him when he visits. And besides, why won't he live at home? He says he prefers living alone, but a bachelor's house is like a devil's den, Dr Bitar is sure of that. Not much he can do about it but offer his advice, which the boy disregards in any case.

As for this revolting job of his, dissecting corpses, that is . . . well . . . What to say, but *al-hamdulillah* that the war broke out as it has more or less spared him from having to continue with it. Forensic pathologists aren't needed these days: everything's fallen apart, people are killed and tossed into their graves just like that, no autopsy, no nothing. No more phone calls in the middle of the night, no more officers requesting his presence. So he sits at home doing nothing.

Once in a while, Dr Bitar goes over to the American University Hospital to visit his former student, Dr Saleem Idreess, now Head of Surgery. Dr Bitar trained him personally and he has become an excellent surgeon. Whenever he goes to see him though, Saleem grumbles about the chronic shortage of doctors.

"They've all left! Sometimes a surgeon will perform ten operations in one day! Occasionally more than that; the doctors are exhausted!"

And when he asks Dr Bitar about his new line of work, the old surgeon tells him there's not much to do nowadays.

"Forensic pathologists don't have much of a role to play anymore. The courts are closed and no-one needs us."

Once Dr Bitar put a proposal to him. He suggested that

dissections could be carried out on some of the corpses that are brought into the hospital from the fighting.

"It would certainly be better than working on corpses that have been preserved in formaldehyde, the way we used to when you were still a student. It would allow the medical students to see for themselves spinal cord injuries, cranial traumas, liver ailments, all manner of things."

But he was stunned by Dr Saleem's answer.

"They're of absolutely no value to us, those corpses. Nowadays, we train our students on the real thing: they participate in real-life surgical operations. You know how it is, we get a lot of hopeless cases, and we let the students practise on them. Some of them even do brain surgery, and you know how difficult that is."

"What's that you're saying?"

"Dear Dr Marwan, you're of the old school. We have new training methods nowadays."

"But that's criminal," Dr Bitar replied. "It's illegal. I didn't teach all those years for you to end up doing this sort of thing! It's a complete violation of our professional ethic. A surgeon's not a butcher, Saleem. God is my witness, butchers are less barbaric!"

Dr Bitar left the hospital and never went back. He will not visit Saleem anymore . . . that man's no student of his, he's just a common criminal . . . how can they let students play around with people's brains and organs like that, even if they are hopeless cases? And anyhow, there aren't any hopeless cases. Doctors do everything in their power and the rest is up to the Good Lord. It's an act of blasphemy against the Creator. What a generation!

And so it was that Dr Bitar spent all his time at home. The telephone no longer rang for him and he no longer went out. Doctors aren't what they used to be . . . Where are the likes of the famous Prussian doctor who could diagnose a patient's ailment just by looking at him? This new generation doesn't know a thing!

The war's over, that's what people are saying. But where are the authorities? Every sort of army in the country but the legitimate one . . . Still, at least work has picked up again and he is getting paid five hundred lira for every report he produces. It's better than nothing . . . How he wishes he were in charge though: he'd have brought out the gallows and hanged all those doctors! But in charge he isn't, and five hundred lira is better than nothing: the building doesn't bring in a piastre anymore, it's full of refugees and he won't take money from Ghassan, he couldn't, not from his own son.

Ghassan came to him one day saying that if they paid one hundred thousand lira, the political cadre would get the refugees out. But Dr Bitar's not having it, he's not paying anyone off, and anyway, he doesn't need money. The refugees will leave eventually, he will get the building back, and then Ghassan will inherit it and become the landlord of several properties. But the boy really should marry . . . if he doesn't, who is going to come into all this wealth? We have to get him married off, he kept telling his wife. She should be on the lookout for him, but she doesn't give a damn . . . she spends all her time playing poker – and losing! So, here he is, chasing around after corpses while she gambles. He wonders where she finds the money. She must get it out of Ghassan. Still, he wishes she'd take an interest in marrying him off . . . she's his mother after all. But she's not interested in anyone but herself really: all she cares about is putting on her make-up in the morning and waiting for evening to come. She often invites him to join them but he doesn't like playing cards, he'd rather go to bed early. Staying up late shortens life expectancy and it's not good for your nerves.

The telephone started ringing again and there was work to do . . .

It is 7.30 one morning when the telephone rings. Lieutenant Yasseen is on the line. Dr Bitar dresses quickly, runs a comb through his hair, and, without even bothering to wash his face, grabs his doctor's bag and hurries down the stairs. He turns the ignition, waits a little while for the engine to warm up, and drives off. When he reaches the U.N.E.S.C.O. roundabout, he parks the car a little way from the statue of Habib Abi Shahla, and walks over to shake the officer's hand. He briefly bends to peer over the mound of rubbish, straightens up and goes back to the car, puts on his white doctor's coat and a mask over his nose and mouth, and returns to the corpse.

He once again bends over the corpse, then, squatting down, pulls back the white sheet covering it, lifts one of the hands, and lets it drop. He rolls the corpse over slightly, notices the red ants crawling on the back of the neck, and tries to brush them aside, but they stick to his hands. He straightens up, rubs his hands together and blows on them, then blows on his white coat, and gets back to the job. He turns the corpse over onto its stomach and inspects the back. He stands up again, steps back, squats down once more, turns the corpse over one more time, and finally covers it with the white sheet.

He walks away, reaches his car, opens one of the back passenger doors, takes off his coat and mask and tosses them onto the seat. Lieutenant Yasseen comes up to him. The doctor tells him the murder must have occurred at least four days earlier, as the corpse has begun to putrefy and decompose, and there are clear traces of beating and torture. Lieutenant Yasseen nods.

"When was the corpse found?" the doctor asks.

"Just now – about half an hour ago."

"That's impossible . . . unless, the corpse was dumped elsewhere initially and then was moved here."

"What should we do?"

The doctor says the corpse must be moved to the hospital morgue.

"The autopsy should be conducted immediately, before the body decomposes any further and it becomes impossible to determine the circumstances of the crime." The doctor gets into his car, the officer leans against his rolled-down window, and they finish the conversation. "You should advise the hospital administration that I'm on my way so that they get everything ready."

The doctor drives off while the paramedics lift the corpse onto a stretcher and carry it to the ambulance. Onlookers gather to watch as the ambulance sounds its siren through the busy streets. "It's just for show," ventures a passerby. "Ambulances switch on their sirens even when they're empty. There's never anyone in there . . . just the drivers who're in a hurry to get somewhere, or want to show off!"

Below is the verbatim text of the report by the forensic pathologist Dr Marwan Bitar that appeared in the Beirut papers on the morning of 23 April, 1980.

Outward appearance:

1 The principal difficulty in examining the body at the site of discovery was due to the extensive burns to the body, inflicted after decease.

2 The naked abdomen is covered in burns, while the trousers over the lower limbs are wet and torn in several places, the tears being caused possibly by large stones or by gunshots. Owing to the absence of gunpowder burns, the projectiles would have been cast from a distance of more than one metre. There are clear traces of blood on the back of the neck.

3 *Rigor mortis* has begun to subside. It sets in within hours of decease, and starts to diminish two to three days later, with the onset of decomposition manifested by bloating from internal gases and the appearance of greenish patches on the abdomen.

Lower abdomen:

1 Bluish haematoma found on the lower left side.

2 Superficial grazing on the stomach and traces of deep cuts, presumed to be from the use of a sharp implement.

Thoracic cage:
1 No bone fractures.
2 Bruises and grazes on the left side of the waist, with narrow longitudinal lacerations, caused by a whip or cane. These must have occurred before death, as the bruising remained after the wounds were opened and cleaned.
3 Circular burn marks on the chest. These clearly occurred before decease, as they are full of pus.
4 Redness on the front of the neck, and the upper frontal third of the chest. This is known as post-mortem lividness, or liver mortis, and is due to sedimentation of the blood, which starts one hour after death and is complete within six hours.

Left hand:
1 Bone contusions and cartilage fractures.
2 Ring finger severed at the base with a sharp implement.

Head:
1 Swelling of the forehead, and jagged gunshot wound measuring seven centimetres long by four wide. No burns or traces of gunpowder around the wound. Fractures to the frontal cranium bone and deep cerebral lesions.
2 Nasal deviation, with bruising and swelling, an indication of occurrence before decease.
3 Gunshot wound on the outer right-hand side of the neck, five centimetres below the earlobe, piercing the right cheek. The wound is only skin-deep and could not have been fatal.

CHAPTER V

The Interrogation

*Fahd Badreddin, 26, single; a combatant with the Joint Forces, he is
also a third-year student at the Arts Faculty of the Lebanese University.
He sleeps on the premises of the party office in Wata Mussaytbeh, as he
has no relatives in Beirut. His only part in this story is that he once met
Khalil Ahmad Jaber, for all of ten minutes. Being neither a family friend
nor an acquaintance, he did not attend the funeral or make the tradi-
tional condolence visit to the house. Whenever we met, he spoke
eloquently about the case, but he clearly had some kind of problem with
his eyes. He always kept his left eye covered with the palm of his hand as
he spoke, and it was obvious that he had a glass eye on the right-hand
side. He is very articulate, as might be expected of a student of Arabic
literature. He says that he cannot read for long, and that is why he has
suspended his studies.*

It was the morning of 12 April. I was in the party office, making tea
and listening to Western pop music on Radio Monte Carlo; I was
getting myself some breakfast – a boiled egg, a few olives, a little
cheese – and wasn't particularly expecting anyone to come in or
anything to happen. Everyone was gone and I hadn't been following events very closely. We spent all our days sitting around the
office waiting for our orders, and I was waiting for mine.

That's when they walked in, with him in tow. He was soaking
wet from the rain, even his scrawny little beard was dripping.
They led him to the small room and I joined them. The man was
shivering from head to foot, and he said absolutely nothing when

they questioned him. I went over to where he sat and looked into his dilated eyes; he shivered inside the coat seemingly glued to his frail body.

I hadn't been following the story – actually, I knew nothing about it. I'd been out of it for a while ... all I did was sit and wait in that office, and I wondered why they'd brought him in. He looked like one of those beggars the city is so full of nowadays. To me, he looked like something out of my childhood – you know, the character from the ditty we sang, "Abu Hashisheh the drunkard, who sold his wife for a tankard." But it couldn't be him, because his clothes weren't all ragged like Abu Hashisheh's, and he didn't look like he'd been drinking.

But, boy, did he smell! That smell was the worst thing about him. When he took off his pith helmet, I saw that his white hair was black with grime, and the hand he smoothed it down with was no more than a claw of bony fingers. When he sat down, he just collapsed into the chair with a thud, as if there were no muscles in his legs. One of the boys offered him a cigarette, but he indicated that he didn't smoke with his index finger pointed up.

And then they took him away – I'd left the room by then, I couldn't stand the smell. Anyway, they took him and I never saw him again ... and no-one talked about it again ... not much, anyway ... but that smell, oh, the smell was so awful, like the smell that time on the mountaintop, so faraway ...

We were trudging through the snow. Our feet sank with every step and we were giddy with laughter as we could practically touch the clouds with our outstretched arms. We tried to break into a run, but couldn't. It felt like we were holding the sky between our very fingers, as Mohammad Saleh said – he died over there in the snow, and they never did find his body. I don't remember how the sky looked that day, but every time I see Mohammad's picture hanging on the wall, with the word "Sanneen" scrawled across it – I feel like crying. Though even crying isn't the same anymore . . . I can't now, the tears just don't seem to come.

I don't know exactly what happened, but one day, there on the mountaintop, I found myself suddenly being dragged by the scruff of the neck across a huge expanse of gravel and stones – at least, that's what it felt like. I wanted to tell them to stop, stop it now! The pain was excruciating, it felt as if my head had been severed from my neck and was rolling away. But no-one heard me, as if they'd all gone deaf. There was no other sensation besides the pain and this terrible echo reverberating inside my head . . . every sound multiplying endlessly inside my ears. But I couldn't hear. I kept saying, please . . .

And then, somehow, I found myself somewhere else entirely. No, not quite . . . I don't know how to describe it, when I moved my head it felt like the gravel and stones were inside it now, so I cried out, "*Ya immi* – oh mother of mine, where are you?" And then I opened my eyes . . . or I thought I did. But there was nothing there, everything was black. I tried to sit up. So I'm dead, I thought, this is what death must be like, I must be dead. I felt a terrible stab of grief, like something sharp was piercing my gut. I said to myself, it's over for you, Fahd. And then I saw my mother's face as she said "it's all over" . . . and then planes were circling overhead like locusts, white planes, blowing dust into everyone's eyes. So I lay completely still. I was dead.

Since there are no tears in death, I didn't cry. When I tried to sit up, however, I found I couldn't move . . . So I was in a grave! That was it! A grave is shapeless . . . a grave is just, well, a grave . . . nothing but blackness, you can't see any colours . . . but then I started seeing these little dots, black ones and brown ones and red ones, growing larger and then smaller. I could see the dots really clearly.

Then someone's hand was shaking me. What was that? And there was a woman's voice, it sounded really muffled, like it was wrapped in cotton wool. And then this hand touched my head.

"He seems better, Doctor."

I tried to move, to say something, but the dots disappeared and the voice went away. That woman's muffled voice was gone. Everything vanished! I tried to speak, and felt a hand on my lips.

"It's alright, you're O.K." I wanted to ask her where I was. Again, she repeated, "It's alright." And then, "You've only lost one eye. The other one is fine."

She sat me up and started to feed me . . . I wanted to talk to her, to say . . . but she gave me this hot drink, and said I should sleep. So I slept . . . no, actually, I didn't . . . I had been asleep all this time, it felt like forever. And then, it dawned on me: I was blind!

I began to howl in the dark. I had finally woken up, and all I could do was shout and scream. There were hurried footsteps and voices.

"A tranquillizer . . . Give him a tranquillizer . . . where are they?"

I screamed until I was hoarse. I don't know how those screams came about, I don't know where the sounds originated, but then something pricked my arm and everything became calm. The doctor explained in his quiet, steady voice that I had been hit by an "Energa" missile and that I had multiple burns on the face and eyes. He told me that they had operated on me, that only one eye was permanently damaged and that the other one was "perfectly alright."

Then he said, "We'll take the bandage off in two weeks, you must be patient . . . you're a fighter."

"I don't believe you," I replied, now hoarse. I told him I didn't believe him and that I was sure I was totally blind. He swore by every one of the prophets, he reassured me, he cajoled me, he tried convincing me, but I didn't believe him. After that, I said nothing at all, I refused to speak. I just sat up in bed so they could feed me and let them hold my hand to guide me to the bathroom.

Lying in bed, I'd listen to every noise and try and picture my mother's face . . . Sitt Zakiyyah's face . . . so reminiscent of

Jerusalem, with its maze of wrinkles like the streets criss-crossing the city . . . I had never been to Jerusalem, and I didn't think I'd ever go there. But to me, the furrows on her face seemed like the narrow streets of Jerusalem that Kamal described to us before he left for the States. Kamal left without ever experiencing the taste of fire piercing his belly. After he left, I never heard from him, until I called him from Madrid that day. "I'm married!" he said, his voice brimming with laughter, just as it used to when we were kids at the American School of Saida together.

I told him about my eyes. And he told me about Lily's. He said she had long hair that fell across her face and twinkling eyes. "The whites of her eyes envelop me as they stretch all the way from there to here," he told me. "She lives here, in America, and I paint pictures of her every day. I'll send you one."

Lying in bed and picturing my mother's face, I thought I saw it crumple as she embraced me. Like the streets of Jerusalem, old Jerusalem, with its warren of narrow alleys and painted crucifixes everywhere, its processions of bishops and clergy, and the Holy Sepulchre glows with light. That's how Kamal had described it. "The sepulchre aglow with light," he had said. And in my mind's eye, I could see that light . . .

One day, when I was little, I came home from school and told my mother about Cana. I told her our divinity teacher at the American School of Saida said that Jesus Christ had performed his first miracle here, in our village, when he turned jars of water into wine.

"No, son, it wasn't our village," she said.

"Yes, it was. The teacher read from the Gospels, and he read the word Cana. I told him we were from Cana."

"Damn these Americans," she said, "and all their humbug about Jesus and the miracles – it just gives the Jews one more excuse to invade and occupy our villages!"

"No, Mother, no. It just means that . . . that Cana is the best place in the world to make wine! Can't you just imagine him standing there, in fear and trembling, with his mother saying, 'Don't be afraid, son.' And despite his fear, Jesus goes towards the jars full of water, and the water turns into wine. He picks one up, tilts it slowly, and the wine begins to flow. All the wedding guests can drink now: they come up to Jesus one after the other and every time he picks up a jar and tips the liquid into their cups, the water turns to wine. Now the bridegroom is drunk, and he struts up and down the alleys of the village, inviting everyone to join the wedding celebration, while Jesus stands by the jars, sleeves rolled up, a mass of curly hair framing his forehead, picking up one vessel after another, to fill every glass or even the naked hands of those surging towards him."

That's how Cana was. Now it's razed to the ground.

And in my mind's eye, I can see Jesus walking the streets of Cana, turning to each and every person he meets. I see him striding in his long grey robe, gazing into the distance, a jar of wine on his shoulder. Dust is swirling in the air, around his head, around his long robe, and around the jars he holds aloft. And I see him as he bends down and drinks, and the water turns to wine.

Jesus is alone. He could be in the hospital . . . In this hospital, all by himself. Oh, it's been so long since I've seen my mother! A year, maybe, or more . . . She might be dead for all I know. Why don't I go and visit her? She doesn't know . . . no, of course not, and I don't want her to. How would I get there? Anyhow, she might be dead . . . no, she can't be! She promised she wouldn't die before she saw me married . . . but I don't want to get married. My brothers are – all three of them. They're all civil servants, "public servants", as we say. My mother is still waiting for me to tie the knot. But I've dropped out of university, I just quit. I told her I was still attending classes, but I'm not. I'm a combatant, that's what I do. I want to reach for the sky and hold it between my fingers, like I've read about in books . . . I want to ravish the sky . . .

Then I heard the nurse's gentle voice. I couldn't see a thing. I asked her why they didn't take the bandage off my left eye since it wasn't injured.

"Doctor's orders," she said. "The doctor said that's what we should do."

"So I *am* blind," I cried out. "Blind, that's what I am!"

Then I heard the Yemeni who was in the bed next to mine.

"You know what they did to me? They removed my eye completely! I told them not to. They'd admitted me to the hospital with a bleeding eye and they took me straight into the operating theatre. I was fully conscious and I told the doctor before he gave me the anaesthetic, please don't remove my eye, just leave it; I don't want to become one-eyed! But he still took it out . . . he put me to sleep and removed it," the Yemeni said, gnashing his teeth and cursing.

Then the nurse came in and led me away by the wrist. The doctor fussed about, and then they took the bandage off my eye. And I could see! No, not see exactly . . . everything was blue; their faces were elongated and bluish, and all the hands flitting around me looked blue. Then the blue gradually receded and the nurse had to steady me as I began to keel over. As the blueness continued to recede, she led me to the mirror and there I saw the crater that had been my right eye . . . But I could see! I was overjoyed and I ran to embrace both the nurse and the doctor! Then the doctor started to work in earnest: first he bathed the crater with antiseptics and then he sealed it off with white gauze.

"We will fit you with a glass eye."

"There's no need for that," I replied.

I went back to bed, thinking I would wear a black patch over my eye, like Moshe Dayan did. Then I could go back to being a fighter. I had thought I was finished, but no: if Moshe Dayan could defeat the Arabs with one eye, then I too could be a fighter. That's what I told the doctor.

He said they were sending me to Spain for an operation to get fitted with an artificial eye. "They'll also do some tests on your left eye, which is slightly at risk. It has been affected by the shock, and the doctors in Spain will have a look at it."

Once I got to Madrid I called Kamal from the hospital. Then he called me every day; Lily called me too, she had a beautiful voice; they'd comfort me and tell me I had to join them in America. But what would I do in America? As far as I was concerned, America was our enemy. I wouldn't go, no way.

There were four of us, in one room, in a hotel called "La Pallas". We'd set off for the hospital with our minder every morning and usually returned at midday. The Yemeni cursed constantly and told us about *qat* and how foreign women liked it because sex was always better after chewing some.

"And *qat* tastes so good, too!" he'd say. "Mmmm . . . *qat* and tea, then beer, and you're up for it the rest of the night!"

He would feel around the gauze-covered depression that used to be his eye and curse the doctor. There was also Nabeel Amer, a short little man who went on and on about Germany, with its steel mills and turneries. And there was Sameeh al-Ashiab, who hid his eyes behind dark glasses and never once addressed us. He spoke only to our minder. And there was me.

One day, Nabeel Amer came back to the hotel, jumping for joy. He hollered all the way down the hotel corridors that he was loaded with pesetas! I don't know where he got hold of the money, but that night we all went out to a restaurant to celebrate.

At the restaurant, the Yemeni said he'd have a beer because wine made you drunk. Nabeel made such fun of him. "You don't know what being drunk is," he told him. "This wine won't make you drunk, this Spanish wine, pfff . . . ! Do you know what 'annay-beh* is? I'll tell you! In al-Khalil, the town of Hebron, where I come from, wine is prohibited – it is *haram*. So we drink 'annaybeh* instead: you take grapes and sprinkle them with water and sugar and then put them out on large trays in the sun. After a few days in

164

the sun, when the mixture has turned into *'annaybeh*, you go out there and scoop up the grapes swimming in their juice with great big spoons and, oh boy, do you feel giddy! Now *that's* getting drunk. Our religion prohibits drinking, but it doesn't prohibit *'annaybeh*. And believe you me, just one spoonful of *'annaybeh* is enough to knock out even the most hardened drinker!"

Nabeel drank steadily as we sat in the restaurant, in the din of Spanish voices and the clatter of cutlery on china. All of a sudden, he bellowed, "My eyes! If only it weren't for my eyes!"

"We're all in the same boat!" the Yemeni told him.

"Yes, but if it weren't for my eyes, I could go back to Germany! Now, I can't go back to the factory in Berlin. A turner has to have perfect eyesight, and I have none at all. When the doctor said I was completely recovered, I told him I couldn't even see as well as when I was blind drunk on *'annaybeh*! Things looked blurred, all the colours seemed wrong, everything was enveloped in a veil of fog. The doctor said I should go to Spain and gave me a referral. And so here I am in Spain. But you tell me, what can Spain achieve when Tall al-Zaatar‡ achieved nothing? Nothing is as precious as our eyesight! . . . Oh, brother, how come you can all see?"

Later, when we left the restaurant, the Yemeni went back to the hotel, and Nabeel and I walked together through the Madrid evening. We came across a couple of girls, Nabeel suggested we try and pick them up. "European girls are different from ours, they're always game." But as we approached, three guys emerged from the darkness. They were loud and brash and made menacing gestures, spoiling for a fight. Nabeel braced himself but I pulled him away.

"You didn't survive Tall al-Zaatar to die here! Women can

‡ A Palestinian refugee camp on the northeastern outskirts of Beirut, which grew to be a slum-like settlement and then became an armed stronghold that was eventually overrun by right-wing Maronite Christian militias, following a protracted siege. Numerous atrocities were committed during and immediately after the fall of the camp, causing many Palestinian fighters to escape into the surrounding woods and mountains.

also be a cause . . . ours is not the only one. But don't get the two mixed up!"

Nabeel had been so seriously wounded, it was a wonder he was alive. Yet here he was, practically blind, leaping around the streets of Madrid as if it were outer space.

"Tell me about Tall al-Zaatar," I said, "tell me how you escaped."

"We just did," he said, adding that the hardest thing was the march through the hills. "Dozens of us, fighters, left the camp and found ourselves walking through the wilderness. We were completely lost: the gunfire was so intense, bullets were flying everywhere, screeching past us, whizzing around our heads, and still we could hear the women's cries ringing in our ears. And even though the whole sky was lit up, we had no sense of direction whatsoever. We stumbled along, falling into ditches as we went, uprooted wild plants as if we'd done it all our lives, and bumped into corpses – the corpses of fighters like us who had also tried to escape – their faces swollen, arms spread wide, weapons nearby. We never made a stop. Even when we thought we recognized someone, we didn't stop to bury him, there was no time . . . we just ploughed on through the inky night of the forest-turned-graveyard. And we would have all been killed were it not for God creating darkness. It was terrifying: every rustling noise, every footstep you heard, you never knew whether you were coming up against a foe or a friend. Still, we walked on, without bearings, until at some point, in the midst of all of this darkness and terror, I wanted a smoke. Feeling around my shirt pocket, I found a packet of cigarettes – it was all scrunched up, like someone cowering with fear. I thought maybe it happened when I bumped into a tree and hadn't noticed or maybe I'd scrunched it up myself and returned it to my pocket, Lord only knows. Anyway, I didn't smoke until after we'd arrived.

"When we got there, the city was teeming with people, there

were refugees screaming and shouting everywhere, and the streets heaved with people's cries and honking horns. I wasn't hungry in the slightest. In Tall al-Zaatar, I was never hungry: all we had was stale bread and cigarettes; the people of the camp had eaten all the lentils because they had run out of bread. I'd been assigned to a hilltop, and after we were completely encircled, we withdrew towards the mountains. It was only when we got to Beirut that I saw the state people were in. You know, when you're fighting you don't see anything, you can't see, but once I got over there after the fall of the camp, I really saw them for the first time. And it was terrifying: here I was, an eager volunteer returned from Germany, standing before our party office in Beirut, absolutely terror-struck.

"They took us to Shiyyah, that's where I was injured. Did you know that when you're hit, at first you don't feel anything? . . . I was setting up a mortar position on the third floor of a building overlooking Ain al-Remmaneh, when I saw this huge flash of light. There wasn't an inch of me that was unhurt," he said, pulling up his pants to show me the scars from the bullet and shrapnel wounds.

We kept walking, and Nabeel dreamed of returning to Berlin.

"The operation on my eye will succeed," he'd say, "and I'll go back to Berlin, to my job and to . . . Anna-Maria. She's a salesgirl in a toy store, I met her in a disco; I'm going to go back, we'll get married and I'll take her to al-Khalil. She never believes the 'annaybeh story when I tell her . . . now she won't believe that I've been hit by so many bullets and I'm still alive!"

What was Madrid like? Madrid was full of medical words we didn't understand the meaning of and which our hunch-backed minder made heroic efforts to translate. Madrid was the shafts of light that streamed through my healthy eye; it was the voices of nurses and doctors, the long corridors, the faces with bandaged eyes – we were all eye patients; and the doctor telling the hunched-backed minder that they would operate tomorrow . . . Tomorrow, he said, they would fit me with a new eye . . . an eye that wouldn't cry, because it was a glass eye, and glass doesn't cry. After the operation, it felt like I had a mountain inside my eye socket! I wanted to rip it out, it felt so leaden and heavy, it was stupid and immobile! Like having another person inside my eye who could see me but whom I couldn't see. All I wanted was to rip it out. But I got used to it. It stayed put and now I don't even feel it, it's as if it weren't there.

I never saw the Yemeni or Nabeel again. The hunch-backed minder said they'd been sent to a hospital in Barcelona, because their cases were difficult, and I would be returning to Beirut.

Beirut . . . Beirut seemed an eternity away. I'd spent an entire month amidst the whispers of nurses, the smell of anaesthetics and medicines, with one glass eye and one healthy eye, which wept and stung and filled up with fog . . . Beirut was so far away, it seemed another lifetime . . .

An entire month had gone by, in which I'd completely forgotten Beirut, and the sound of the shells booming across the city; during which I'd forgotten even the colour of my clothes. Here I was, alone in Spain one day and back in Beirut the next! I was going back the following day!

I'd said I'd be back. I'd told Sameer and Aatef, "I'll be back." Sameer said I would be a retired fighter.

"No," I told him, "not retired! I will come back and hold the sky between my fingers!"

Just the way we said we would when we filled the streets with our noisy demonstrations, when we chanted that we would hoe the earth and plough it anew and be the seeds of a new beginning.

And here it was: Beirut, a jumble of buildings, the sun glinting off its cement high-rises and its blue sea. The very same sea that filled with sailors searching the deep . . . As beautiful as the women, whose shimmering bodies lay on the sand that stretched all the way from Beirut and back, like the midriff of the world.

I took off my dark glasses, the city glistened white. I was sure they'd be waiting for me. No, I wouldn't go back to Cana, I'm no Jesus Christ, and the yearning ache in my belly for Beirut had been coursing through me, like wine through my veins.

And so there I was, back. Descending the steps from the plane, I can see that no-one is there waiting for me; inside the airport terminal, people suddenly begin scurrying around and jostling each other as shells begin landing in the vicinity. A steward groans and predicts the airport will close. I go to the party office . . . no-one there either. I'm told they've left for the mountains, far away. Marwan says they're all up there, where everything is covered in snow. "Then we'll go skiing down the slopes!" I said.

Boy, and what a steep descent it's been!

I'm the only one left here now. My old buddies have all gone. Sameer is in France, finishing his studies; Aatef went back to his old job at the Social Security Department; and I'm left with this new bunch of recruits who don't even know the meaning of the word war. They just strut around toting their guns, talking about war. They don't know what it means to die, how terrible it is. They talk about it as if it were something beautiful. But death is terrible. When I tell them, they don't believe me. I don't go with them on their patrols. I stay here, no, I don't go . . . I'd rather just stay here and wait.

Samar's advice was that I should go back to university. I told her I wouldn't. Samar was a student at A.U.B., who also worked at the film institute. That's where we first met in a big room covered in a pall of cigarette smoke. I was there because someone who knew about it told me they were making a film about the war and wanted it to include a fighter's testimonial. The director – whose name I forget, but he spoke like such a know-it-all – wanted a fighter to stand up in front of the camera and recount what he had experienced while the camera panned from place to place.

During the meeting, the director introduced me as a war

casualty who was also an intellectual and therefore someone able to speak articulately on the subject of war. He said he'd already prepared the text of what I'd need to say in front of the camera. He gave me the paper and I started to read it out loud.

"My name is Mohammad as-Sayyed. I'm a combatant with the Joint Forces of the Palestinian Revolution and the Lebanese National Movement. We are fighting to preserve the independence and unity of an Arab Lebanon, for the liberation of Palestine, and against the forces of imperialism, Zionism, Fascism and reaction! Pause. Behold the crimes of the Fascists! Pause. As for the war, let me tell you that we are peace-loving people, and we make war for the sake of peace. Pause. The forces of Fascism are committing untold atrocities and we are defending the lives of innocent women and children. Pause. Many of my friends have died. I held them in my arms as they breathed their last with the chant of freedom still on their lips. Pause. I was wounded, I lost my eye, do you hear me, my eye. Pause."

I asked the director about the word "pause." He told me that every time it occurred, the camera would cut to documentary footage of Tall al-Zaatar, the shelling of West Beirut and other battle scenes. I told him I thought it would be a terrific film. Everyone in the room, all those people smoking, agreed.

Then the director stood up.

"Listen, Brother Fahd," he said, "you have to put a bit more feeling into it, as if what you were saying was coming straight from the heart. Relax in front of the camera – don't be so stiff, you can move around a little, you know, act, if you see what I mean. Put some emotion into your voice, let your body go. You get me?"

I told him I understood. I picked up the paper again and tried moving as I read the first sentence. Then he started again.

"No, no, no! Look at me!" And he snatched the text from me and began to read, skipping the word "pause".

"My name is Mohammad as-Sayyed, I'm a combatant with

the Joint Forces of the Palestinian Revolution and the Lebanese National Movement. We are fighting to preserve the independence and unity of an Arab Lebanon, for the liberation of Palestine, and against the forces of imperialism, Zionism, Fascism and reaction. Behold the crimes of the Fascists! As for the war, let me tell you that we are peace-loving people, and we make war for the sake of peace. The forces of Fascism are committing untold atrocities and we are defending the lives of innocent women and children. Many of my friends have died. I held them in my arms as they breathed their last with the chant of freedom still on their lips. I was wounded, I lost my eye, do you hear me, my eye."

His entire body swayed and his voice shook with emotion. "Now do you understand? You have to do a little acting."

I felt completely overwhelmed and incapable. I told him I couldn't do it.

"I can't act," I said.

"Sure you can. What do you do for a living?"

"I'm a freedom fighter."

"I know, I know. I meant before that. What did you do?"

"Nothing," I said.

"O.K., but try and do a little acting." And he handed me the text again.

"I don't know how to, I already told you. It's difficult."

"Try," he repeated.

I took the sheet of paper and I tried again, as he sat opposite me, his mouth agape and his eyes following my every move.

"That's great," he said afterwards. "It's already much better. Now, Fahd, listen, whenever you reach the word "pause", that's the end of that particular thought: so there should be some change, maybe alter your tone, or even wear different clothes. But on the very last sentence, 'I was wounded, I lost my eye, do you hear me, my eye,' you should remain absolutely still before the camera. You must not move as we film you."

"What will you be filming?"

"We'll be filming you taking off your dark glasses . . ."

"What did you say?"

"We'll be filming your eye, and there'll be a voice-over with a commentary by a Red Crescent doctor on your injury."

For a moment, I was speechless in front of that roomful of people. Then I told him I wouldn't do it. I said I wouldn't let them film my glass eye. No way.

"But don't you see, Fahd, it's really important. There's no harm in it for you and it'll further the cause."

I could see everyone nodding in agreement, but I reiterated my position.

"I'm not an actor," I said, "I'm a fighter. Maybe you should get yourself an actor, someone like Mahmud Yasin or Omar Sharif. They're sure to do better than I could. I won't be ridiculed."

That's when Samar stood up. "No, Fahd, you don't understand," she said.

"You explain to him," the director told her. "It was your idea. Go on then, convince him."

A cacophony broke out in the meeting hall with everyone talking and arguing at the same time while I stood there like an idiot. Samar came up to me.

"Fahd, we don't want you to act. All we want is the truth."

"What truth is that, sister? The director has just asked me to act so they could film my glass eye. I wear these shades so that no-one can see it. It's not an exhibit item for display. And you expect me to let you show it on film!"

I repeated that I wouldn't act, not the way the director wanted at any rate. In actual fact, I wouldn't have minded being an actor, but not like that. Goddamn, this wasn't play-acting anymore! They wanted me to behave like some laboratory rat!

And so I walked out. I hurried down the stairs, without turning back or saying goodbye. Hearing her footsteps behind me, I slowed down, and we walked down the street together.

"How about a cup of coffee?" she asked.

"Alright, why not?" I said.

We drove to Hamra Street in her little white Renault and went into the Modca Café.

"What got into you?" she said.

I told her I was all for acting, that I thought the screenplay was really good, but that filming my eye was out of the question.

"But that was precisely why we selected you!"

"Well, then you'll have to find someone else. There are lots of people out there with eye injuries."

"We chose you because you are also an educated person, an intellectual."

"Listen to me, Samar. It is something I feel embarrassed about. It is painful, the glass is painful, and I feel ashamed."

"Wow, that's terrific! It's really good. Why don't you say that in front of the camera?"

"You're so tactless," I told her. "You expect me to talk about my eye in front of the camera as if I'm some kind of freak!"

But then she gave me a lecture about "the cause" and the role of information.

"I know you! You fighters are all the same! You despise knowledge and intellectuals. But information is incredibly important and film is the best medium of information, maybe the most important. Imagine, thousands of spectators in Europe and America seeing an educated freedom fighter with a glass eye talking articulately about the justice of our cause, about the plight of women and children, about all the martyrs, against a backdrop of shots of Tall al-Zaatar! It would have an incredible impact! It would shift all of public opinion in the West! You underestimate the importance of information as a weapon at our disposal!"

Watching her speaking animatedly, I found her pretty. If only she'd agree to sleep with me or love me, I thought. I was ready to love her, to be smitten with her, and her small eyes, but not to appear on the screen the way she wanted.

I told her the issue was a complicated one and I would have to think about it.

"The cinema is such a fabulous thing," she went on, "the way it can lend grandeur to events. Imagine, for instance, a sequence on Tall al-Zaatar: women, children, wailing and sobbing, the camera panning from face to face, zooming in on this cute child with large black eyes and curly hair who's picking his nose; the child is totally unaware of what's going on, as if he were unseeing, unhearing. Now wouldn't that be fabulous?"

"Yes, that would be very powerful, it'd be really great," I replied.

"And imagine," she went on, taking out her Marlboros and lighting one for each of us, "just think in what original ways we could portray death! Let's assume, for instance, that we're filming a corpse somewhere in the old town centre: the corpse is surrounded by overgrown weeds and grasses and a high earth embankment. The camera rolls silently, stops at the corpse, then cuts to a wild flower growing among the weeds. Wouldn't that be absolutely beautiful?"

"Yes. Yes . . . but what about the smell? . . . The smell would be intolerable!"

She just smiled.

"Oh, I see! Of course! The camera wouldn't capture the smell, only the picture!"

"So you see, even death can look beautiful!"

I looked at her. Light music played softly in the background.

What does this girl know about death? She talks about it as if we were talking about the movies . . . What does she know about it? If I told her about what happened to Sameeh, what would she say?

*

We'd gone up to the Zaarour heights by cable car, which sat under Sanneen's silent gaze. There was snow everywhere and we were posted in one of those snow-bound two-storey chalets. We'd lit the wood stove and the five of us sat around keeping watch at the windows. I didn't understand why I'd been stationed with them, they were all older than me, in their thirties, and I didn't know any of them. But they were professional fighters and I felt safe with them and expressed my admiration for them as they told stories of missions they'd carried out inside occupied Palestine. We had practically forgotten there was a war going on, sitting there day after day, eating and drinking tea, playing in the snow together and listening to the radio. It was all very peaceful.

And then, all of a sudden, everything blew up. There was a huge explosion, the snow turned a deep red, and from our positions behind the windows we saw them, advancing in line formation, like a pack of wolves. Despite the fierce shelling, we were able to watch them firing and advancing, getting closer and closer. I had my Kalashnikov, so I opened fire, but still they came, and when some fell to the ground others surged forward in their place. I don't know where I got the courage to do it . . . it was the first time I'd ever fired a gun in my life, and my bullets were lethal . . . I could see the advancing men falling and dying. Shells were raining down on us now, blackening our faces and hands with soot, and still we fired, round after round after round . . . The advance suddenly halted, giving me enough time to refill my magazine and release its contents, even though the shells kept coming down. I left my post at the window to look for the others. No-one. And then, there, by the wall under the westerly window, two bodies. Looking closely, I saw Sameeh slouched against the wall in a pool of blood oozing from his waist.

"Where are the others?" I asked him. He gestured that they'd gone.

"We must retreat," I went on. He nodded in agreement. I

told him to lean on me.

"I can't," he said. "I'm really bad, I can't move. Leave me here and you run for it . . ."

Then I saw his tears . . . a grown man, with a thick moustache, and tears silently washing down his blackened face.

"You go on, I'm not going to make it."

I picked him up and hoisted him onto my shoulder. His body was a dead weight and he was having trouble breathing. We left the chalet and I started up the mountain. I knew that our side was stationed on the eastern flank, so I walked eastwards . . . Just him and me, miles from anywhere, with nothing but mountains and snow around us, and the cloud-studded sky . . . Climbing up that mountainside, with him slung across my shoulder, I was gasping for breath. I could hear my heartbeat ringing in my ears, and I thought I was going to collapse. My legs felt like a solid aching mass gradually spreading upwards, and with him pressing down against it, I thought my chest would burst.

I stopped, and eased him down to the ground gently. He lay motionless against the snow, with the congealed blood around his stomach dark and thick. I sat down beside him. He asked for water, and I thrust my bottle towards him, but he couldn't hold it, so I opened it and held it to his lips. He took a few sips and said, "Leave me, it's too far, we're not going to make it." Then he began to shiver, his teeth chattering from the cold. I took off my jacket and covered him, he was shivering so much his entire body shuddered and his teeth clattered in my ears. I sat beside him in silence and, gradually, the shivering subsided.

"We can go on now," I said.

"Leave me," he repeated. "I'm dying. It's a long way, and you won't make it."

I put my jacket back on and hoisted him once more onto my shoulder – the hills stretching endlessly before me, I carried on with him dangling over my back, hot and feverish. I kept climbing upwards, as snow filled my boots and my feet turned to blocks of ice, and he continued to shiver from the fever running through his body. When I felt I couldn't go on, I stared at the ground doggedly and kept going. But then I had to stop, I just couldn't go any further. I could see a little hollow that had been carved out by heavy artillery, so I put him down and he crawled towards the hollow. I covered him with my jacket again.

"Listen," I said.

His face was the colour of chalk, white as the snow, his lips yellow, his eyes shut.

"Listen," I repeated. "I'm going to . . ." He murmured something inaudible. "Louder," I told him, "a bit louder, I can't hear you . . ."

He repeated the same words . . . just that one little sentence . . . nothing else . . .

"It's been a long day . . ."

"Listen," I said again. "The water bottle is here next to you and I've covered you with my jacket. Stay still, don't move. I'm going on to the next position to fetch some help."

"It's been a long day . . ."

"Listen, I'm going. Do you need anything? Sameeh, do you hear me, we'll be back soon, don't worry, we won't leave you here. I'll be back with them in less than an hour and then we can carry you properly. Did you hear me?"

"Such a long day . . ."

"I'm leaving now. Do you need anything? I'll be back. Stay right where you are and don't move."

I set off, leaving him lying in the hollow, shaking under the khaki jacket, with the water bottle next to him. I realized I was thirsty and had a long way to go, so I came back, picked up the water bottle and drank. I drank greedily, almost finishing the bottle, and still my thirst wasn't quenched. But I had to leave him some, so I stopped, and put the bottle back next to him. I leaned down close, he was still breathing, with his head propped against his chest, his body all curled up on itself.

"Sameeh," I said one more time, "I'm coming back, wait for me." And I set off again.

I was climbing nimbly now, hurtling along, jumping where I could, as if I had rid myself of a great burden, going steadily eastwards. I didn't feel frightened, I was sure I wouldn't lose my way in the hills. Only now, when I picture myself on that solitary eastwards journey through the hills, after leaving Sameeh in the hollow, do I feel frightened. What if I had got lost with no food or water? What if I had stumbled on their positions, not ours? And why had I drunk from the water bottle? The mountain was covered in snow, and I had drunk the water in the bottle and left him so little!

I walked and walked, and after three hours without a moment's rest, I finally reached our positions. I could see my comrades in the distance and could hear their voices.

"Fahd is here," one of them said.

First Lieutenant Omar led me to his tent. There, I drank my fill, then tea was brought and he started questioning me about the numbers involved in the attack, the weaponry they had used, and the ensuing skirmish. I told him they'd attacked in waves, that the skirmish was over quickly, but that the shelling had continued and I withdrew under fire.

"That shelling was from our side," he said. "We assumed the position had fallen to them, so we shelled it."

Then I told him about Sameeh.

"Poor bastard," he answered.

I told him we had to go back for him. "Where did you leave him?"

"Three hours from here."

"That's impossible."

"What's impossible?"

"We can't go back."

"What do you mean we can't? We're just going to leave him there to die?"

"Yes. I can't jeopardize the lives of ten men for the sake of one. The hollow where you left him is now in enemy hands."

"But I promised."

"I'm sorry."

"What do you mean, you're sorry?"

"He'll be a martyr to our cause."

I began to scream.

"Listen, Fahd," he said, "this is a war, we're not playing cops and robbers here. Fighting a real war means sacrifices have to be made."

I was almost in tears, desperate to get back to him. "But I promised, Comrade Omar! I left him in the hollow, covered with my jacket, and I promised I'd be back."

"Take it easy, Fahd. He'll become a war hero and live forever in the glory of martyrdom."

"That's outrageous!"

"O.K., enough now. It's over."

And that was that. I would not have gone back had I been asked to do so, but I was screaming because I knew that no-one would make such a request.

It was all over.

It had been a long day.

Samar was still talking with that strange excitement of hers. "Listen," she said, "you're not listening! We have to publicize the justice of our cause and expose their fascistic practices: the killing, the rape, the looting, the house demolitions and dispossessions. That is the role of progressive cinema! It's our job to document such atrocities!"

"But we do the same," I told her. "We too are guilty of crimes, of killing, of . . ."

"That's not true! What you're saying isn't true!"

"It's true. I swear to God! Remember Damoor? When we were in Damoor . . ."

"Don't you start up about Damoor! Why don't you tell me about Maslakh and Qarantina, about Naba'a and Tall al-Zaatar instead!"

"Please. There's no need to use that tone of voice. I'm only speaking the truth."

"What truth? That's not the truth. The truth must serve the revolution. That kind of talk just undermines our cause."

"The truth must serve the truth. Full stop."

"And war is war. Full stop."

"Don't I know it! As God is my witness, you think I don't know that 'mistakes' are made in all wars, and that it's all about 'strategic momentum and political gain'? All I'm saying is that we too are guilty of 'mistakes'."

"No, you're overstating the case. How can you be a freedom fighter and speak like that?"

"Well, Comrade, I can, and I will continue to be a freedom fighter. But that has nothing to do with what I know to be the truth."

So that's it, and I'm still here. What else could I do, where was I to go? Samar's advice was that I should go back to the university. What for? How could I study with my useless so-called good eye? It becomes inflamed and painful as soon as I start reading. There's no way I can resume my studies, and I don't know any other trade or occupation. And anyhow, why should I? Half my friends have been killed in combat, should I simply forget about them, let them rot in their graves and run away, like I did with Sameeh? No, I wouldn't do that.

I stood up to go and the waiter brought the bill. She insisted on paying.

"I've got it," she said.

"So have I."

"But I invited you."

"No, no, really, it's O.K."

She paid and we walked to her car.

"Where shall I drop you?"

"At the party office."

We drove in silence, with foreign music playing on the radio; when we arrived, I invited her in.

"Thanks, but not today."

"Shall we meet again?"

"What for?"

"To continue the discussion."

"Alright," she said, and we set a date.

We met like that several times. We always went to the same café, and said almost the same things, but I was never bored. She was pretty and lively, and I wanted to tell her I loved her, but I didn't dare.

Then, one day, we went to her place. It was in a secluded building, somewhere off Bliss Street, close to the American University of Beirut. We went there because she wanted to read me the draft of a screenplay she was working on with the filmmaker Jalal Abul Huda – the same guy who had tried to "direct" me.

The apartment was nice, with a large living room, bedroom, bathroom, kitchen . . .

"You live alone, how odd," I said. "Rents are so high."

"This apartment's been requisitioned," she said. "Comrade Abu Habib worked his connections and I don't pay any rent."

She got the screenplay and began to read aloud. But I wasn't listening. She was sitting so close to me on the sofa, smoking as she read, I was trying to think of a way to take her hand. Then she stopped to comment on a sequence.

"Isn't it just lovely here? The scene of the woman toasting the lentils and reminiscing about Palestine . . ."

"It's great . . . ," I said, and grabbed her hand, which was lying on a cushion next to me.

She didn't say anything; she didn't pull her hand away or object, and just carried on reading. She took her hand from mine to turn the page and did not put it back on the cushion.

"Would you like some coffee?" she asked.

"Yes, please."

As she went to the kitchen, it occurred to me that I should follow her . . . I remembered that in all the Arabic novels I had read, the woman goes to make the coffee and the young man follows her, then he catches her from behind and swings her round to face him, and instead of describing what happens between them, the writer gives a detailed description of the coffee boiling over. I got up and followed her into the kitchen. She was standing facing the stove and the coffee was already boiling over. When she turned to face me, instead of doing what they do in novels, I told her about novelists and their descriptions of coffee boiling over.

Shaking her head, she blew on the coffee froth and said: "That's what comes of a poor imagination and a reactionary attitude to sex." Then she put the coffee pot down on a tray and we went back to the living room.

We drank our coffee and made small talk. She'd gone to buy a new pair of trousers, she said, but found that everything was made in Hong Kong, and there weren't any originals on the market anymore.

I got up to leave. She stood and followed me to the front door. I gave her my hand and she shook it. Then I took a step towards her, bent down slightly and kissed her on the cheek, then edged a little closer. "No," she said, "please don't." I kissed her on the lips, she kissed me back, and this time she didn't say, "No, don't." I wrapped my arms around her, but she pushed me away gently.

"Not now. I'm busy now."

So I left. And I didn't see her again after that; or, rather, I did, about a week later – in fact, we went to her place, and I slept with her. But she was like a block of ice. She didn't move or seem aroused, and I felt like I was raping her, so I got up and dressed and I left.

We'd made another date to meet at the café, but she didn't show up and she never called. I even went to the film institute to ask after her, but they told me she wasn't coming in that day.

And so, she vanished, just like that! I don't know why she broke off with me. That day, when I was undressing, and she lay naked on the bed, I felt suffused with love: her brown body glistened against the white sheets as I bent down and kissed her, and as I fondled her breasts I told her I loved her and wanted to marry her immediately. But she turned into a block of ice. When I tried to break the ice, it wouldn't even chip! And now, I hear she's married! She never even contacted me, she's married and living on Verdun Street. She hitched herself to some big merchant, some fat cat in the sugar business!

I wonder why she lied to me like that. She was forever going on about "the system" and "bourgeois hypocrisy" and yet when-ever I criticized the situation, she said I was a niggling, narrow-minded petit bourgeois . . . And now, she's gone and married a sugar merchant! Extraordinary!

Naturally, I refused that part in the film they were making, but she wasn't upset; she did try to persuade me to change my mind but she wasn't upset, she said she respected my point of view. And then she disappeared.

So here I sit now . . .

Actually, before they took him away, I heard them questioning him. What did they want with the poor guy? It was plain he had nothing to do with all this. He seemed like he had a screw loose maybe, or was some kind of a simpleton, but they buzzed around him like bees with no end of questions. I didn't interfere – I don't like getting mixed up in that sort of thing. The poor man was standing with his hands up in the air, as if a gun were being pointed at him, and then he began circling around the room, and they around him. I couldn't figure out why he was going round and round like that, with his hands up in the air. I wanted to tell them to take pity on him, to leave him alone and let him go. I tried to approach him as he circled, and that's when I noticed his smell. I thought he must not have washed in a long time to smell like that. Then he stopped dead in his tracks, and he made this rattling, rasping sound: he was trying to say something, but I couldn't catch the words because he was muttering, so I got closer. I still couldn't make out anything he said, he looked like he was chewing his words, then spitting them out, with a rattle from his throat. The others were also trying to make out his words, and one of them was even taking notes. When I asked the officer what he thought the man was saying, he said, "I don't have time for you now, I'm busy, the report needs to be ready soon."

"But what's he saying?" I repeated. "It's unintelligible."

"Comrade, please, I beg you, I beg all of you comrades, just leave me alone with him."

So I left the room. But that smell followed me, it was – how shall I put it – like the smell of a corpse. I held my nose, I even splashed my face with water, but the smell wouldn't go away.

My father always said that if you wanted to honour the dead you buried them. Why don't they ever bury the dead these days? I think that the dead should be buried even smack in the middle of a battle. The fighting should be suspended, and each side should bury its dead. It's terrible how they just leave them . . .

When I'd said as much to Comrade Omar, back in the mountains, he'd told me that I was having a rough time. And looking fixedly at my good eye, he said, "You're a war casualty, and your injury has undoubtedly affected your morale. Go back to Beirut and rest up, Comrade." And so he sent me back here.

It's not true I was having a rough time in the mountains. Only once did I say I wanted to give up and go home. It was long before that, and I didn't leave. I just said it, and went and spent two days in my tent. But then I came out and resumed combat with the others. Why did he say I'd been through a lot and should return to Beirut? I'm just fine . . .

All I did was want to know why they killed the boy. I begged Omar to spare him. I was really serious this time, but they executed him anyway. I didn't even tell them his name. I'm the only person who spoke to him . . . there was no reason to kill him.

They just shot him in cold blood, right there in front of me. He stared at me with eyes full of terror and reproach; I lowered my gaze, but I saw how they killed him.

I'd been the first one to spot him. He was lost in the mountains, with his rifle slung over his shoulder. He seemed to be searching for something and I just went up to him and grabbed him. He offered no resistance as I led him away.

"You alone?" I asked.

"Yes."

"What are you doing here?"

"I lost my way."

"Where are your people?"

"Over that way."

"Come on. Walk ahead of me."

We set off, him stumbling in front, with me behind, holding his rifle, and my comrades bringing up the rear. I noticed his knees were knocking. "Please, leave him," I told them. "I'll carry out the interrogation."

I took him into my tent and he told me about himself, in a trembling voice, over some hot tea. He said he was from Dowaar, that he had been raised by the monks in Bikfaya, and that he had lost his way.

"But why are you fighting?" I asked him.

"I fight just like everyone else."

He was very young, with a pretty face. I told him not to be frightened.

"You're going to shoot me!" he said.

"No, we won't, don't worry."

"But you people kill."

"No, we don't. We don't kill wantonly, like you. How many in your unit?"

"Five, we were on a reconnaissance patrol, and all of a sudden I found myself alone."

"No. How many in the entire unit?"

"Oh, lots."

"That is?"

"That is . . . I, I don't know. A large number."

"A hundred?"

"More than a hundred. Perhaps . . . yes, more than a hundred."

"Weaponry?"

"Same as yours."

I hit him.

"You'd better talk," I said, striking him on both cheeks. "This isn't a joke." He began to shake.

"I beg you," he pleaded, "don't kill me."

"Weaponry?"

He added up their weapons for me, then said:

"Honestly, that's all I know. I haven't been to every one of our positions; I'm just an ordinary militiaman. Please don't kill me."

"We won't, you don't understand a thing. Are you hungry?"

"No. Thanks."

I handed him a Marlboro, which he smoked greedily, in total silence. I heard Comrade Omar asking where the prisoner was. I stepped out of the tent and presented my report.

"That's great, really great," he said. "He spilled the beans quickly. Bring him out, I want to see him."

I went back inside and asked the prisoner to follow me. "Here he is, Comrade Omar."

"You scum, you fascist bastard, you savage!" And he started to strike him; then, moving in even closer: "You're frightened . . . real men aren't frightened . . . a combatant doesn't tremble like a child . . . Stand up!"

The boy looked so desolate, I had wanted to go to him and reassure him, when I heard the gunshots. It was Omar, with his pistol; the boy keeled over into a sea of blood while the others fired machine guns and revolvers at the twitching body.

Once they had stopped, I went over to where he lay and turned him onto his back. Two glassy eyes stared back at me.

"Take him far away from here," Omar said.

And they took him away.

"But why," I asked him, "why did you do that? I promised we wouldn't kill him."

"You promised, huh! We did what we had to do."

"But why? He was just an innocent young boy! And he was our prisoner."

"You don't suppose that if they'd taken you prisoner you would have remained alive, do you?"

"But, even so . . ."

"Do you think that if he'd captured you, he would have spared your life?"

"Still . . ."

"Have you forgotten what they did to Saïd when they got him near the Nasra Tower in Ashrafiyyeh? How they roped him to a Land Rover and dragged him alive through the streets, as people gawked? Have you forgotten?"

"But I still . . ."

"Have you forgotten how they hurled the children off the Nahr Beirut Bridge?"

"But even so . . ."

"Even so, even so . . . Just shut up, will you. We have to kill them!"

"But we, too . . ."

"But we, but they, but this, but that . . . shut up philosophizing and get off my back!"

"Comrade Omar, I promised him, he was just a boy, without even the first signs of growth on his face. And he had nothing to do with the bridge or the Land Rover!"

"Cut it out, will you? By your logic, no-one has anything to do with anything and everyone is innocent. What does it mean to have nothing to do with it? He knew what there was to know and was a fighter like the rest of them, and this is a war. We're not playing games here, and nor are they. They kill us and we kill them."

"But . . ."

"But . . . nothing."

I went into my tent and didn't come out for two days. I tried to forget the whole episode and to convince myself that Comrade Omar was right, that what he said was true and I was just being sentimental. And I managed to put it behind me; until the day I felt the maggots swarming over my arm.

It was dark, and we had left our dugout for more forward positions, engulfed in gunfire and shelling. As great flashes of light punctured the darkness, the very stars seemed to tremble in the sky. I was inching forward, on my belly and firing, when I suddenly collided with something. To begin with I couldn't tell what it was. My arm had hit something taut, like inflated rubber, and then in an instant there were maggots everywhere, on my hand and up my arm. I drew back quickly, dropped my rifle, got onto my knees and started brushing my arm off frantically: from my forearm, the maggots had reached my waist, just above my cartridge belt. And then the smell exploded in my nostrils, and I froze. I was rooted to the spot, as if paralyzed. I considered retreating and returning to my tent, but I didn't.

It was only the following morning – when the first sliver of light is still trimmed with darkness – that I saw him. It was the young boy, his body all bloated, with the first stages of decomposition already evident on his face, especially around the lips. I couldn't help myself, I started howling. Immediately, the gunfire resumed. Still howling, I beat a retreat.

When I got back, I was raging.

"Why couldn't you have buried him?" I screamed at Comrade Omar. I threw my rifle to the ground and went into my tent, swearing.

He followed me and said he thought I was no longer fit for combat and should return to Beirut. It wasn't true, I was perfectly fit for combat – it was just that he couldn't accept what I was saying. My request was simple enough: I was only asking for the boy to be buried. I didn't see what the problem was – God alone knows how unbearable those maggots and that smell were!

So I returned to Beirut and set myself up in this office – and I have never left it since. I'm always combat-ready, but no-one ever calls me up anymore; even when Israel invaded the South in 1978, I wasn't asked to go to the front.

But what I want to know is where the maggots come from. People say they come from inside you, but I think they come from the smell. I remember the feeling to this day – it was as if I'd plunged my hand into a rubber pillow of writhing, wriggling maggots; they crawled up my chest, reached my neck and then my nostrils, and then they exploded into that smell.

It was the same smell, when they brought in Khalil Ahmad Jaber. Why didn't they wash him – after all, he could've been infested too – before they questioned him? That interrogation was such a sham!

And now, here I am, I can't say anything or go anywhere, I just can't. They might be able to, but I can't.

There was this guy . . . I don't know his real name, Issam we called him, that's what he said his name was when we were in the mountains together. Anyway, I ran into him here in Beirut one day and people were calling him Ibrahim. I wonder what became of him. I saw him on the street once and he walked right past me, as if he'd never laid eyes on me before! As if we'd never been comrades-in-arms and shared those times together!

He was one of those men who spent the length and breadth of the day talking politics. He was our political mentor, actually, and we used to gather round for hours listening to him tell us about Mao Tse-tung and about Pol Pot, who abolished the cities and liberated the imagination; he would talk to us about the people's war, about guerrilla warfare, revolution and liberation. I'd never met someone like him before: he was a university lecturer and a fighter! I used to think that all academics were just armchair revolutionaries, you know, bespectacled and pot-bellied, sitting in their offices, full of hot air and flamboyant gestures. Ibrahim wasn't like that at all, you should have seen him that time he was injured. He'd been hit in the foot and he didn't even flinch.

I wasn't far off and I shouted over to him, "Comrade, you're wounded!"

"I know," he said.

"Retreat, I'll cover you."

"No, we must get Talal."

"Talal? Where is he?"

"He's over there. He was hit in the head, I think he's dead."

His voice was steady as a rock even though Talal lay there dead! He suggested we belly-crawl towards the body and drag it back.

"Be careful," he went on, "the attack's going to be vicious, but if we don't retrieve his body now we'll lose him."

I tried crawling on my belly but found I didn't know how to.

"What's with you?" he asked.

"Nothing."

"Go on, I'll cover you."

"No, you go back and I'll get Talal. You're wounded, leave me."

But he wouldn't, and we retrieved Talal together – Talal, handsome as a rain-filled cloud in spring, Talal for whom every girl in Arabia would have given her eyes, Talal who now lay beside us, his face drained of life. Issam, at my side and still bleeding profusely, said: "Don't cry . . . we die so that life may go on. Men don't mourn martyrs."

That was Ibrahim.

He asked me what I was up to these days.

"Oh, I'm just around," I told him, "and what about you?"

"Me? Nothing much," he answered. "I'm back at the university, teaching."

"What about the revolution?"

"Well, what about it? . . . Everything's fallen apart . . . hasn't it? It's finished. It's all over."

"Ibrahim, no, how can you say that! What of Talal, then? Have you forgotten?"

"Talal is a martyr. And we suffer."

We went to his office, and there he started talking religion, telling me about praying and fasting.

"Is that you, Ibrahim, talking like this? Where have all our revolutionary ideas gone?"

He said he thought that a return to religion was the only solution.

"But, but there's a war out there, sir, what should we do?" I asked him.

"Nothing. It isn't our war."

"Where is our war then?"

"It has yet to start."

"You mean to say that when this war's over, you expect us to start fighting all over again?"

191

"Yeah, you got it! Once this war's over, then the real war will start."

"Well, don't count on me. This war has just about exhausted us. One war is enough, sir. Please, no more."

He said I should come and visit him at home and gave me his address. I told him I was much obliged.

"No, really, come over tomorrow evening at seven. We'll be doing some religious study."

"You're really serious?"

"Really, Fahd, come on. It's over, man, don't you realize?"

"What is there to realize?"

He just raised a finger skywards and walked away, limping. Remembering his injury, I wanted to ask him about that foot of his, but he was already gone.

So here I am, alone . . . and I've had it up to the eyeballs with the murder of Khalil Ahmad Jaber! It was just one of those senseless, meaningless incidents: they brought him in for questioning, I saw him, then he left, and then nothing. I don't know why Abu Jassem – our unit captain, his real name is Sameer Amro – is making such a song and dance about it. We're sick and tired of his endless investigation, of him making a mountain out of a molehill! I'm sure the boys didn't do anything to him, it was just a straight-forward interrogation and then they let him go. Could it be that they . . . ? No, they couldn't have killed him. Then who did it? Could it be . . . ? No, no, it's not possible . . .

As for that Fatimah Fakhro woman, she's just witless! He had no such thing as a bucket or brush when they brought him in. Why she's been saying that he trudged around whitewashing walls and tearing down posters, I honestly don't know! I'm convinced he was just an ordinary guy, a poor soul . . . maybe he was a refugee. Perhaps he'd lost all his family and he just liked to wander about, isn't that what tourists do? Surely there's nothing wrong with that!

Who killed him? Some kind of gang, maybe . . . Abu Jassem says that's impossible, that he's got the place sewn up and no-one can move a muscle without his knowledge. And it's true. He's been able to track down the people involved in most of the crimes being committed – it was him that uncovered the murder of the Armenian doctor and his wife. At least that's what he says. And if it's true, then why can't he find Khalil Ahmad Jaber's murderer? In any case, I don't think it merits this huge fuss, and the interminable talking, and Khalil's wife coming here constantly for never-ending meetings with Abu Jassem.

And why was Fatimah Fakhro dragged in here and threatened? She had nothing to do with this! Her husband divorced the other woman and stole the bracelets – well, maybe he did and maybe he didn't – and then they killed him. What's the point of interrogating her, of threatening her and beating her like that? I really don't understand anymore, why we're getting sidetracked by all these petty incidents! And, in any case, why shouldn't people be allowed to whitewash the walls and remove posters if they like? *Ya akhi*, we human beings are born free, and the walls don't belong to us!

Personally, I don't think that he was doing anything suspect around those walls. There's this engineer, Ali Kalakesh, who came in here all high and mighty, complaining about it in connection with his daughter. What could that poor man do to his daughter? In any case, at the end of the day, it's none of my business and Khalil Jaber is dead. He has found his rest, what more could anyone want? Though not before he was tortured . . . He was badly beaten up, that's for sure, but he's dead and gone, and it's over! In a country like ours, where such a staggering number of people have died, is the death of Khalil Ahmad Jaber really an issue?

People say he was the father of a martyr . . . Don't ask me why, but there are martyrs sprouting everywhere these days: as far as I can see, everyone's become a martyr, or belongs to the family of a martyr. Where did the son die? He wasn't killed in combat, I'm sure, so how could he be a martyr?

And now Khalil Jaber's a martyr too. I bet I'll be the only one that gets killed without anyone calling me a martyr. And anyway, what difference does it make? Does it matter once you're dead, whether or not they produce a poster of you?

Poor Khalil Jaber, honestly, I feel so sorry for him, nobody should have to die like that. They just dumped him there, like some piece of trash or bit of flotsam . . . Is that any way to treat a person? I don't like to meddle in things that aren't any of my business, but it's because of that smell . . . I smell it on myself all the time, I carry it around on my own body now. Even though I wash and shower and use soap and shampoo, I still come out smelling like that! Tell me, how can I get rid of this maggot smell?

And, anyhow, why didn't anyone consult me? They interrogated him alright but no-one asked me what I thought. I'm sure Comrade Omar said I was a coward. But I'm not. He's the coward. No, no, how could I say that, I saw him with my very own eyes lead the offensive with such bravery . . . but I'm not a coward, either – I'm a fighter, just like them. I'm better than they are – at least I stayed the course. The others all drifted away, but I'm still here. I live in the office and do anything that needs doing – the thought of women never even crossing my mind, not after the episode with Samar and the film!

So here I am. Anyway, how to leave and where to go? How could we abandon our martyrs?

I go to the graveyard and I talk to them. Whenever I have a serious problem I go there, and stand beside Talal's grave and talk to him. And he answers me. He says, never mind, let it go. And I believe him. He always says everything's fine. And I believe him. Why wouldn't I? He was my commander. He was the one who persuaded me to join the revolution. He was the one who took me off to the training camp, the one who said the revolution had started when the war broke out. We were in his house when we heard about the Ain al-Remmaneh bus.[†]

"It's started," he said. "The revolution has started!"

That night, we went downtown, to the old commercial centre, and we blew up the *Kata'eb*[‡‡] party offices. It was my first time doing explosives. The streets were completely deserted, it was really eerie. He asked me something and I hesitated before answering, I didn't want him to hear how breathless I was. And Talal explained, with a smile, that it was because it was my first time. He didn't tell me I was afraid, he just rested his hand on my shoulder as I drove, getting out of the car every now and then to lay down the explosives. On the way back, we heard them going off, one after the other, but he dragged on his cigarette calmly and said that it had begun and we had to be prepared for war.

When I go to his graveside, I don't take flowers or anything with me. I go and ask him questions, and he tells me to be patient and that things will change.

"But they're changing for the worse, Talal."

"No, they're not, you think that, but things are getting better. Everything gets better."

Once, I told him that I wanted out, that I wanted to give up this whole business and find myself a job. He burst out laughing – I swear I heard him! He laughed so loud I had to look over my shoulder to make sure that the people who were in the cemetery, looking after the graves of their dead, hadn't heard him. He told me to go back to the party office and wait there.

"And if you feel bored, ask them to send you to the units down south," he said.

[†] The incident that signalled the outbreak of the civil war. On Sunday, 13 April, 1975, a bus full of Palestinians drove through a militant Christian neighbourhood of Beirut and shots were exchanged outside a church. Both sides claimed the other attacked first.

[‡‡] *Al-Kata'eb* is Arabic for the Phalangists, the right-wing party that spearheaded the coalition of Christian militias antagonistic to the Palestinians and the "National Movement".

I asked but they refused. They told me it was because of my eye. "Just wait," Talal said.

So I sit here waiting, and I feel as if I'm bearing the weight of the world on my shoulders, like that mythical centaur: it feels as though all the stars and the moons, every one of the planets, the very heavens are on my back, and I am beginning to stoop under the weight of it all. I'm scared of what might happen if my back breaks, the heavens would come crashing down, as the saying goes ... But they haven't fallen, and here I am sitting tight, immovable. Didn't he promise me that I would hold the sky between my hands? The sky is so distant, and my back is almost breaking.

I'm going to stay put, I'm not going to move; I'm just going to wait. Talal said I should, and so I am: I'm waiting for my mother, I'm waiting to get married, I'm waiting to die, I'm waiting for the revolution, I'm waiting for . . . nothing in particular, just here, waiting for nothing.

They're all the same! The difference is that when they say they're brave, they're lying. I'm brave but I don't expect anything, I'm brave because I know and expect nothing.

Ladies and gentlemen . . .

I put on my dark glasses, then I take them off, and I tell you that the end does not exist. I am the only actor in the world to admit that that there is no such thing as an end. You may go now, but don't expect an end as there isn't one. Have you understood? No-one understands. Still I wait. I'm the one who expects nothing. I'm the one who expects everything.

Captain Sameer Amro, or Abu Jassem, as he is known by everyone, is thirty-five, short, stocky, and powerfully built. He uses a cane, which he holds with his right hand, and from his waist bulges a leather cartridge belt, with bullets for his Smith and Wesson. Though his left arm is amputated at the elbow, he is quite unselfconscious about it.

The man's reputation is legendary. His hand was severed

during Black September, the month of pitched battles between the *feda'iyeen* and the Jordanian Army, in 1970. He was sent to one of the Eastern bloc countries for treatment, but refused to have a prosthesis fitted. "It's better this way," he says, and so his arm ends in a stump at the elbow. People say that even though the severed limb went on being terribly painful for over a year, he was stoical about it, displaying exemplary fortitude and never complaining.

Abu Jassem is the stuff of legends. He was among the very first to join the revolution in 1966, abandoning his studies in electronic engineering at a university in Germany. He is reputed to have been part of Abu Ali Ayyad's inner circle, and makes constant references to the man. Recalling the military training camp at al-Hama, off the Damascus highway, he emphasizes Abu Ali's harsh but fatherly manner with the young recruits. If it weren't for his fatherliness, how do you suppose we could've become *feda'iyeen*, he likes to say.

The story has it that in 1966 Abu Jassem was wounded in an operation against the Israeli army, but that he somehow managed to crawl back to the Lebanese border with seven bullets lodged in his abdomen. After a patriotic border officer picked him up and dispatched him to a hospital in Saida, the Deuxième Bureau[‡] got wind of the matter and Abu Jassem was arrested. Held for over a year in the Helou Barracks with his wounds unhealed and open, he bore the pain with outstanding courage.

They say he was held there with Jalal Ka'wash, the *feda'i* who died in custody after he was dragged around the compound roped to the back of a vehicle. At the time, the Lebanese government issued a statement alleging that Jalal Ka'wash had taken his own life by throwing himself off the third floor of the building. Abu

‡ The notorious secret service agency that, under the "reformist" regime of General Chéhab in the 1960s, suppressed political freedoms. Surviving into the 1970s, the Deuxième Bureau became synonymous with extra-judicial abuses.

Jassem never talks about Jalal – if you ask him, he just shakes his head and gazes into the distance. He will only talk about the period of his interrogation.

A terrible period.

Only three days after the operation to remove the bullets from his abdomen and while still running a raging temperature, soldiers of the Lebanese Army surrounded the hospital and notified its director that they had explicit orders to arrest Abu Jassem.

The director, who was also the operating surgeon, said it was out of the question. The man was wounded, his life was still in danger, and there was not a law anywhere in the world that permitted his arrest. "You may," he told them, "station a guard outside his room." But arresting him would be criminal, he would die.

They paid the doctor no heed, stormed Abu Jassem's room, wrenched the I.V. out of his arm and carried him out on a stretcher. The officer in charge said they were taking him to the Military Hospital in Beirut. The doctor did not believe him. "The man will die, and I will raise hell about it," he said. "It's outrageous!'"

But the doctor did nothing of the sort, and news of the incident was not carried in the local press. It only appeared in an underground publication with limited circulation in Gaza City.

In actual fact, they took him straight to the Helou Barracks. Realizing that they wanted him dead, Abu Jassem refused to answer any of their questions. The interrogation had started, to all intents and purposes, inside the ambulance that transported him from Saida Hospital to Beirut. One of the soldiers had asked: "Where were you wounded? Where do you get your weapons from? How many of you are there? Where are your bases in South Lebanon?"

In enormous pain, Abu Jassem just stared up at the ceiling of the ambulance. The vehicle sped down the potholed tarmac, and every time they hit a bump, he was sure that his stitches were going to burst open. That was when he made up his mind that he would die without opening his mouth.

When they arrived at the barracks, they told him to get up and walk. "I can't just jump out and walk . . ." he began, stopping in mid-sentence after seeing the ruthless glint in the officer's eyes. He realized that they would shove him out of the ambulance and then claim that he had died attempting to escape. "O.K., I'll walk."

Bracing himself against the side of the vehicle, he doubled over and slowly rose to his feet. He felt his abdomen was ripping open – dizzy with pain, he fainted and fell to the ground with a thud, like a solid plank of wood. The soldiers picked him up and threw him into a dark and dank cell, without even a blanket to lie on. He lay like that on the bare ground for another twenty-four hours, before regaining consciousness.

When he came to, his head was pounding and his body was racked by shivers.

"Where am I?" he cried. No response. Then a man came in with two tin cans, one full of water and the other empty, for him to urinate in "and keep the place clean". He crawled to the can with water and drank, then tipped its entire contents over his head to try and bring down the raging fever. The following day, they gave him dry bread in addition to the water.

Abu Jassem became delirious, and he remained so for an entire week, drifting in and out of consciousness. A soldier at the barracks – who subsequently enlisted in the Joint Forces after the split and collapse of the national army – would later recount Captain Sameer Amro's odyssey with nothing but admiration, always referring to him as Captain-Sir.

As he told it, loud banging, punctuated by occasional rasping cries for help, could be heard coming from the lower part of the barracks where the hallucinating Abu Jassem was being held. And although these muffled cries troubled all those who heard them, no-one dared ask the commanding officer what the source of the noise was.

Ali Tabsh, the former soldier, says that after three days of this, he was detailed to clean the cell, and that when he went down, he found Abu Jassem, convulsing and delirious, in a pool of excrement and urine. When he approached the prisoner and spoke to him, there was no response. When the soldier looked more closely, he could see greenish patches dotting the flesh of his abdomen, and when he brushed against him, Abu Jassem's entire body shuddered. After cleaning out the cell, the private went up to the duty officer's room.

"Sir," he said, "the man is dying." The officer looked up scornfully. "Sir, I cleaned out his cell. I saw him with my own eyes, he's covered in pus and is so feverish he's practically unconscious."

"Let the dog die!" the officer answered.

"Sir, he's in agony!"

"Get out of here, and mind your own business, will you!"

"Sir, I think he should be in a hospital."

The officer jumped to his feet, cursing.

"Calling themselves *feda'iyeen*! Conducting their dirty little wars, they deserve to die! They're nothing but agents, and death is all they deserve. I'll finish him off myself!"

Private Ali Tabsh left the room, and after he told his fellow soldiers what had passed between him and the officer, no-one dared take any initiative whatsoever. They could hear Abu Jassem's agony and all they could do was wish him a hasty death. They knew the poor wretch would never get better in those conditions.

Ali Tabsh even thought he might go to him in the middle of the night to finish him off and relieve Abu Jassem of his suffering, but he never did. He was too scared, that they would consider him a criminal, and he would be expelled from the army.

But Sameer Amro, aka Abu Jassem, did not die.

The soldiers could not believe their eyes when they saw him up and about one day, walking around the compound. He was slightly stooped, it is true, but there he was, wearing a clean set of clothes, on his way to the examining magistrate's office.

After the rasping rattle had stopped, everyone had forgotten Abu Jassem was in that cell.

But he had not died, and when Ali Tabsh met up with him again ten years later, he almost leapt to his neck and embraced him. However, Captain Sameer's steady gaze, calm tone and amputated arm all restrained the soldier from showing his feelings to his officer-hero.

No-one knows for certain how it came about that Sameer Amro returned to life. According to rumours circulating at the time, Gamal Abdel Nasser had pressured the Lebanese president to ensure the prisoner received proper care and was not abandoned to his fate. Some people attributed it to sheer luck, it was a miracle they said, the result of untold suffering and fortitude, as his body slowly expelled the poisonous pus and the wounds began to heal, though they continued to ooze blood. Others still said it was the doing of Khodr Abul Abbas, who had appeared before Abu Jassem in the dead of night and had touched the wounds with his spear, leading Abu Jassem to recover.

Whatever the truth, the point is he recovered. And whenever people ask him about his recovery, he says nothing. He smiles enigmatically, baring a gold tooth. In actual fact, he himself doesn't know how. Whenever he tries to remember that time, he cannot conjure up anything but a film of white gauze . . . but he remembers the interrogation very well.

Entering the examining magistrate's office, Sameer Amro, the *feda'i*, is met by the contemptuous gaze of the officer who remains seated at his table. Sameer ignores him and scrutinizes the maps hanging on the wall behind him. The officer invites him to take a seat and offers him a cigarette.

"Thanks, I don't smoke."

"What will you have to drink, tea or coffee? It's been a while since you've had any, surely?"

"Thanks, but I won't."

The officer rings a bell and orders coffee, one plate of *osmalliyah* and a bitter coffee for himself. While they wait for the coffee, the officer busies himself with a stack of papers before him. A soldier brings in the two cups of coffee and puts them down on the table. The officer takes a sip, sucking his lips in noisily and licking off the froth that has stuck to them. He lights a cigarette and inhales deeply. Sameer leaves his coffee untouched.

"Drink, man," the officer says.

"Thank you, I don't drink coffee."

"You're stubborn, aren't you?"

"I am."

"Listen to me," the officer says, rising. "A softly-softly approach is useless with you people. But let me tell you that it is within our power to break you. We can put you through hell, if we so wish."

"You've already done it, down in that cell."

"You think I'm joking?"

"No, I think there isn't anything you can do."

"Listen, we want one thing, and one thing only, from you . . . Just a little information on your bases in the South."

"I know nothing."

"You mean you won't talk?"

"I mean I know nothing."

The officer rings the bell again. Two large, heavily built men enter, muscles bristling. Holding him up by the armpits, they just lift Abu Jassem out of his chair.

"The chicken treatment, sir . . . ?"

They took him out of the room and led him to a kind of elevated scaffold, where prisoners were suspended by their hands and feet, like a chicken on a rotisserie spit; after a few moments, they brought him back into the room.

"Looks like nothing works with you," the officer said.

"You've used every method you have, and I still know nothing."

The officer's voice softened.

"You're young and healthy, why waste your youth like this? ... You're all traitors, you're a ... you're nothing but collaborators."

"You must be mistaken, sir. It is you who are the collaborators and the agents."

The officer got up and slapped him. Facing him squarely, the *feda'i* Sameer Amro spat in the officer's face. The officer wiped off the spit with a tissue and barked an order to the two strongmen to give him the "spit," which they did.

During the next and final interrogation session, the officer said what he had to say in a couple of sentences. "Be informed," he told Sameer as he led him to his cell, "that you shall spend the rest of your days here. Your people have split up, and every government in the Arab world is accusing them of treason." Sameer Amro remained in that cell until the June 1967 war. When he was released, he went straight back to al-Hama camp and lay low for a while.

Stories abound of his courageous exploits inside the Occupied Territories. According to one of many such accounts, he single-handedly put an Israeli tank out of commission with an RPG missile.

Abu Jassem is now the apparatchik in charge of the party office where Fahd Badreddin "works," and he is the only person who treats Fahd with any respect. He even consults him on occasion. Besides his participation in many leadership organizations, he is responsible for special operations – including, it is rumoured, the 1972 Munich Operation (although no-one was able to confirm this information); he is a very senior apparatchik in West Beirut with many duties attached to his position. He remains, however, a man of few words.

Since the outbreak of civil war in Lebanon, Abu Jassem has

become rather irascible. During the War of the Mountains[‡], he was very vocal about the need for decisiveness, arguing in favour of prosecuting the war to the bitter end, to victory. But, as is well-known, the "decisiveness-in-battle" principle was eschewed in favour of Arab and international intervention – in Abu Jassem's words, a mere diversionary tactic before the *coup de grâce* was delivered. Waving his stump in the air, he curses the pass we have come to.

Gradually, and in spite of his reluctance, he was assigned a car, a driver, and then a bodyguard. He did not want them, but he was told they were "unavoidable security measures" in the changing situation and that "given the positions of responsibility we are now in, you can't refuse." So he agreed. But he agreed reluctantly. He dismissed the driver early as often as he could, and would find some mission or other in the South on which to dispatch his bodyguard, simply in order not to be accompanied.

The captain has not changed much over the years. He has put on a little weight, maybe, but he remains a solid man. People say he drinks – everybody drinks – but he has never been on a mission drunk, so it's not a problem. He is adamant about the subject of border security, because, in his words, there is a very real danger of enemy infiltration. But when it comes to political analysis, he raises his stump in the air as if to say that he knows nothing.

The captain has not enriched himself. That is a fact. There are those who have displayed such ostentation that it cannot pass unnoticed. But he remains unchanged. Although this place is awash with petrodollars, Abu Jassem has lost none of his probity or integrity. Everyone knows that Captain Sameer Amro could have gone the way of many others and filled his pockets, but he obviously has not had that inclination. Or perhaps it is for

[‡] A subconflict between the 1982–3 and the 1984–9 phases of the Lebanese Civil War, which took place in the mountainous Chouf District located south-east of Beirut.

some other reason we don't know about; or even, simply because he has remained faithful to his principles.

When the subject of looting and other abuses is brought up, Abu Jassem is quick to retort that such incidents constitute the exception and not the rule: "These are passing aberrations which will disappear, leaving only the true combatants."

His role in Khalil Ahmad Jaber's case is somewhat unclear. Khalil was initially taken in for questioning at the party office when Captain Sameer was not there, and it is possible he may not even have read the report submitted by his aide, First Lieutenant Salah. But after learning that the victim was the father of the martyr Ahmad Jaber, he went to pay his respects at the home of the deceased. He listened patiently to Khalil's wife, mobilized his assistants and personally initiated and supervised the inquiry: he had Ali Kalakesh summoned, he interrogated Fatimah Fakhro, he read the coroner's report closely, and he considered at length the factors which led to Khalil's detention.

"I said only to arrest him . . . Why did he die like that?"

They assured him that none of them had been involved in the murder, that they had released him the same day.

"Then who is the brute that kills a poor tramp for his gold wedding ring? Whatever happened to his manhood?"

He told them he suspected them, his very own men. But then he dismissed the thought. It couldn't have been them – they wouldn't kill a man for his wedding band. After all the banks that were looted, no-one out there would kill a man for a petty little gold ring, worth no more than a couple of hundred lira!

Faced with such an impasse, he halted the inquiry and closed the file.

He supervised the funeral arrangements personally, he went to the deceased's home and let Khalil's wife know that henceforth her late husband would be considered a martyr. He oversaw the provision of food for the occasion and regularly visited the home of the deceased, and he never tried to obfuscate the fact that Khalil had been arrested for a few hours, on his orders, four days before the body was found. He vowed to lay his hands on the murderers and have them publicly executed.

Abu Jassem took the posters of Khalil Ahmad Jaber to the house in person, and he stood in the reception line alongside the widow and other relatives for the condolences. And when the mourners questioned him on the details of the interrogation, he sipped the bitter coffee placed on the table before him, sucking his lips in noisily and licking off the froth that stuck to them, inhaled deeply on the first drag of his cigarette, and answered with his customary cool-headedness.

"It is clear," he said, "that we cannot allow our ranks to be infiltrated. What is going on here is a war, not a game. It is not child's play. Khalil Ahmad Jaber was detained for security reasons. Are we supposed to let 'irregularities' escape our scrutiny? There was this man, whom no-one seemed to know, trudging through residential neighbourhoods, sleeping on the street and ripping down posters. He may have been booby-trapping cars or placing explosives outside the homes of law-abiding citizens. We had no idea who he was, but when we ascertained his innocence, we let him go . . ."

Everyone nods in agreement.

"We were merely doing our duty. Should we allow the posters of our war heroes to be defaced? You yourselves know the value and importance of their sacrifices: if it weren't for them, none of us would be here today; if it weren't for them, you wouldn't be able to sleep in your own beds; if it weren't for them, your homes would have been overrun and you would have been driven out of them; if it weren't for them, we would have been subverted from every tenet of our religion and faith. How could we let the posters of our martyrs, our war heroes, be torn down? You know how precious such pictures are to the relatives and friends of the dead, don't you? Didn't Khalil himself exhibit an almost passionate concern for his son's posters? Didn't he come to me over two years ago with a request to print another batch?"

The wife butts in to say that that was true – he always wanted there to be pictures of Ahmad hanging on the walls.

Abu Jassem continues.

"You see, even though Ahmad died four years ago, his father still wanted to see the pictures of his son kept on the walls. What should we tell the parents and relatives of the new martyrs? Should we tell them that their loved ones' posters are being torn down? How could we? It would be unacceptable. Will the revolution last forever? No, of course not. Speak up, if you think otherwise."

"No, no, of course not," everyone replies.

Mr Munir Itani, an old friend of Khalil's, is getting quite worked up and he proclaims that the revolution is there to protect the walls and that the walls are there to protect the people. But then he glances over towards Abu Jassem and asks the comrade when he thinks all this will be over.

"When all what will be over?"

"This calamity . . . This war . . . !"

"It's going to be a long war, our enemies want to see us vanquished, and resistance is necessary. We are resisting by all the means at our disposal: we are fighting in the South, we are on a war footing in Beirut, and for the sake of the resistance we must try and lead as normal an existence as possible."

One of the mourners – Khalil's wife does not know his name, he is one of Ahmad's old buddies from the sports club – mentions the various protection rackets and other abuses of power.

"It's intolerable, Comrade Abu Jassem," he says.

"Absolutely . . . ! We will not tolerate such practices, and you must help us uncover them. Name anyone extorting protection money and I will take care of him."

No-one says anything.

"Well, why don't you speak up?"

"Oh, no reason, no reason," says the deceased's son-in-law. "We were speaking in general, there's no need to go into parti-culars."

Abu Jassem picks up where he left off.

"But in order for life to return to normal, schools, restaurants and cinemas all must reopen, everything should be operating normally. We have a duty both to resist and to go on with life. Do you think we should let people tear down advertisements and posters from the walls on a whim? People came and told me they'd seen a man doing just that. Should we just have sat there and done nothing? Maybe the man had been planted in our midst, we didn't know it was Khalil, may he rest in peace, so we took him in for questioning. We made public pronouncements about the return to normalcy and here was someone who was hampering the process. It's a fact, everyone is getting back down to business, offices and restaurants are reopening, the situation is improving, and there's no need for people to feel any kind of pressure."

"Well, what about the shelling then?" someone asked.

"That's not our responsibility . . . you should ask someone else about that. Our responsibility is to look out for ordinary citizens to an even greater degree than for ourselves!"

"But all we see are politicians in fast cars, living it up like the rich, while we grow poorer by the day."

"Nonsense! You find me a pauper, and I will find him an honorable job."

"But what about the politicians, then . . . ?"

"What's wrong with them? Ask me, I should know. By God, they don't even have enough time to eat! Ensuring their protection is absolutely essential . . . security precautions are indispensable in the current circumstances."

Abu Jassem drones on, and the people let themselves be

convinced. That's what people want – to be convinced that there's a reason for all this, that their fortitude, long history and good reputations are not in vain.

"I will not let Khalil's murder go unpunished, I will discover the guilty party, and then we'll see. But we won't forget that Abu Ahmad died a martyr's death, and a family that can offer up one of its own is capable of any sacrifice or act of generosity. Unto them is paradise promised. 'Think not of those who are slain in the way of God as dead. Nay, they are living. With their Lord they have provision.'"

Abu Jassem rises to take his leave. Everyone stands up respectfully, even the deceased's wife who, as the person befallen by tragedy, would not normally stand for anyone in such circumstances. One of the women wishes him every success.

Someone else asks the wife a question about the whitewash story; she denies everything:

"Nothing but lies! The captain assured me it was nothing but lies and gossip."

"Then, who killed him?" Nadeem, the son-in-law, asks.

"Degenerates . . . a gang of degenerates, that's who."

"Really . . . !"

"Everything's possible these days."

"It is a sign of the times," the wife says.

"It is the wrath of God, as we near the Day of Judgement, the end of times," says the sheikh sitting in the corner of the living room.

The fact is Abu Jassem does not have the time for this kind of thing.

His obligations now discharged, he has dropped the case – although he was never anything but courteous to Khalil's wife, on her periodic visits to the party office. Still, tongues are wagging that he is travelling to Europe rather often these days. Fahd Badreddin thinks he goes on missions. Others say that his stump has become very painful again and that he goes for treatment. And the malicious say he goes for rest and recreation.

"But where does he get the money from?"

"Oh, money's not an issue! Beirut is awash with money."

"But the Arabs don't grow oil, so where does it keep coming from?" Fahd asks.

"You're so naive," a brash eighteen-year-old fighter answers him

"God blessed us with oil so we could be rich."

"But it is our plague!"

"Well, without it there would be no war," eighteen-year-old Sami goes on. "Don't you understand, it is oil money that bankrolls all the factions in this war."

"And that's why we don't want it," Fahd says.

Sami smiles: "I don't know what's happened to you. People say you were traumatized in the mountains."

CHAPTER VI

The Posters

*Mrs Nada Najjar, 28, the deceased's younger daughter, wife of
Nadeem Najjar, mother of two young children, aged five months and
five years respectively, and a resident of Aysheh Bakkar. Her husband
runs a pinball arcade on nearby Independence Avenue. Nada Najjar is
tall, dark and full-bodied, with small close-set eyes. She's considered
to be highly intelligent as she went all the way through school, graduat-
ing with a Baccalaureate in the Sciences. She did not pursue further
studies. She married Nadeem, a family friend who was a member of
the same sports club as her brother, Ahmad. Unlike Ahmad, however,
Nadeem never enlisted in the Joint Forces. Seven years Ahmad's senior,
he owned a business, which he hoped to transform into a large trading
house one day, and he was married. This is what he repeated to Ahmad
whenever the subject of taking up arms was broached. Nadeem
was categorical about it: he was not prepared to die "just like that", as
he put it. This rift in their views caused a noticeable cooling in the
men's relationship.*

Nada happened to be at her parents' home the day news of
Ahmad's untimely death arrived. People said her wailing and
keening could be heard all over the neighbourhood. Ululating
and rocking with grief, she ran out to the street, her head uncovered and her feet bare. Her sorrow seemed inexhaustible, she
spent all her time at her parents' house and even slept there.
To begin with, Nadeem Najjar didn't mind. He had never felt
this sad either. Never before in his life had he felt like this.

"Poor Ahmad . . . so young and innocent . . . He'd gone to

fight, not to die . . . It was his destiny, that's what it was . . . It was written," he told Nada.

He wanted her to get a grip on herself and come home. But all she did was cry. So Nadeem left her at her parents' and took care of the children; initially, he sent them over to his sister's, in Ras el-Nabeh, but after a while it wasn't feasible to leave them there any longer. The children should come home, he said, and so should she. But she wouldn't.

Nadeem Najjar found her behaviour puzzling. There she sat in her parents' house all day, drinking coffee and chatting non-chalantly with visitors as if nothing had happened . . . But no sooner did he say something to her than she started to cry.

One day he yelled at her, saying this really had to stop.

Nada had been sitting beside her mother, next to the blind sheikh who had just reached the end of the Qur'anic recitation, when all of a sudden she burst into tears. Just like that, out of the blue, with the living room full of people. Tears streaming down her face, she got up and went into her brother's room and came out carrying pictures of him, sobbing.

This really had to stop. It was becoming contagious: the mother was starting up, and soon the other women in the room, none of whom Nadeem Najjar had ever seen before, were crying too. Her face puffy and flushed, Nada started keening. One of the women went and fetched a bottle of orange blossom water, and as she dabbed some across Nada's face to soothe her, Nada's moaning only intensified. A whole week had gone by since the boy had died, and she still wouldn't come home or stop this endless wailing!

All the men in the room had their eyes on Nadeem.

Turning to him, one of them exclaimed, "Poor child!" and another enjoined: "As God is my witness, that's a real sister! She's got a sister's heart. A gem of a sister she is!"

Then another chimed in: "*Ya Allah*, such an emotional girl, she's going to die of grief!"

And a fourth added, "It's all over for the one who's gone."

Nadeem saw how they were all looking at him. He jumped to his feet, grabbed her by the wrist, and tried to pull her out of the armchair. As she clung on, he began shouting at her.

"Get up! Get up, damn you! Enough of your crying, enough of dying! Come on! Get off this armchair! You're coming home with me, you stupid woman!"

The mother took no notice, she seemed indifferent. The father, Khalil Ahmad Jaber, carried on with a political discussion he was having with two other men. One of the mourners, a friend of Nadeem's, remonstrated with him.

"No, Nadeem, don't do that . . . Leave her alone. It's her brother . . . come on, man, let her be, let her cry her heart out, it's good for her; it's cleansing."

"This isn't crying! This is idiocy! Get up, woman, get up! I said we're going!"

"Leave me alone!" she screamed.

All eyes turned to Nada.

"Home, I said. We're going home!"

"Good gracious, he won't let the poor woman cry . . ."

"I have nothing against crying," Nadeem shouted back, "but brother, this isn't crying. This is a torrent of tears, it's a travesty of grief . . . This is *haram*! The woman has lost her senses."

And he yanked her out of her chair.

Dazed, Nada stood up and followed her husband out of the room, as everyone looked on. And so it was that she went home. But ever since, she has felt totally estranged from "that man", as she now calls him . . .

How could he do such a thing, and in front of all those people? What did he expect, that I wouldn't cry over my brother? Since when was crying forbidden? He was my brother, after all! Had it been his brother, I can assure you, the world in its entirety would have heard the crying. But he acted like that because it was my brother! And why wouldn't he let me wear black? He says one shouldn't for a martyr, a so-called war hero . . . I'd like to know what that is anyway! What does it mean to be a martyr? Does it mean Ahmad's not dead? Martyr or not, you're dead, regardless. I didn't agree, but he wouldn't let me say what I thought, or anyone else for that matter. How, how could we leave the corpse in the hospital like that and not bring it home? They didn't even wash him, they buried him the way he was! And we were made to feel like strangers. It was Nadeem who spoke with the *shabab*, as if he were Ahmad's family, while my father stood there like a complete stranger. And after all that, he expected me to stop crying! The truth is, he was jealous of Ahmad . . . Imagine, being jealous of a dead man! To think that I have a husband who is jealous of my dead brother! What a husband! Oh God, what a husband!

Well, of course I love him . . . can a woman not love her husband? And he used to be such a fine husband, too; he was hard-working and life was good, *al-hamdulillah*! My mother had had her doubts, though. She thought a pinball arcade was basically gambling. "I'm not marrying my daughter off to a gambler," she said. But it was Father who settled it – "He's a good boy," he told her, "from a decent family, and he's also from the neighbour-hood." I agreed with Father. Nadeem was a handsome young man, he was full of life. I'd see him driving about in his little car, and when he offered me a ride to school one day, he looked at me in that very special way, all smiles and charm. So I agreed. He was better than my father, a civil servant. Civil servants have such an insufferable life! All Father ever did was tell us about telephone exchanges and the new electronic systems the new minister had ordered. He was obsessed with telephones! And then there was no more work for him during the war. Whereas with Nadeem, business went right on, people didn't stop playing pinball. Even when there was no electricity, business carried on – I don't know how, we had no electricity for six months! He told me he'd bought an electric generator, and that he was also selling ice cream on the side. Things were even better than before, he said.

He was rarely at home though. And when he came back late at night, he reeked of arrack . . . and something else . . . the Lord alone knows what! He was different somehow. I knew what he was like when he drank araq, but this smell that was on his breath, this was different. But I didn't dare ask.

The truth is he was smoking hashish. When people said he was passing joints around with "the boys", I didn't want to know. According to him, business had improved, things were good, and he wasn't going to be scared off by the war and the shells falling on our heads.

It was Ahmad who told me. He was back from the frontline, he'd come home to a hero's welcome.

"War is war," he said, "and it is our duty to fight."

I told him I didn't agree and that Nadeem was right. Why was it our duty to fight? We're not fighting a war, we're rushing to our deaths. I wanted to say something else too but he cut me off and gave me this little lecture . . . I don't know how he came up with it.

"That was true a long time ago," he said, "in the days of our forebears, under the Ottomans, when Father's uncles all perished in Safarbarlek – they died of hunger and squalor, not from the fighting. But all that's over now, we're no longer led to our death like sheep to slaughter. We are the masters of our destinies, we are fashioning our own future."

So I said to him, "You know how it is, Nadeem being a family man and all . . ."

That really set him off. "Your husband's no man!" he ranted. "He's just using the children as an excuse not to join up. If that's what it really is, why is he spending all his time hanging out with those guys?"

"Which guys?" I asked.

"Forget it, forget I ever said anything."

I asked again, and he said the same thing.

"I want to know," I insisted.

So he began telling me about this bunch of so-called combatants who were nothing but hooligans and gangsters and who hung out in Nadeem's shop smoking dope. "They're the ones who do the looting," he said, "during the fighting." Nadeem didn't accompany them, he added, but he had opened his doors to them, and the shop had become a den of iniquity and vice.

"Not only is that wrong," he said, "but it's shameful. Once we take over, they'll all go to jail."

"Including Nadeem?" I asked.

"He'll be the first to go."

Now I understood why Ahmad rarely visited us anymore, and why he and Nadeem had fallen out, but as a woman what could I do? I had tried, once, to tell him . . .

It was the middle of the night, and I wasn't able to sleep. I was sitting up in the hallway, I'd settled our little boy there, the shelling was so bad that night . . . It was two in the morning, I thought the shelling was never going to end . . . I was so afraid . . . Every time I heard a shell ripping through the sky with that high-pitched whistle and then landing with a wailing thud nearby, I would huddle over my little boy to try and protect him with my body. Nadeem wasn't at home, and I was really worried about him that night. I was sure he'd been hit. But there was nothing I could do except wait, and weep. As I lay huddled against my little boy, crying, he finally arrived. He opened the front door and walked in humming, as if nothing was wrong, as if all those shells were nothing at all. He refused to lie down with us in the hallway and said I should come to bed as usual.

"And what about the boy?" I asked.

"Leave him there if you like."

"But I'm afraid."

"There's no need to be."

So I followed him into the bedroom. He undressed, put on his pyjamas, and lay down. The room reeked of that strange smell. I snapped, I felt I couldn't take any more – what kind of a life was this, by God, my mother was right!

"I won't have it," I told him. I swear that's all I said. I didn't say anything bad; all I said was that he was smoking dope, that the shop had become a hashish den, and that he wasn't looking after us properly. Honestly, I didn't say anything.

He went ballistic! He hurled himself against me and started hitting me with his fists and gnashing his teeth like a madman. How dare he . . . He'd never done that before . . . this was the first time . . . I couldn't cry out, I was afraid to wake the little one. He just kept hitting me and hitting me, and, in the end, I couldn't hold out any longer, I bit down on the pillow and began to sob. The blows kept coming as he screamed and cursed and carried on, saying things I would be ashamed to remember, let alone repeat!

Now, honestly, do I look like a whore to you? He told me, his wife, that I was a whore! He said all women were whores, and he could do as he pleased. And, then, he took me, you understand what I mean, he had sex with me! Can you imagine? I didn't want to, I told him, but he just did as he pleased. He slept with me, and then he sat up in bed and told me to make him a cup of coffee!

"Coffee now . . . At three in the morning . . . ?"

"Yes, now. I want a coffee, now."

Going to the kitchen, I thought I would collapse . . . my legs felt like jelly and my eyes were stinging. But I made him his coffee. He lit a cigarette and started talking – I could hardly understand what he was saying, though, because he was slurring all his words. He rambled on and on, and I told him I agreed with everything he said, even though none of it made any sense to me. I had to force myself to listen to him and was having a hard time keeping my eyes open.

"This is the beautifullest war!" That's what he said. And then: "It's shit! Yes, war is shit. But it's beautiful. Oh my, the women out there! And the guys, you should see those young guys, may God protect them all! Such a war, praise the Lord, such a beautiful war! . . . I'm all in favour of it now . . . I'm into the big time . . . you know what I mean . . . the kingpin! Yes, me! You understand? . . .

"Bah! You understand nothing! No-one understands anything! Those guys are real tough, they're brutes. You know the butcher, Abu Saïd, yes, our butcher? Well, listen to what he just did . . . He closed the shop, rounded up a few of the guys, and with his assistants from the shop, they all set off together. His is a nice, tight little operation, those guys only go where the going is good, they only fight where there is the really good stuff, you know, fridges, couches, ovens, gold, silver . . . Now, there's this guy, his name is Sami al-Kurdi, and – and, if it weren't for your dear brother, the son of a . . . they call themselves honourable men, he and those boys of his! Honourable, my eye! Me, I'd like to know what that means! . . . Honourable! . . . Like a dog . . . or a donkey, perhaps? It's honourable, is it, that they do the dying and others rake it all in! Well, let me tell you, with Abu Saïd it's like this: he rakes it in and he doesn't die. Here's to you, Abu Saïd!" And raising his cup, Nadeem slurps some of his coffee and asks: "And you, madam, what do you think of that? I haven't heard your view on the matter, Sitt Nada."

Me? I wanted to go to sleep, that was my view.
So, back to Sami al-Kurdi . . . Tonight was Sami's night. God knows where he gets his stuff from . . . He walked into the arcade and asked me where Abu Saïd was. I told him he hadn't arrived yet, so he sat and waited for him. He poured himself a glass of arrack and said Abu Saïd was late.

"He must be on his way, where's he gonna go?" I told him.
"You sure he's coming?"
"Of course I'm sure. He was probably just held up somewhere.

He's bound to come. Where's he gonna go?"

An hour later, Abu Saïd shows up, with four of his best boys in tow. Some of the finest he has. The best, I swear, the very best . . . they pay up and get to do as they please! Not like your idiot brother. You heard me, milady, yes, that idiot who pontificates about principles! I'd like to know where he picks them up, those principles of his . . . I'll tell you where he gets them from . . . from the open sewers on our streets! Principles, my eye!

Anyhow, where was I . . . oh yes . . . Sami al-Kurdi. I don't know where he gets stuff from . . . He must have some kind of inside information. Anyway, there he was sitting, whispering into Abu Saïd's ear, and then, all of a sudden, the chief jumped to his feet, fully alert, with this serious look on his face.

"I don't believe you! You're nothing but a liar, you son of a Kurd!"

"No, Chief. I'm not lying."

"I swear I'll shoot you if you're lying!"

"You do as you wish, but I'm telling you, my info is one hundred per cent correct."

"Let's go, boys!"

"What's going on?"

"A quickie and we'll be back. The court will assemble here, in the shop. O.K. by you, Nadeem?"

"O.K. by me. What court?"

"You'll see. And I don't want any customers around here when we get back, do you hear? Come on, we're off. We'll be back soon."

"The place is all yours, Abu Saïd."

They grabbed their rifles and left.

"What about your drink, Abu Saïd? You haven't finished."

"We'll be back, I tell you. We'll only be a few minutes. It'll wait. And you wait too."

I waited. They were gone more than an hour, but you should've seen them when they got back! They were a sight for sore eyes!

If it weren't for that . . . son of a bitch brother of yours! No, he wasn't with them, and he didn't interfere personally . . . but his boys did. It may just as well have been him.

Anyhow, Abu Saïd came back with his boys, all puffed up like a peacock, and Sami al-Kurdi looking like a godfather, and they had these two guys with them: an old man, with a head of white hair, and a younger man, who seemed to be his son. The boys had blindfolded the two of them and were leading them along like little dogs. It was too funny for words . . . the old man in front, the young man behind, feeling the ground with every footstep, as if he were climbing some mountain or making his way through a thick forest, shaking like a leaf! Abu Saïd poked him with his rifle butt.

"You're nothing but a woman!" he mocked . . . "What's all the shaking for? Where's the man in you, boy?" while the older man intoned *al-hamdulillah*, dear God, it is your will . . . And the younger man repeated Oh Lord after each of his invocations. That is how they came into the place.

Seated in his chair, with all the rifles pointed at the two prisoners, Abu Saïd says: "The court is now in session and I want nothing but the truth. First, let's have the evidence."

So Sami al-Kurdi steps forward and places this rusty little semi-automatic Carlo, with forty rounds of ammunition and an empty magazine, on the table in front of Abu Saïd. The chief takes a sip from his glass and clears his throat.

"The truth, do you hear, I want nothing but the truth. The truth alone will save your lives. Come on, Grandpa . . . say something!"

"Yes, yes."

"Look here, Grandpa, you're an old man, and I have nothing but respect for that white hair on your head. You live here, don't you, in our neighbourhood? And none of us here is fanatical or sectarian in any way, right? And all our religious teachings affirm the brotherhood of man and fraternal love, don't they? So tell me, sir, what's this machine gun for? It seems that you are living in our midst and shooting at us."

"I swear, son, it's nothing."

"What do you mean, nothing? If it's a joke, it's not funny."

"Honestly, it's nothing."

"Who gave you this machine gun?"

"Really, it's nothing. I've had it ever since the '58 uprising. And I'd forgotten all about it. I'd forgotten I owned a machine gun."

"Why buy one in the first place?"

"We're not involved in any fighting; we have nothing to do with this war. I told you it's a relic from '58!"

"You mean you were against the people's revolution in 1958?"

"My dear sir, I wasn't against anything. I bought it for self-defence."

"You mean to say we're harassing you? That can't be, we're not sectarian."

"No, no, quite right. But in 1958 it was different. At that time, it was sectarian. But you're right, this time it's not like that!"

"You bought the gun to use against us."

"No, honestly, I don't even know how to use it!"

"Oh, now I see. You bought it for your son, so he could use it against us."

"But my son was only a child then, he was three years old in 1958. How could he carry a gun at that age?"

"Where do you work?"

"Right here – I work for the Stico Pharmaceutical Company."

"Where's that?"

"Not far from here, off Hamra, on Maqhool Street."

"Where?" al-Kurdi asks.

The younger man started to answer him. "It's close to here . . . it's . . ."

"Maqhool Street, I know where that is. Right by Sandy's Bar," says Abu Saïd.

"Sandy's?"

"Yeah, Sandy's . . . You know, where Warda works. Or have you forgotten Warda?"

"Anybody ever threaten you, Grandpa?"

"No. Never!"

"Well, then that means you're against us. You're fifth columnists, agents!"

Then Abu Saïd gets up, goes towards the younger man and slaps him right across the face. "And you?" The young man is shaking from head to foot. "I'm guessing you're the spy, the one who writes the reports."

"No, no, mister. I swear, it's nothing to do with me."

"What about the machine gun then?"

"I didn't even know we had one."

"I know your sort. You've been sniping at us with that machine gun, haven't you?"

"Me? No, sir. I swear. And anyway, it's not good for sniping."

"How do you know? . . . It seems you know something about guns after all . . ."

"Please, don't get me wrong! It's just that, well, I mean, everyone knows that kind of thing! All you have to do is read the papers!"

"The nerve of him!" al-Kurdi says. "You've got a nerve!"

Abu Saïd lights a cigarette and clears his throat one more time.

"I know your sort! You're all the same. Anyhow, the court has ruled . . . Oh, no no, before that . . . In the name of the revolution, in the name of the people, and after examining the incontrovertible evidence at our disposal, the court has ruled that the two gentlemen . . . er . . . er . . . your name?"

"Munzer, Munzer Nahhas."

"Munzer Nahhas and his son . . . er . . . your name, boy . . . !"

"Jean. Jean Nahhas."

". . . that the aforementioned gentlemen, Munzer Nahhas and his son, Jean Nahhas, have been found guilty of acting as agents on behalf of imperialism, Zionism and the Isolationist Forces. Having heard the suspects' defence and reviewed the documentary evidence presented by the freedom fighter Sami al-Kurdi, the people's court, sitting at Mr Nadeem Najjar's arcade on Independence Avenue, has handed down the following sentence: summary execution by firearms, with immediate effect."

There was complete silence. "Applause, where's the applause?" thundered Abu Saïd.

So I started clapping, and then they all joined in. I've never been to a public execution, this was my chance! And it was going to be two-for-the-price-of-one, like seeing two films at one sitting! My, what a fine performance Abu Saïd and those boys put on!

Then, Abu Saïd takes the two men and locks them in the bathroom. And al-Kurdi asks him, isn't it a bit risky to kill them in cold blood, just like that.

"Well, how else would you have us do it?" Abu Saïd replied. "It's a death sentence, isn't it?"

"I tell you, Abu Saïd, it scares me."

"Bah! You're just a chicken. And a thief to boot! You're the one who took all the jewellery from their house. You couldn't care less about the revolution!"

Sami al-Kurdi said nothing. Abu Saïd glanced over to the boys.

"Well," he said, "who's going to carry out the sentence?" No-one stirred.

"Alright then, I'll do it, but I need an assistant," and as he scans their faces, every one of the boys averts his eyes, lowering them to the ground.

"Not a man among you, eh?" Abu Saïd had hardly finished saying, when we heard all this commotion outside. The boys reached for their guns and Abu Saïd peered out to see what was happening, when a tall young man strode into the arcade and placed his hand over the machine gun lying on the table.

"Where are they?" he asks Abu Saïd.

"I don't know what you're talking about!"

"Listen here, Abu Saïd. This isn't on. Our orders are clear: no abductions or kidnappings! We want them released. Now!"

"No, no, you've got it all wrong. You're mistaken. This isn't an abduction or a kidnapping. We are responsible people. They are agents, and by capturing them we are discharging our responsibilities to the revolution."

"Responsibilities? Bullshit! Don't give me that crap! I want them, Abu Saïd, and I want them now!"

"But . . . brother, you don't understand. We're the ones in charge around here, and we know what's best. And anyhow, what do you mean 'no abductions'? If you can do it, so can we!"

"Abu Saïd, you'd better stop your little game. This place is surrounded, and it'll be my pleasure to start the bonfire!"

So Abu Saïd gets up cursing and goes to the bathroom to fetch the two men. Then, as the tall young man picks up the machine gun from the table, Sami al-Kurdi steps forward.

"Sorry, brother, but that's ours. It's war booty."

The tall young man pays no attention to him. He takes the machine gun and walks out of the arcade with the two captives. He leads the old man by the arm, with the son following behind, both of them still blindfolded.

"Get in the car, sir."

"They're going to kill us!" the young man cries, falling to his knees.

"Come on, get in, sir."

"It is the will of God," the old man says, his voice breaking. Still on his knees, the son is pleading, I beg you, spare us!

"Don't worry, you're going to be alright," the tall young man says, helping the son to his feet as the father gets in the car. "We're releasing you."

"They're bluffing, Father. They're going to kill us and throw us in the sea."

"Almighty God, spare me this ignominious end," the old man exclaims. "May the Lord protect you and reward your mercy!"

Then the engine started and the vehicle disappeared.

Inside the arcade, everyone was fuming.

"What business is it of theirs?"

"They said they weren't going to kill them, but I bet they will!"

We all thought they would. Sami al-Kurdi chuckled.

"Some chief you are, Abu Saïd!" he said. "In fact you're nothing of the sort, you're just fooling around! You didn't even try standing up to them. They did as they pleased. Where's all that muscle and might of yours, huh?"

"Shut up, you dog!"

"Me? A dog! . . . No, sir! More like you're the dog . . . and the son of one too . . . and a coward to boot!"

Abu Saïd drew his gun and fired, hitting Sami al-Kurdi in the belly.

"Come on, Chief, can't you take a joke?" he cried, falling to the ground. "See what you've done? . . . Stop shooting, will you? You're killing me!"

And the boys picked him up and took him to the hospital.

Abu Saïd stayed in the arcade with me. He sat there, drinking, smoking and cursing. He was furious. And me, I thought he was right. Yeah, what was it to do with them? Why was it off limits only for him? Because his boys loot? Who doesn't? No, it's just because he's the neighbourhood boss and he's a local. They're just thugs! But now he's done for, and so are we . . . I think the business is going to go down the drain . . . all because of this shitty war . . . if it weren't for this damned war, we wouldn't be where we are . . . I won't be able to carry on the same as before, I can't anymore . . .

Nadeem rambled on like that, and I think I fell asleep while he was still talking. Anyway, there was nothing I could do – he was my husband after all. It was best to keep quiet and put up with him. And that's exactly what I did, until Ahmad died.

Oh, how could he, how could such a fine young man like Ahmad go and die, just like that! Why did he have to join up? The war has nothing to do with us but we're the ones who die! I told him, I told him he would die! At night, I would dream that he was dead. And he died! And then Nadeem expects me not to cry over my own brother . . . He's my brother, how could I not cry! How could he shout in front of all those people like that, how dare he!

Ahmad was my little brother, he and I used to sleep in the same bed. I would tell him stories and he loved listening to them. We'd lie in bed and pull the covers up over our heads, and he'd ask for the story about the Russian priest, and I would tell it, over and over again, until he fell asleep.

"Listen up, Ahmad," I'd say. "There was once a Russian priest who had a cat he loved very, very much. One day the cat stole his piece of meat, so he beat her and killed her and then he buried her. And on the gravestone, he wrote: There was once a Russian priest who had a cat he loved very, very much. One day the cat stole his piece of meat, so he beat her and killed her and then he buried her. And on the gravestone, he wrote: There was once a Russian priest . . ." And Ahmad would be asleep.

Why, it seems like it was just yesterday . . . even though he'd become a boxing champion, and I was married . . . he would come and sit beside me and ask me to tell him the story of the Russian priest.

I can't remember who told us the story, but we used to sing it as a ditty at school, and the nun would get so angry with us, saying that it was wicked, and would chase us across the playground in her white and brown habit. She was pretty, that nun. I told my mother that I wanted to be a nun when I grew up, but when I draped a white towel over my head and walked around the house rattling off French words, Ahmad on my heels, it upset her.

She told my father about it, and he hit me. I nearly died he hit me so hard. The following year, he moved me from the convent to the local government school. But I liked the nuns' school better.

I haven't become a nun, and whenever I think about him now, I can't help picturing Ahmad as a skinny little boy, brown as a nut, with a mass of curly hair, dripping with molasses! My mother is screaming at him in the kitchen for pouring a jar of molasses all over himself, and I run and scoop him up into my arms and whisk him off to the bathroom, where I undress him and splash water over his head and back and neck, and feel like licking the molasses off his eyes and face! And him holding his fists out in front of him like a boxer, running around the bathroom to make me chase after him, and my mother yelling. His head dripping wet, his lips blue with cold, and my clothes soaked from washing and scrubbing his skinny little body, and still the molasses won't come out of his hair. So I get the scissors and snip this way and that, and his thick dark curls cascade to the ground, and there is water everywhere, and then Ahmad slips. I finally take him to my bed to get him to go to sleep. He asks for the story of the Russian priest but I want to tell him about Jebina who's lost in the forest and is attacked by wild animals, and how the wolf chases her so that he can ravish her.

"But that's a scary story," protests Ahmad. "I don't like stories that make me cry."

I begin the story, and he immediately starts to cry.

"But in the end everything's alright," I tell him. "Jebina gets married and the wolf doesn't get her."

He won't stop crying, so I switch to the story of the Russian priest, and then he laughs and laughs and finally he falls asleep.

Hey, brother! That's how he would call me. I don't know why, but even as a grown man, he'd always say, "Hey, brother." He was the only one who truly loved me in the family: my father loved

227

Su'ad, my sister, because she's fair-skinned, but he hated me.

"Little soot-face," he'd say, "we found you in a sack of charcoal!"

But he always spoiled Su'ad because she is fair, even though she never lifted a finger for him! When Father was ill that time, she came down from Tripoli just for two days and then went back home. The roads aren't safe, she told Mother.

Whereas I stayed day and night – even though he wouldn't talk to me, and Mother said I should go home. "Your husband will be upset, girl," she'd say. But it wasn't that . . . she doesn't like me either, because I'm dark. I think dark is nice. Everyone says I'm prettier than my sister, except for my mother . . . All she ever wants is news of my sister . . . She treats me like a servant. Yes, a servant . . . ever since I was little. . . . First, I was a servant to them at home and now I'm a servant to Nadeem.

But Ahmad . . . how could he die?

I told him, I begged him not to! I still can't believe it. I barely saw his body for one minute. They brought him home in the coffin, they put it on his bed, and they opened it for just one minute and then they took it away. There was blood on his neck, it was horrible. And now, he's dead. Everybody's dead. Abu Saïd is dead too.

The war was supposed to be over. That's what people said. The Deterrent‡ had come in and everyone said it was over. But it was nothing of the sort. Wars are like cats, it's one litter after another . . .

One day Abu Saïd is standing outside his butcher's shop, with the freshly slaughtered carcasses hanging from their hooks, and this car speeds by, guns blazing . . . and, boom, he's dead.

Nadeem was really upset. When he saw Abu Saïd sprawled out on the pavement with the strung-up lambs in the shopfront, he came home crying like a child. Why did they kill him? I don't

‡ Widely used term to refer to the Syrian-led Arab Deterrent Forces that entered Lebanon ostensibly as peacekeepers.

know, Nadeem wouldn't say anything. All I know is that ever since Abu Saïd died, Nadeem has started coming home early again. He'll watch T.V., have a glass of arrack with a plate of *labneh* and some sliced tomatoes, and then go to bed.

Mother said they closed down the gambling den after Abu Saïd died. Which means Nadeem was involved. But I never asked – I don't want to know. The important thing is he no longer hits me, and he doesn't rant and rave and turn the house upside down. And he no longer gets apoplectic every time he sees Ahmad's picture in its black frame hanging in the living room. And he's stopped getting upset when I tell the children stories of Ahmad dancing in the ring and beating his opponent in every boxing match he was in.

Basically, he's calmed down. Ahmad never did, however.

He used to come home from school, toss his books on the bed, and go straight out again to the sports club; and he wouldn't return until after dark. Mother complained that he wasn't studying hard enough but Father always said the boy had a future full of promise. Some future! What promise? He's gone now, dead and gone.

They're all dead. Even the son of our neighbour Abu Khalil died. The war was supposed to be over, that's what everyone said, but they still kidnapped him; when his body came back, it was mutilated. Poor old Abu Khalil, sitting on a chair outside his front door, day after day, waiting for people to come and condole with him! Nine months he didn't move off that chair, sitting there waiting all day, drinking endless cups of coffee and listening to the radio.

They're all dead now.

What I'd like to know is why this shelling doesn't stop, now the war is supposed to be over. When I asked Nadeem, he said it was the Jews.

"The Jews are shelling the south," I told him, "not here in Beirut."

But he said the only explanation for the shelling was the Jews.

"Why are they still shelling?" Abu Khalil would ask the mourners coming to condole with him. "Looks to me like they want to kill every single person – like that, there won't be anyone left who's witnessed this war to do the telling: if someone survived to tell the tale there'd never be another war. It seems that this country's destiny is to spawn a new war every twenty years. That's why everyone must be killed."

"But who would do the fighting then, Abu Khalil?"

"People . . ."

"But they would have all died."

"Others would replace them. The human race is resilient, it's not easily annihilated. God created Man to hold sway over Nature, to burn it all up if he so wishes! And that's what we've done, we've torched every field and every orchard, and if it came to it, we might even set the sea alight."

Abu Khalil is always waiting for visitors and I feel scared. I've been scared of the shelling ever since the war began – unlike Nadeem, who was totally unfazed by it. He'd come home at all hours and never seemed scared of anything. But he's changed. Now, whenever he hears the shelling, he doesn't stir. He stays at home all day, and sits quietly in a corner like a child who's afraid he's going to be punished.

Everyone's scared now, even my father was. And he too died . . . Who would have thought that you would meet such an ignominious end, Abu Ahmad! They killed you and threw you in a heap of rubbish . . . it was a complete fluke that anyone found you at all. In the rubbish, Abu Ahmad! First your son, then you!

What the hell is going on here?

Right from the beginning, I never understood what was going on. I mean, why did my father lock himself up in his room like that? It must have been because of my mother, she's so insufferable! God help you, Abu Ahmad, with her for a wife! Whenever I went to visit them – even though I never saw him – the smell was unbearable. If my mother was cleaning the room every day, as she claimed, where then was this smell coming from? Maybe it was the cat. Honestly, I don't know how she ever agreed to this cat business. But even cats don't produce such a foul odour! And then why did she let him out of the house? She should never have let him go. "But what could I do?" she lamented afterwards . . . What could she have done? She could have stopped him . . . she could've asked the neighbours for help. But she worried about what people would say . . . And now we're in the papers . . .

What's more, how could he disappear for three whole weeks, without us knowing anything of his whereabouts, when, afterwards, everyone said they kept bumping into him on the street? It's all Nadeem's fault: he tells me that since Abu Saïd died, he no longer knows "the boys". How could they leave him like that after he died in such a gruesome way, how could they bring his body home, with that stench, and put on such a boisterous celebration at his funeral!

As far as I'm concerned, it's utterly incomprehensible. None of it makes sense, and I can't bear to think about it anymore. I don't even care to know who the killer is. And if we did know, what could we do? Take our revenge? And who would do it anyway? Nadeem, who's terrified? Or maybe the husband of Sitt Su'ad? Those people are all armed to the teeth, how could we possibly take them on? An eye is no match for an awl, as the saying goes. But why, that's what I want to know, why did they do it?

Because he went around painting the walls? That's nothing but a lie! The walls in Beirut are not painted, full stop. If he had whitewashed them, the city would look nicer. So then, was it to rob him? He wasn't carrying any money, no more than twenty lira anyhow. That's what Mother said. Or was it for his worthless wedding ring?

At least, I'm not afraid for him anymore: he died, and found his rest. But it's my mother. She's been through so much, and Su'ad doesn't seem to care. She says her husband won't let her come to Beirut because the coastal road is too dangerous, and driving down the other way, the inland route, takes so long – more than six hours. If truth be told, I don't have much time for that husband of hers, even if he is a rich contractor! All he's got to show for it is his pot belly and his affectations of piety! His is the worst sort, as Nadeem says, appearing holier-than-thou but stopping at nothing to get what he wants . . . completely under-handedly of course! He talks like some character out of that T.V. soap, *Abu Milhim*, all morally superior and sanctimonious, as if butter wouldn't melt in his mouth!

So he won't let her come to Beirut, and she won't move herself, and I've had enough: I can't take anymore, I can't shoulder the entire responsibility by myself! Nadeem says I could stay with her, he even suggested she should live with us, but she wouldn't hear of it:

"And leave the house? Over my dead body. This is my home." When Nadeem insisted, she started shaking she was so upset. "I know what it is," she said, "you want your inheritance while I'm still alive! You want to take the furniture and the house and the money I collect for my dead husband and son."

Nadeem is so furious, he won't visit her anymore. But he says I should. He wants me to stay on good terms with her – he's worried that she's going to leave everything to Su'ad!

"Money loves money," he says, "and that fatso would love to add your mother's to his."

Me, I'm not worried about the inheritance – it's her that worries me.

When they brought my father's body home, my mother went into a trance-like state. She wouldn't see anyone, she just sat in the room by the closed coffin, keening and begging us to open it.

Nadeem told her we couldn't. But of course Su'ad's husband had to say that it was her right, and that she should be allowed to see her husband one last time.

"The corpse is already decomposing," Nadeem told him.

"So what . . . It's still her right . . . !"

So they opened it – oh my God, you can't imagine the stench that enveloped the house. It was the same kind of smell as when my father used to lock himself in there, but much, much worse. It was literally unbearable. Everyone left the room, except for my mother. Then Nadeem went back in and shut the coffin.

"Ma, no more . . . It's enough."

And then, all of a sudden, out of nowhere, the house swarmed with gunmen and gunfire filled the air.

After the funeral, their leader came to see us. I don't remember his name anymore, but one of his arms was just a stump, and he bristled when he spoke. After seating himself in the centre of the living room, he began while everyone listened with rapt attention.

"The martyr's father has himself become a martyr. Khalil Ahmad Jaber has sacrificed his life for the revolution. What happened to him is unimaginable and we hereby declare him a martyr. Truly, he is a martyr!"

Everyone dropped their head and invoked the Lord's mercy for the deceased while my mother looked at him with utter consternation.

"But we've got to find out who did it," Nadeem said.

"Yes, absolutely. And that is our responsibility. All of you please take note, please, that I am personally taking personal responsibility for this: the murderer will be arrested and will be hanged from one of the famous Beirut pines."

Then he launched into a eulogy of my father, extolling his support for the revolution, his affection for its combatants, and the encouragement he gave his son to join the ranks and even make the ultimate sacrifice. He said that after Ahmad had died on the battlefield, his father had praised the Lord and bidden his wife to trill with joy.

My mother nodded heavily.

"That's right! She ululated! It shouldn't surprise you! Isn't a martyr on earth a prince in heaven? 'Think not of those who are slain in the way of Allah as dead . . .'" Then he looked to us to finish the Qur'anic verse, and Su'ad's husband intoned: "'Nay, they are living. With their Lord they have provision.'"

And he got up and left.

And the visits started. At first he told me they had decided to give my mother a stipend of one thousand lira a month, as a sort of living allowance. Then on the seventh-day memorial, he came in carrying big red and blue posters.

"They're even bigger than the ones they made for Ahmad," my mother remarked.

"Yeah, we've changed the format," he said. "We're making them larger now."

And he started telling us how he had plastered the walls of the city with them.

"Everybody must see the martyr's picture – especially a martyr as unique as Khalil Ahmad Jaber. It's not every day that a fifty-year-old man is killed in such a barbaric way – God forbid! Everyone must see his picture. We've hung it everywhere. The walls of Beirut are plastered with his picture."

My mother smiled. It was the first time since my father's disappearance that I had seen her smile. She picked up the posters and as she gazed into his face with tears in her eyes, she murmured: "Dear, dear Abu Ahmad, you deserve far more than this."

Then she hung one in the living room, another one in the bedroom, and put away the rest of them in her wardrobe. He'd brought a lot of posters with him, around two hundred of them.

Then he left.

After that, my mother started going to the party office frequently. When I asked her why, she said she was following up with them about the marble gravestone.

"They're going to erect a big marble gravestone. It's going to be the biggest one in the whole of the Martyrs' Cemetery. It's going to be really beautiful! And I've asked them to change the marble on Ahmad's grave. They said they'd consider it. It's not easy, the man in charge told me, because they can't give him preferential treatment. They have to treat him the same as all the others. But he said he'd think about it. So I keep going to see what they've decided. They promised that Abu Ahmad's tombstone would be ready in two weeks."

"But, Mother, that doesn't make sense," I told her.

"What do you mean? Anyway, what do you know? You don't understand anything and your husband's just a dope-head."

I told her Nadeem had changed. She didn't believe me.

"Don't be fooled," she said, "I know him. I know what men are like. Just you wait and see, he'll be gambling and smoking again in no time. But watch those children of yours, young lady, you've got a baby now. Goddamn that husband of yours, why did he have to name him Hassan?"

I had told Nadeem I wanted to name the baby Ahmad, but he wouldn't hear of it.

"We're going to call him Hassan," he said, "after Abu Saïd, God rest his soul in peace."

"So you prefer Abu Saïd to my brother, eh?"

"Abu Saïd was my friend."

And so we called the baby Hassan, and Nadeem even nick-named him Abu Saïd. "I'll do as I please," he says.

Well, let him, and I'll do the same. But, still, I call the baby Hassan. It doesn't make any sense for me to call him Ahmad and for Nadeem to call him Hassan. And since that's his name, I call him Hassan.

But my mother . . . I really worry about her. She frightens me. She's not herself anymore. Whenever I go and visit her, I find her sitting in Father's room, staring at the posters all laid out on the bed. She sits there for hours on end. When I yell at her and tell her it's enough, she jumps up, gathers them together carefully, and puts them back in the wardrobe. As if they constituted her entire worldly wealth! I don't understand how she can think that! It makes no sense: she gets a martyr's stipend of one thousand five hundred lira now. And I slip money her way too, I don't dare tell Nadeem though. He never asks how I spend the housekeeping money, poor dear, that's his one quality – he's generous to a fault. He always gives me whatever I ask him for.

What I want to know is what she does with all that money she's getting. Once I asked her, but she wouldn't tell me. She started saying that life had become very expensive and the *sheikha* charged a lot. What *sheikha*? I said, but she wouldn't answer.

Then, one day she said that Father had asked her to hang his posters throughout our neighbourhood, and she wondered whether Nadeem would do it. I questioned how it was possible for Father to speak to her since he was dead. She said it had been his spirit.

"What spirit?"

"Oh, I had his spirit summoned. And he, his spirit I mean, asked me to do it."

I really lost it then. I told her that if she carried on with all that superstitious mumbo-jumbo, it would be the end of us. But I regretted it when I got home. Maybe she was right, maybe . . . who knows? Everyone says the *sheikha* has miraculous powers. Maybe she really could summon spirits.

So I went back to my mother's. I found her staring at the posters again.

"Didn't you ask him who killed him?" I said.

"I've asked him several times, but every time we ask, the

236

coffee cup stops moving. The *sheikha* says it means he doesn't want to answer."

"More likely it means that he doesn't know," I said.

"No," she replied. "The *sheikha* told me that when the cup is still, it means that the spirit doesn't want to answer. When it doesn't know, it says so, but when it doesn't want to answer, then the cup stops moving across the table."

I thought I might go and visit the *sheikha* myself one day and have her summon my father's spirit. I'd ask him to tell me about the murderer. I know he'd answer me, I'm sure he would. He wouldn't tell my mother because he knows how she is.

But then I got scared. Even though I don't believe in all that stuff, it still scares me. Spirits are spooky and Nadeem would kill me if he found out. So I didn't go.

And now, you know what's happening to her? Someone told me they saw my mother on the street one day with Abu Khalil, the neighbour. They had all these posters with them, she'd hand him one and he'd plaster it on the wall. When I told her this had to stop, she denied it all. But I know that Abu Khalil is always over at her place, whenever I go he's there. And as soon I arrive, he leaves.

People are gossiping about him spending all his time visiting her. He's alone now, his wife's been dead a long time, and after his son died, his daughter-in-law took their little boy and went back to her parents'.

It really scares me. Nadeem thinks Mother has lost her senses, that she cares only about Abu Khalil and those posters and not her grandchildren.

And I'm scared.

Provisional Epilogue

This is no fairy tale.

The fate of Khalil Ahmad Jaber was indeed a tragic one.

But the greater problem remains: the murderer remains unidentified. We have a mystery murderer.

The people I questioned during the course of my investigation felt they could not identify the murderer. Some said they simply did not know. Anyway, had they known, they would not have told me, and had they told me, I would not have divulged anything. And even assuming I had – or could have done so – I certainly would not have dared to put it down in writing.

But is *that* the problem?

Is the identification of the murderer the problem? Would it help us understand the motives for the crime?

I don't think so.

No. Even assuming the murderer was identified, and the motives of the crime were known, even if, finally, the murderer were put to death, it would not change anything. People say that putting murderers to death serves as a deterrent to others but, in reality, no-one is being deterred. Murderers are executed and nothing changes. Take, for example, the two men hanged for the murder of the Ibrahim family – a man, his wife and their daughter – whose bodies were buried in a fallow field near the village of Maghdousheh. The ripple effect was nil. Witness the murder of Khalil Ahmad Jaber.

I find myself completely baffled: this author feels he really does not know what happened in his story and that he is not in full possession of the facts – whereas normally, an author is supposed to know all the details of his story, especially the ending. He is supposed to let the ending unfold gradually and slowly, so that the reader can draw his own conclusions.

But in the case of this story, the author doesn't know anything, and he also hasn't been able to present the facts in the gradual and slow manner necessary to both convince and entertain the reader. And when the author's in the dark, the plot really does thicken. It could have been Ali Kalakesh who did it, or Fatimah Fakhro, or Sameer Amro, or Fahd Badreddin, or Zayn 'Alloul, or maybe Abu Saïd, or even Nadeem Najjar, or even, why not, Elias Khoury, or yet another?

Let us turn the enigma on its head and view it from a slightly different angle: in whose interests was it to kill Khalil Ahmad Jaber? Logically, nobody's, for Khalil Ahmad Jaber had no enemies, nor was he involved in anything remotely shady. He was a most transparent man.

So, then, it could have been suicide. While that is a distinct possibility, it has been set aside on two counts: first, the forensic pathologist's report, which clearly demonstrates that the victim could not have shot himself, given the position of the corpse when it was found. Even assuming that Khalil Ahmad Jaber *had* discovered some novel and unprecedented way of killing himself, it is impossible that he would have mutilated himself in that cruel way. The forensic pathologist's report is quite unequivocal: the martyr was clearly tortured; his body bore the telltale marks.

Second, the rarity of suicides in Beirut: I do not know of a single Arab writer who has committed suicide, aside from Tayseer Subool. Oh, they despair alright, their writings are full of ranting and angst, but they don't commit suicide . . . even though the suicide of a writer might have a huge impact. Anyhow, I should not be going off on tangents: Khalil Ahmad Jaber was not a writer, I mean he did not have the particular sensibility that writers and artists possess, and if writers are not committing suicide, surely ordinary law-abiding citizens – without any of

240

the writer's heightened sensibility – are not about to do so.

That said, I knew a man who committed suicide. But he was not a writer, he was a tailor. I barely remember the story, I was six years old then. I was out playing on the street with the children from my neighbourhood. We were playing *shalleek*, a somewhat complicated game where you start by throwing a sharpened pole, like a stake, right into the middle of a circle drawn on the ground with a stick. The one who succeeds in doing that goes first; he has to hit the stake hard enough with a stick to make it catapult into the air and fall as far away as possible. My father forbade me to play this game because it was dangerous, especially for our eyes. Anyway, there we were playing *shalleek*, when all of a sudden we heard all this screaming and carrying-on coming from the tailor's house. Everyone ran – the entire street, including us children, ran to see what was happening.

As I stepped into the house, I saw, in the middle of a crowd of men and women in tears, my father holding the tailor's wife by the hand. As soon as he caught sight of me, he let go of her hand and came towards me.

"Go home," he said.

When I asked him what was happening, he replied that the neighbour had committed suicide.

"What does that mean?" I asked.

"That means he committed suicide, that he's dead. Now, go on home!"

Later, I heard him tell my mother that the tailor had committed suicide in Rawsheh – he had plunged off the waterfront road and his bloated corpse was found floating off Ouza'ï.

What did he mean, "committed suicide in Rawsheh"? I thought people went there to swim, around and under Pigeon Rock – the way I did many years later, with my beautiful girlfriend Surayya. We would paddle together on a hasakeh to swim around the Rock. Poor Surayya, she is married and fat now, nothing like she used to be. When I ran into her outside the American University Hospital, I hardly recognized her.

The tailor committed suicide in Rawsheh, where everyone swam! I used to imagine my swimming there one day and bumping into a corpse, but when I eventually did, there were no corpses. There was just Surayya. Surayya was everywhere: beside me, around me, with me. She would plunge underwater and swim away, and though I chased her, over and over again, I could never catch her – although Mr Nohad the barber did. He came along and caught her alright, and he transformed her into another woman.

Anyway, getting back to the point, Khalil Ahmad Jaber did not commit suicide: ergo, he was killed. But we do not know who killed him. And if, to this day, we do not know who killed the political strongman and powerful leader, Kamal Jumblatt[‡], how will we ever find out who killed Khalil Ahmad Jaber?

It was not for lack of trying, either. I spent months investigating and reading to try and establish the facts. I must have smoked thousands of cigarettes sitting at my desk, with an aching back, trying to figure out what happened . . . to no effect.

So now, dear reader, you too may feel as bewildered as I do. Faced with the impossibility of discovering the truth, you must doubt, as I do, the reported incident itself, as well as people's accounts. I am sure one of those clever literary critics is going to say that I'm making a mountain out of a molehill. I can just hear him saying, "But surely Beirut is just like any other city, full of ordinary people leading ordinary lives, going to work, eating, sleeping, having sex, having children, dying, celebrating festivals, buying chocolate eggs, sugared almonds, and *maa'moul*." While all of that is true, I do not know how one can reconcile that assertion with my story.

‡ Kamal Jumblatt was the leader of the Druze community in Lebanon until his assassination in 1978. In addition to being a sectarian strongman, he was the leader of the National Movement.

If it were not for fear of being told that I have been blowing things out of proportion, and that I am full of doom and gloom, indeed that I invite misery – and that such a negative stance merely "serves the interests of the imperialists" – I might have told you the barber's tale, or written the story "White Masks". But if I, who have witnessed all these events and lived through them, cannot believe my own eyes, how could anyone believe this story who has not shared our experience of this beautiful city, Beirut? And I will no doubt be accused of exaggerating, of only seeing the tragic side of life, of being unable to behold the sweep of history, the importance of geography, etcetera, etcetera, etcetera . . .

The truth is I now have to admit my mistake: I should have used a more serious incident as my point of departure. After all, how significant is the discovery of a corpse, especially that of an unremarkable man, just an ordinary citizen? And what does the phrase – an ordinary citizen – mean anyway, in light of the government's "extraordinary powers" and the conduct of summary justice? It makes no sense whatsoever, and the critic is right. So it's a meaningless story, I admit it. Had I been looking for meaning, I should have taken a different tack and told the story of . . . Genghis Khan, for example.

However, if after all that has happened to us you expect me to tell that kind of story, you're mistaken – as was I.

Had I been looking for meaning, I should have started differently. I should have told the story of the Palestinian man who was found dead in an airport toilet after committing suicide; or maybe the story of my friend, the doctor Ajjaj Abu Suleiman, and his countless love affairs; or perhaps the story of our neighbour, Imm Mohammad, and how her husband died. Maybe, if I tried again, I could lend some meaning to our story here and bring it closer to the happy ending that we all secretly yearn for: the resolution that would shield us from the debilitating pessimism we all feel – isn't that the whole point of a story?

As for the Palestinian who was found hanging in the airport toilets, well, that is a very ordinary story really, with a straightforward narrative, and no stylistic flourishes whatsoever – no magic realism, flashbacks or literary cadences . . . It is the simple story of a young man who realizes that he has lost everything and commits suicide. Just like the tailor.

But the tailor was rather more fortunate than the young man, because when he hurled himself into the sea, he at least was able to breathe in the fresh air and plunge into clean, salty seawater. Whereas the young man, let's call him Moeen Abbas, committed suicide in the worst possible circumstances: in the stench of an airport toilet, amid throngs of travellers and well-wishers milling around the halls, not to mention policemen, soldiers, immigration officials and the *mukhabarat*.‡

The tailor committed suicide in far, far better circumstances, and one can feel fairly confident that he did not suffer the horrific pain Moeen Abbas went through. According to doctors, when the tailor flung himself over the edge of the road into the sea, he died instantaneously: his death occurred on impact, as his body was propelled onto the rocks in the shallows. Whereas Moeen Abbas must have suffered terrible pain – pain of a rather different sort than that of Ghassan Kanafani's heroes who were left to die in the inferno of a bolted tanker truck under the sun. At least the characters of *Men in the Sun* were part of a group, while Moeen Abbas was all alone – and death shared with others must be easier to face than solitary death. However, the most significant difference is that the characters of *Men in the Sun* are heroes, or archetypes. Moeen Abbas was neither: he was just an "ordinary" young man who committed suicide in an airport toilet. And the terrible pain he suffered was due to the fact that he hanged himself by his leather belt, which he had not lubricated with

‡ The secret police or intelligence services.

soap or any other type of grease, the way executioners do with the noose to ease the hanging victim's pain.

Moeen Abbas was a medical student at Cairo University. His parents and relatives all live in Gaza City, which has been occupied by the Israeli army since the June 1967 war. As they were extremely poor, Moeen Abbas had to make do with a small scholarship he was awarded by the Egyptian government as an honours student.

Moeen Abbas led a very ordinary – not to say substandard – life in Cairo. He studied hard but yearned to finish and return to Gaza to work and settle down.

He was not particularly politicized, beyond simply being a Palestinian: you cannot be Palestinian and not be involved in some form of politics or other. That is to say, he took part in whatever student events were held at the university, put up posters when necessary, and distributed books and pamphlets about the Palestinian cause.

In Cairo, Moeen Abbas began feeling increasingly conflicted: after years of dreaming about her, he found he wished to forget his young cousin, Sana', to whom he had promised marriage, and whom everyone in the refugee camp knew was destined to be his wife. He was very proud of Sana' and of her stunning looks. But now in Cairo there was Mona, a fellow student.

Moeen Abbas had never felt like this before. He was in love and it felt like a huge dam had burst inside him. Mona would talk to him about her studies, about the films she went to see, about her sadness at the death of Abdel Halim Hafez – she said singing was "finished" now that he had died. But as this subterranean river swept Moeen up, Sana' was nowhere to be found in it. What would he say to her, how could he tell her about all this?

Moeen went out with Mona, the black-haired Egyptian beauty. He waited for her and wrote to her . . . One day he found himself scribbling on a piece of paper something that resembled poetry. He tore it up. I'm a doctor, he thought, not a poet. Poetry isn't for me.

Yet here he was living with this ever-expanding wellspring inside him. Mona by his side everywhere: in the lecture room, in the dissecting lab, with her laughter and the dimples dancing in her elongated face. She was the daring one too. It was Mona who urged him on; he didn't want to do it. He always told himself that he would not have sex with the woman he loved until after marriage – because sex is sacred. He had always felt sickened by the sight of those naked or half-clad Israeli girls who roamed the beaches in Gaza and fully agreed when his grandfather fulminated about that kind of conduct being contrary to "our customs".

But look what was happening to him now! Not quite knowing how, Moeen Abbas found himself in his tiny room, lying beside Mona, sprawled out on his bed. And then it all happened, and afterwards as he watched her get up to get a pack of cigarettes, completely naked with her brown back glistening, he felt he must be the luckiest man alive, and he resolved to stay by this woman's side for ever and ever.

She came back with two lit cigarettes, nestled her head against his chest, and started smoking. She talked about everything under the sun, about the loathsome bald professor who chewed gum while dissecting corpses, about the smell of formaldehyde, which made her feel nauseous, about politics and Camp David, and the war. He wanted to talk to her about love, he wanted to tell her that he had set his mind on marrying her, he wanted to tell her about Sana', about Gaza and the hospital he would work in when they went back together to the occupied Strip.

"I have to go home now," she said. He wanted her to stay and sleep by his side the whole night long.

When Mona left, Moeen decided he would write Sana' a letter and tell her the truth – although it would be a blow, he felt he owed her the truth. When he saw Mona the next day, she seemed upset, she told him to be careful because a decision had been made to deport all Palestinian students from Egypt. As he listened to her saying she felt afraid for him, he felt afraid only of losing her, and he wanted to tell her that he loved her and had decided to marry her. On an impulse, he made up his mind to tell her about Sana' and how he was going to end it with her. But Mona did not let him get a word in edgeways.

"Watch out, brother Moeen, they are after you."

He could not have cared less, he was not afraid of anything. He asked her to come back to the room with him, but she said not today, she couldn't.

That evening, as he sat alone trying to write something about love, there was a violent banging on the door. When he opened it, he was immediately seized and dragged down the stairs. "But I need to . . ." Not allowed to finish his sentence, he was thrown into a military jeep and told by the soldier accompanying him that he was being put on the first plane out of Cairo.

"But what about my belongings . . . my clothes, my books?" The soldier said he knew nothing about that, these were his orders.

And, sure enough, they took him to the airport, where he waited for three hours in a tiny room the size of a prison cell and then was made to board a plane. As the plane took off from Cairo Airport, Moeen Abbas felt around in his pockets: he found he had almost five Egyptian Pounds on him and a box of Cleopatras with nine cigarettes left. In a complete daze, he was not even able to ask the stewardess where the plane was bound, and did not hear the captain announce over the P.A. system that they had landed at Damascus Airport. He had nothing to eat, just drank a bottle of Pepsi and felt his stomach burning from its acrid flavour.

Moeen Abbas got off the plane with nothing to his name; he had neither a passport nor identity papers, only his student card. Even so, the airport official was polite to him.

"You're one of the deported?"

"Yes," he replied.

"Welcome, welcome."

And he handed Moeen a piece of paper and told him to report to the immigration authorities within the week. Moeen Abbas left the airport building without a clue as to his next destination. The only possible place to go, he thought, was the Yarmouk refugee camp, where he knew his father had some first cousins. He got a taxi to drive him there, but when he handed over the five Egyptian Pounds he had on him, the driver began to swear and told him that he was not about to accept such a paltry sum.

"But I have nothing else," Moeen pleaded.

The driver continued to shout, curse and threaten, undeterred by the crowd gathering around the car. An old man stepped for-ward and asked what the trouble was. Raising his voice above the driver's vituperations, Moeen explained how he came to be where he was and was candid about the fact that he had absolutely nothing to his name. The old man settled the fare, some fifty Syrian lira, and Moeen could not thank him enough. When the old man asked him if he had any relatives in the camp, Moeen told him about his father's cousins. The old man thought for a while and said that he personally did not know anyone by the name of Abbas, but he invited Moeen into his own home. When Moeen politely declined the offer, the old man suggested he could stay in the camp mosque.

So Moeen went to the camp mosque. One of the onlookers at the taxi scene had given him twenty-five lira in exchange for his five Egyptian Pounds, with which he was able to buy himself a can of sardines and two loaves of flatbread. He ate in the court-yard, and then, feeling exhausted, went inside the mosque, found himself a dark corner in which to lie down, and fell asleep.

Moeen lived in the mosque like this for five days, five whole days and nights during which he did not budge, other than to go and buy himself a little food. He had no idea what to do with himself. It seemed to him that he was going to end up being one of those shaggy-bearded beggars, sitting outside mosque doors with a begging bowl at his side.

Then, one day, a man in his forties who had been watching him all this time and sometimes seemed to be on the verge of speaking to him came up to him and put his hand on Moeen's shoulder. "Listen," he said, "everybody here knows what happened to you, and the camp's welfare association has decided to collect some money on your behalf. They've done it without telling you, but expect a man to come tomorrow and hand you eight thousand lira."

"Thank you very much, but . . ."

"But, naturally, you wouldn't know what to do with that much money. I'll tell you, son, I can get you a passport and a visa to Sweden, as well as a plane ticket. And it'll only cost five thousand lira."

"But I don't know anybody in Sweden."

"You'll meet people. Sweden is a beautiful country, it's a wonder-ful place, it's big and it's got lots of universities and factories and things like that."

Moeen thought about it: there was no other way out. I'll learn the language, he thought, I'll manage to finish my medical studies somehow, I'll send money to my folks, and to Mona, and will come back a doctor!

"O.K.," he told the man. "I'll do it."

The money was handed over to Moeen in a short ceremony with fiery speeches denouncing the "treaty of treason" with Israel and the policies of Arab governments that harmed the interests of the Palestinian people.

Moeen Abbas was overcome with joy: he was leaving, his problems were over.

He thanked his hosts profusely. Choking back tears, Moeen

said he would forever owe the residents of the camp a debt of gratitude, and that he believed the road to victory against the Zionist enemy was now within reach. Then he left the building and went back to his little corner in the mosque. On the way there, he met the man and handed him the five thousand lira.

And then he waited.

Two days later, the man returned with a plane ticket, a passport, the visa and everything. Moeen went to the market, bought himself some trousers, a shirt and a belt, a jacket, some shoes and a suitcase in which to put his belongings, as well as a small leather pouch for his passport and ticket. He converted what money he had left into U.S. dollars, with the help of the same man who had got him his things – that very same man handed him the dollars.

Finally Moeen took a taxi to the airport. As he neared the airport he felt both excited and apprehensive: he was the one choosing to travel and from now on, he was not going to do anyone else's bidding. Entering the airport, he was searched by security men who scrutinized his passport carefully. Everything was O.K., but he had arrived at the airport early. That is what the airline official said, adding that he'd have a two-hour wait until boarding.

So Moeen went to the cafeteria to get a cup of coffee, which he drank standing at the counter. And then it happened. He really didn't know how, but it happened.

Someone asked him a question, and he turned towards the speaker and got into a long conversation with him about the dangers of flying. He realized it was time to pay for his coffee and go and get the white boarding pass from the Scandinavian airlines desk. When he turned to pick up his pouch, he could not find it. He looked around, bent down and searched on the ground, he questioned the waiter, he asked everyone there if they had seen his leather pouch. Maybe he had left it in the toilets. He raced there, going into every stall, looked all over. But he hadn't even gone to the toilet!

Moeen went back to the cafeteria looking for the man he had been chatting with. There was no-one there. So he searched again.

"Maybe I left it in the camp." So he got into a taxi and went back there. He ran into the mosque like a lunatic, searching frantically everywhere. "I know I had it. The security officer examined the passport at the airport. Where could it be?"

Moeen sank into the corner of the mosque, completely stupefied. "I've got to go back to the airport and look again. It can't be ... It must ..." He hopped into another taxi, went back to the airport and ran into the lounge. He was like a man crazed, searching under tables, questioning people, making strange grunting noises. Finally, an airport security officer stopped him. Moeen told him his tale. It was clear from the officer's expression that he did not believe a word of it. Moeen was just about to resume his search when he saw the officer's hand reaching for the scruff of his neck.

"You're just a con man, aren't you? Let me see your I.D."

Moeen had no I.D., he had no papers. He repeated his story, although he did not dare admit that the passport was a fake. The officer just gave him a verbal warning and told him to leave the airport building – immediately.

Moeen Abbas could not go back to the camp, no-one would believe him. They wouldn't believe that he had lost the passport, and the ticket and the money, at the airport.

So he went into one of the bathroom stalls, took off the leather belt he had bought the previous day, hooked it to the ceiling somehow, climbed onto a toilet seat, put his head through the noose, and hanged himself.

His body was found the next day when the early-morning cleaner came in and could not open the locked door. She broke the lock to find Moeen Abbas' now-livid corpse dangling from the ceiling, his neck shrivelled to the size of a child's, his body rigid: a hanging stiff, like the ones you see pictures of in the papers.

But how did he manage to hang himself? He must have suffered terribly! Usually, when someone is hanged, the executioner pulls away whatever the victim is standing on so that he hangs. And usually, simply by instinct, the victim's feet reach for the ground – that is why the victim's feet thrash in that terrible way – and then the body is stuffed into a white sack and the victim is left there, a pale object dangling from the gibbet.

Moeen Abbas, however, must have cast himself aloft deliberately. He most certainly tried to reach the toilet seat cover with his feet, for that is a matter of instinct, it has nothing to do with one's will. And his feet must have slipped, either because the cover was wet or, more likely, because of the new leather shoes he had bought at the souk – the soles were not yet worn, and everybody knows how slippery new soles can be. That would also explain the expression of utter horror on Moeen Abbas' face – he must have reached for the toilet seat cover and grown increasingly desperate as his shoes slipped repeatedly; thus, we could say that he "slipped to his death", with the belt tightening around his neck until he expired.

The people of Yarmouk camp could not fathom why he should have wanted to kill himself. Some of the people who had said goodbye to him earlier in the day had seen him returning to the mosque, but no-one knew why. And when his photograph appeared in the Beirut papers, the reporter who filed the story quoted a woman passenger as saying she had seen him looking for his little pouch. "But no-one knew the secret of the pouch."

I recounted this story to my friend Dr Ajjaj Abu Suleyman, just to make him feel better – he being the sort of person who always thinks that his troubles are worse than anyone else's. "So as you see, Doctor, what happened to you is nothing, nothing at all compared to this. You should thank the Lord, Dr Ajjaj, truly you should be thankful," I told him.

My friend Dr Ajjaj Abu Suleyman is a strange man, he is a

dentist by profession, but as long as I have known him he has never actually practised dentistry. He says it's because he hates the job. "Imagine," he says, "an old woman coming along to have her teeth pulled out, there's all this blood and then you have to make her a complete set of false teeth. She opens her mouth so wide it's like a cave full of djinns . . . and the smell . . . ! What's more, some teeth are white but some are a nasty yellow . . . Also, whenever a patient opens his mouth wide, I think he's going to bite. You know how it is, I am leaning down over a patient's wide-open mouth, poking all these strange instruments inside his mouth, and then suddenly I am sure he's going to bite my nose off, so I stop and pull back . . . the poor patient is totally bewildered! Granted, I have a large nose. When I was little, my brother Imad always teased me about it, repeating Ibn Rumi's famous verse to me. But after I realized that the size of one's nose bears a direct relationship to one's sexual prowess, I got over my hang-up about it.

"It was Imm Shikri who told me; she was a forty-something prostitute that many of us frequented when we were dental students. She lived in a little house on the rue de Damas,‡ right across from the medical faculty at Saint Joseph University. She was impressed that I was so well-endowed, and always attributed this to the size of my nose – she claimed there was a direct correlation between it and my organ; she was always saying I was the best dentist she'd ever had, with an excellent bedside manner!

"Anyway, back to my story . . . scared as I was of all those white teeth and cavernous mouths that gave me the feeling my patient was going to jump up from the chair, rip my nose off my face and devour it, I closed the clinic. I just closed it down and became a journalist.

"Journalism isn't easy, but at least I'm not frightened of anything. Editors are a mediocre lot by and large, and you can get

‡ A historic street, as it became the "Green Line" that divided Beirut in two during the civil war.

away with pretty much anything. You know how it is these days, with all those Arab petrodollars, editors are a dime a dozen. All you have to do is praise an article – which someone else wrote but the editor signed – and his rancid little face will break into this big smile . . . yes, rancid, that's what their faces are . . . and then he'll leave you alone!"

The truth is I have had my doubts about some of the things this strange friend of mine says. I mean, how is it that a dentist, a high and mighty doctor, can close his clinic and become a journalist overnight? What is more his nose is not that big . . . mine is larger, and I feel neither ashamed of it nor endowed with unusual sexual potency.

I eventually found out that my friend Dr Ajjaj Abu Suleyman does indeed work for a newspaper, but he is in the archives section. I went to see him one evening – the first time ever that I paid him a visit at work. When I got there, the watchman told me the doctor came in only in the mornings, as he worked in the archives. Later, at the café, I chided him.

"You're misleading me, Doctor."

"Me?"

"You work in the archives!"

"But I told you I did . . . In any case, it's the best place to be. What do you think reporters do, anyhow? They only translate foreign news agency reports. That's all reporters are, mere trans-lators. A reporter these days isn't a writer anymore, he's just a machine. But I'm a writer, or at least I aspire to be one . . . Did you know that some of the greatest writers were doctors? Chekhov, Yusef Idriss, Abdel-Salam al-'Ujeyli, to name only three! They were doctors and writers! That's what I am going to be – a writer – and that's why I'd much rather work in the archives. Listen, my friend . . ."

"I'm listening, Dr Archives!"

"I'm not joking, in the archives I'm in charge of all this

humdrum stuff. Where do you think novelists get their material from. You don't suppose they make it all up, do you? Not at all, nobody makes up anything! It's all right there for the taking, either in press archives or directly out of people's mouths! You'll see, I'll write a great novel yet . . . it's just that I'm . . . exhausted . . . My nerves are frayed, this can't go on . . ."

And then, leaning across the table, his voice dropping to a whisper: "I'm in a fix . . . a real fix. And I'm scared. They want me to marry her! Can you believe it? I can't . . . no . . . I won't marry her!"

I told him it seemed pretty simple to me, that if he was being blackmailed, he should pay them off and he'd be rid of them.

"What do you mean, pay them off? No, sir, I'm not parting with a piastre!"

I had been aware that my friend was involved in "those kinds of relationships". I knew he was having an affair with a girl, although he would not reveal her name or introduce her to me. He said she was ugly and stupid.

"All she reads are romance comic strips! She comes over once a week, I sleep with her and then she leaves. She hardly says a word, nothing more than small talk. She's just a slut!"

He had laughed recounting how as a result of their relationship he had taken to reading cheap celebrity tabloids and also those photo-strips she got. They were really entertaining, he said, and certainly better than all those newspapers which never told you anything. I told him I was both impressed and intrigued by his relationship to this girl. Was it really possible to experience that kind of unadulterated passion, without words, without promises, without courtship? And then came the shocking realization that he was in way over his head.

"You don't understand . . . she's only fifteen, she's a schoolgirl. She comes over in the afternoon after school, between two and four, and all I pay is four hundred lira . . . It's a fabulous deal! I am having this torrid, passionate liaison, of the sort you read about in romance novels, but without any of the commitment. And she's as fresh as a rose . . . it's as simple as that. You know Nazeeh al-Tabesh?"

"No."

"What do you mean 'no'? He's that neighbour of ours, the one who runs the café."

"Oh, him!"

"Yes, him. Well, he's the one who brought her to me. He said: "Be good to her, Doctor, she's very young, and she must be home by four." And he took my money and left.

She just stood there in the middle of the living room like someone lost. I shut the door and bolted it, and slid a tape of light Western music into the cassette player. She asked me if I wanted something to drink. Coffee, I told her. And she went straight to the kitchen, as if she already knew the house – she seemed to know where everything was. When she came back with the coffee and sat down beside me, I suddenly felt ashamed of myself. It was impossible, if I had married young she would have been the age of my daughter. But the devil was out and about, the very devil was in the house! So I took her and slept with her. She was so docile, and warm, she never said a word, and she was beautiful, beautiful . . . like an actress or a model . . . She closed her eyes, and I watched her, like that, with her eyes closed . . . She was warm as a loaf of bread . . . I couldn't get enough of her. Then I heard her whisper that I should get up because she had to go home.

She got up from the bed, went into the bathroom and washed, then she put on her clothes and left. I tried to arrange another tryst. "No," she said. "You have to ask Mr Nazeeh." When I asked her what her name was, she told me to choose a name for her.

"Najma," I said.

"Najma," she repeated. "That's a pretty name."

"That's because you're a star, my Najma. Will I see you tomorrow?"

"Ask Mr Nazeeh," she replied.

So I started asking Nazeeh for her. She would come over and I would pay. I didn't know anything about her family. I tried to find out once, but she cupped her little white hand over my mouth and silenced me.

"But why are you doing this?" I asked her. "You're so young."

"It's better this way, and we'll live well."

"What about your parents? What do they think of this?" She covered my mouth again. "And what about love?" I asked. She threw her hands up in the air, smiling. And I led her to the bed.

Nazeeh al-Tabesh suggested I try someone else besides Najma. He had lots of girls, of every age and colour. All I had to do was choose. But I told him I liked Najma.

"You've fallen for her, man," he said, chuckling through his chipped teeth.

"God forbid! It's just that she's beautiful!"

And so Najma kept on coming to my place, and I paid. It took more than half my salary to keep her coming! But, honestly, how had Nazeeh al-Tabesh got hold of such a stunning bunch of girls? I asked him if he wasn't afraid of the authorities, of . . . you know . . . being caught.

"And what authorities would those be?" he replied. "We are the authorities, we're in charge," he said. He explained he was under some sort of protection and that I was to be discreet.

And then the problems started . . . bad, bad problems . . . I got this anonymous phone call at the paper. The guy said he was Najma's brother. I played dumb, pretending I didn't know what he was talking about. Then he came to see me in person. He was this fortyish-something man, with deep-set eyes, telling me he knew everything and that Najma was his sister and I had to marry her.

That was ridiculous! How could Najma be his sister? Since

Najma wasn't Najma at all, it was just my name for her – I didn't even know the girl's name. Najma didn't exist as Najma, and it was obvious that I had been the object of some sort of extortion racket – right from the off. I was about to tell him that he was lying, that Najma wasn't Najma, but then I saw the gun bulging under his jacket, and I held my tongue. He said he'd give me five days, or else ...

"Or else you know what'll happen, don't you?" he added before leaving the room.

Then he started to call. He's been phoning every day, both at home and at the office, "to remind me", he says. And the five days are up tomorrow, and I don't know what to do. I can't marry her! That's out of the question! Who would I go to and ask for her hand anyway? To Nazeeh al-Tabesh? . . . And start pimping for him, maybe? No, sir, I will not marry her. Let them kill me! This time tomorrow I'll be dead. Tomorrow, they will kill me!

When I went to see Nazeeh al-Tabesh, he acted as if he didn't know me, the bastard! He's the one who got me into this mess! Can you imagine, pretending he didn't know me or the girl? "I have no idea what you're talking about," he said! And all that time, he was pocketing the money! He'd be waiting at my door for his four hundred lira, like a panting dog . . . And now he knows nothing! I'm telling you, I won't give in, I will not marry her. What can they be thinking of, me marrying a prostitute? I wouldn't marry anyone – the very idea of marriage is abhorrent – and I certainly won't marry a professional whore! Let them kill me! I'd rather die than marry her!

I could see that Dr Abu Suleyman was very distraught. I told him I thought the problem was simple. "All you have to do is pay up: that's what extortion is about. They just want your money."

"What do you mean just pay? Suppose I offer her 'brother' money and he then considers it an insult to the family honour and kills me!"

"Let's go and see Nazeeh," I suggested.

"If he knows 'nothing about this', how am I supposed to give *him* the money?"

I told my friend I would go with him. The truth is I wanted to go, partly for his sake, but also partly because I found all this talk about young, nubile girls titillating. I thought it was pretty hot stuff, especially if the girls were virgins. So we went together.

Nazeeh al-Tabesh greeted us courteously and asked what he could do for us, acting for all the world as if he really had never seen my friend Dr Abu Suleyman. We took Nazeeh to one side, I did all the talking.

"It's about Najma, Mr Nazeeh," I said.

"I'm sorry, sir, but I don't know what you're talking about."

For a minute, I believed him. Perhaps he didn't know, perhaps this friend of mine Dr Ajjaj Abu Suleyman was playing games with me. Maybe he was making the whole thing up, like he did with his teeth fantasy, and his work as a journalist, and his . . . But I quickly dismissed the idea . . . it's not possible, I thought.

"I know that it's nothing to do with you, but we'd like you to act as a go-between, a go-between who will help bring about a positive outcome," I said.

"Go on."

"We'll pay."

"It's nothing to do with me."

"One thousand," I told him.

"See you around, sonny. We're busy here."

"Three thousand. What do you say?"

"Three thousand isn't worth discussing. Sorry, but the brother won't be impressed."

"Four thousand then."

" . . . "

"Alright, five thousand . . ."

"A little bit more than that," he urged.

"Five is all we can manage. It's five thousand or . . . or, do as you please!"

"We don't stop at murder."

"And we don't have any more than that."

"Alright then, it's a deal. Let's have it."

"Tomorrow."

"Uh-uh. Now."

"Tomorrow. We'll be here, with the money, early in the morning. O.K.?"

"O.K."

Dr Abu Suleyman asked, "I have your word?"

"Absolutely. My word of honour, Doctor."

"That means the phone calls will stop."

"That's right. The whole thing will be over, and with five thousand lira we'll make sure the girl has a decent future."

As we left the café, Dr Abu Suleyman grumbled that he didn't have that kind of money. I urged him to get hold of the necessary sum by the next morning.

"And what if I don't?"

"You're a dead man. Don't you understand, we're at their mercy! They run the show round here. Pay up and you're safe."

The doctor was of course able to get the money together somehow, the threats stopped, and Najma disappeared from his life exactly as she had appeared.

Still, what I find difficult to understand in all this is how these people manage to set up such specialized prostitution rings. Maybe it's because there are so many refugees, and a general breakdown in family relations – actually, that's not true, because family ties have, if anything, strengthened during the war. So how are they doing it?

My friend Dr Ajjaj Abu Suleyman could no longer bear to even hear about the subject. One day, he announced that he was planning to go abroad.

"I'm going to Mexico," he said. "I've got relatives there, and I'll start a dental practice."

"What about your writing?" I asked him.

"What writing, man? I haven't got what it takes to write! Would I be able to write about my episode with Najma? Of course not! So why write if I can't write about my own life? Writing doesn't make any sense otherwise."

I told him I thought he should get married and stay in Beirut.

"Expatriation is hard. We're used to Beirut in wartime . . . Once you've got used to Beirut you can't live in another city. It's hard to imagine cities without war – because you know that all their civilities and niceties would fly right out of the window at the drop of the first bomb."

Still, the real problem is not Dr Ajjaj Abu Suleyman – by the way, he never did leave; he stayed on in the archives department, he never became a writer either, and it looks like he's planning to get married.

No, I think the problem – the real problem – is exemplified by Imm Mohammad. She is the sort of woman you cannot set eyes on without cursing your very existence! Honestly, death seems preferable to that woman's life! A widow with ten children, the eldest only eleven, and she the sole breadwinner. She is always on the move, working as a maid, a cook, a laundress, and all the while her children are constantly hungry.

"The problem, sir," she tells me, "is us, not the refugees. They'll all go home as soon as the war is over. But us, where will we go? . . . It's my fault, I wouldn't let him do what he wanted, and that's why he died. I killed him. Like everyone else, he could no longer go to work because of the fighting. But he wasn't an employee either, so there was no salary coming in at the end of every month. He was a longshoreman down at the port, and they're dailies, they don't get a monthly wage. And with the port becoming a war zone, who would dare go down there and work?"

*

He wanted to do what everyone was doing: we'd see people going down there – we saw them with our very own eyes – loading up T.V.s and fridges, selling them and making a living. Not him though . . . It was all my fault, I tell you . . . I was afraid, and he listened to me. May you rest in peace, dear Abu Mohammad. Why, oh why, did you listen to me?

Whenever the shelling started, I wouldn't let him leave the house – no way! So he stayed at home. And whenever it was quiet, he'd work as a day labourer on one of the few remaining construction sites close by. And I helped out . . . I cleaned people's houses, and we managed. We barely had enough to eat, but *hamdulillah*, we were able to have another four children, praise the Lord!

He was a man though, and like all men, he wanted to go with the others . . . He tried to persuade me, but I wouldn't be persuaded. "No, it's ill-begotten wealth," I told him. And he agreed with me. Dear man, he always agreed with me! May the good Lord rest his soul!

Then everything calmed down. People said the war was over, the "Deterrent" intervened, the shelling stopped, the streets were crowded once again, there were tanks and soldiers everywhere, it was over. I told him it was time to go back to the port. "You should go back to work now," I said.

He said that he didn't like his job anymore . . . that it wasn't for a man of his age. I told him that was ridiculous, it was the only job he knew and surely he wasn't going to learn a new trade now.

"Or are you going to stay at home, then, and let me do all the earning?" I asked him.

So, because I insisted, he went back to the port.

I felt sure it was safe and I looked forward to working a little less and spending more time with the children. And so he went back to being a longshoreman. Gradually he regained his strength . . . he was like a young man all over again! I thanked the good Lord he was happy with his job! And everything went back to the way it was.

Not a month went by, I swear, maybe less than a month, and he was dead. He wasn't hit by a bullet or a shell, no-one abducted him, so that we could say he died in the Lord's service, no, he just dropped dead. How could he . . . and me with all these children! I can hardly manage, I swear to God, I simply can't manage any longer . . . I'm exhausted, weary to the bone and worn to a thread, look at my hands . . . And the shame! . . . And no help from anywhere . . .

God will provide . . . He's dead, they said. Just like that, dead. He was helping to unload a fridge, they told me, you know one of those enormous refrigerators . . . he was bent forward, with his back braced against the truck, his arms extended behind him to steady the load. And he slipped, or the fridge slipped, honestly, I don't know, anyway, something slipped, and the fridge fell on top of him, and he was crushed to death. It landed on him with an almighty thud, they said. They all heard it.

He went without a peep, they said, and when they brought him home he was dead as the dead. What was I supposed to do? Yes, of course I wept, but I had to carry on working. I've a family to keep. People said I should go and have him registered as a martyr, a war hero, you know. They said go to one of those militia offices and register his name, and get the stipend. Nothing to it, they said.

So I went. But the men at the militia office wouldn't do it. They said he wasn't a martyr because he wasn't a combatant.

"Consider him one!" I told them. "Did he not die in the line of duty, that we might live, that the port may prosper, that this country may be glorious, that the Devil knows what . . . for crying out loud, consider him something, anything!"

But they wouldn't, and we got nothing, not a piastre.

Then they told me to go and see Nazeeh al-Tabesh, the owner of that café on the street corner. People said that with his "connections in high places" he would be able to "obtain something" for me. So I went to see him.

He was very polite, he gave me one thousand lira and told me to come back in a week and that he'd have "something arranged". Well, of course, the one thousand lira just evaporated – it was as if I'd never had it. You know what it's like, sir, with all the expenses when someone dies . . . the funeral, and then food and coffee and cigarettes for everybody.

When I went back to the coffee shop a week later, Mr Nazeeh wasn't there. They said he'd be back soon. I had just made it home when he arrived. He greeted me and sat down. Then he started explaining how difficult everything was.

"Things are difficult, my dear, and the monthly stipend is an extremely complicated matter. But listen, sister, yes, you're like a sister to me, and I would like to be able to help you . . . you're still young, and you're pretty, you know that . . . and making a living could be the simplest of matters. If you did just three hours a day, you'd get one hundred lira, that's more than a doctor makes in a day. What do you think?"

I didn't understand what he meant. So I asked him to tell me more.

"There, take this five hundred now, get yourself some new clothes, fix yourself up a bit – a little powder, some rouge, a touch of kohl, you know what I mean."

"What for, Mr Nazeeh, sir?"

"They're the tools of the trade, my dear. If you get yourself ready, you can get started in a couple of days. I'll go with you to the client's house, he'll hand the money to me and I'll give you your share – you are not to take direct payment."

Now I understood! Shame! Shame on him for even thinking that I could do such a thing!

I threw him out, and tossed the five hundred lira in his face! Imagine, suggesting that I should do such a disgusting thing! The nerve! Doesn't he fear the good Lord? Does the Day of Judgement mean nothing to him?

He was armed, but arms don't make a man. Honour, and honour only, makes a man and that Tabesh fellow has no honour! And he threatened me.

"Where's that thousand lira, then?" he said.

I told him I'd give it back to him but that he'd have to wait. The bastard tried to slap me, and when I began screaming, he ran off . . . May he burn in hell!

And now? How are things now? *Al-hamdulillah*, I work for decent folk.

You know, people like yourself, sir. We have just enough to eat, and my eldest, Mohammad, is an errand boy at our neighbour's shop. I said it before and I'll say it again: praise be the Lord! Life is just one big game of chance, isn't it . . .

"You are pretty, Imm Mohammad," I told her. I meant it too.

And why not give it a try? Life would certainly be easier for her, and, well . . . one way or another it was work – and very lucrative work at that! "You're a handsome woman," I repeated, "and you could do it if you wanted to."

"Even you, sir! They told me you were a polite and courteous young man, and that's why I agreed to see you, even though you're a bachelor. Even you! No, sir, and the Lord is my witness!"

"Come on, Imm Mohammad, I was just joking! I didn't mean it! And I am a polite and courteous young man!"

"We're much obliged to honourable, decent people like yourself, sir," she said.

I left her to her housework and went back to the airline office, and to my ticketing machine.

But, getting back to the problem . . .

You see, I was trying to "change the air" as we say in our part of the world, to . . . lighten up the atmosphere, to . . . to lift up our spirits . . . and instead of fixing it, I broke it, as the saying goes . . .

But I digress. Back to the problem once more. So, what is the problem?

Look, I am a realistic man, and realistic people keep their eyes open and their ears to the ground. I have watched and I have listened, but I still cannot figure it out. What you see is what I see: Khalil Ahmad Jaber was murdered, and by rights, we should be able to come up with a reason for his death. Isn't that what we were taught? That to each problem there is a solution, to each effect a cause, for each birth a death ... That's what we were taught, and the lesson has stuck: what goes up must come down; whoever digs his brother's grave falls into it; the less said the better; kiss the hand you cannot break, and pray for it to be broken; whoever marries your mother call your stepfather; when the winds of change are blowing, keep your head down; the middle road is the best; let sleeping dogs lie; if speaking is of silver, then silence is of gold; secrets shared are secrets bared; who dares, wins, etcetera, etcetera, et cetera, et cetera, et cet era, et cet era, et cet era, e t c e t e r a, e t c e t e r a . . .

My well-meaning attempt to "lighten up" has failed, even though I was only trying to follow the dictum that says you can find a seed of mirth in every reversal of fortune. When I tried to be daring and "change the atmosphere", the story got worse. So where's that seed of mirth?

O.K., let's start again: let us now assume that Khalil Ahmad Jaber did not die, let us assume, just for the sake of argument, that the newspapers fabricated the story and that the coroner is lying – just like the novelist writing this story. If we assume all of that, then our problem is solved.

Yesterday I was struck by a devilish idea: why shouldn't Khalil Ahmad Jaber have died just like the rest of us? That's it! After all, a human being can't die in any way other than the way the rest of us die!

Suppose, for example, that he was sleeping in the hallway of a building, and some burglars came along, armed with guns and knives, and went up to the sixth floor and robbed the apartment, taking all the valuables they could carry with them. Just as they are about to leave the building, they notice a man sleeping under the stairs, he seems restless and he's snoring – as though he were just pretending to be asleep. They think he might have noticed something, so they panic and kill him.

The thing is, however, that this kind of an ending is not possible, because we are not supposed to write illogical endings. And it would be illogical given the one certainty we have: that Khalil Ahmad Jaber was tortured. His left ring finger was severed, and his one and only valuable, the wedding ring he had bought in the gold souk thirty years earlier, was stolen from him.

Now, the wife confirmed that the ring had grown tight on his finger since, like most of his fellows around the Mediterranean, Khalil Ahmad Jaber had put on weight after marriage, and it had become increasingly difficult for him to slip his wedding band off. This almost led to a potentially serious situation, as Khalil's finger started to feel numb. When he told the doctor that he thought the circulation in his finger was being impaired, the doctor agreed, and suggested that a jeweller snip off the culprit ring. But Khalil would not hear of it. He was, after all, a conservative man, that is, a man of ingrained habit: he always slept in the same position and sat in the same place at the table. That is why he refused. The wedding ring stayed on his finger, he seemed to get used to it being tight, and he never, ever, took it off.

Given that it is crystal clear that he was tortured and his ring finger was severed, the aforementioned hypothesis is obviously false.

So, what then?

What indeed?

The truth is, I don't know; and even if I did, it wouldn't change anything. Suppose we did know that X was the murderer, would that make things better? Would it enable us to try X in court? Would it make Khalil's wife happy? Surely not, it would only compound her misery.

Moreover, I am absolutely convinced that the whole thing is not worth more than the effort required to read about it, and even that is a moot point. An astute reader will probably consider it a waste of time to read stories everyone knows about, while another kind of reader will think that there are better and more exciting stories than this one. And they would both be right, and so would you, and so would each and every one of us . . . as likely as it could be your fault, it could be ours, it could be anyone's, or everyone's . . . And truth is indivisible, they say!

This whole thing isn't worth any more than the effort required to read about it, and with all due respect, Khalil Ahmad Jaber was only one of millions of honourable citizens in this country who risk death on a daily basis. So, should his death be of any greater import?

Investigating his story, I have had no other aim than to "entertain, please, and pass the time", to borrow a phrase from Abu Hayyan al-Tawhidi, our revered storytelling master – the very same one who threw all his books into the river after burning them, such was his despair over the human condition, his disenchantment with the world, and his scorn for his epoch and its rulers.

However, what if we assume that Khalil Ahmad Jaber did not die, that he is still alive now, trudging through the streets of Beirut, trying to erase and whitewash the walls? Well, what if we did?

Some might say there'd be no harm in that, why should anyone want to kill him for it? Others might say the exact opposite. And yet others might be baffled by the whole business and feel unable to say anything.

There are then three possibilities. And the Lord alone knows.